Surrender to Scandal

BOOK 5: THE SINS & SCANDALS SERIES

KELLY BOYCE

The Sins & Scandals Series

While there are those who spend their time in modest pursuits, upholding propriety befitting the lords and ladies of the ton, it would seem that for others scandal is just a sin away...

The hero of SURRENDER TO SCANDAL was introduced in Book 1 of the series, AN INVITATION TO SCANDAL. Benedict was the big brother of my heroine, Abigail, and from his first appearance, I loved this character and the influence he had on Abigail. Having a big brother of my own, I've discovered a thing or two about the influence they can have.

This book is dedicated to my own big brother, Craig, who reminded me early on that every great heroine benefits from having a big brother who helps keep her feet firmly planted on the ground, while challenging her to reach for the stars. Thanks for being that for me.

Chapter One

"Have you heard a word I've said, Glenmor?"

Benedict Laytham pulled his attention away from the window and returned it to Marcus Bowen, who had come by to discuss several investments they'd made and future ones he had in mind. The man's brain never sat idle.

"Forgive me, I had just..." He let his words trail off. He had just what? Been staring like a lovesick schoolboy at the carriage conveying Miss Judith Sutherland up the drive to Sheridan Park? Hardly respectable behavior for the Earl of Glenmor, now was it? He cleared his throat and straightened. "Never mind. You were saying?"

He'd had a devil of a time concentrating on Marcus's report. A most disconcerting situation, given the current state of the Glenmor finances. But the fact was, he had not been expecting Miss Sutherland to stop by this afternoon and her sudden presence had left him with an unwanted sense of disquiet. He really needed to get over this. It was inevitable that he would run into her with relative frequency, given he was staying at Sheridan Park while the Glenmor countryseat, Maple Glen Manor, underwent much-needed—and frighteningly costly—repairs. According to his sister, Abigail, Miss Sutherland was assisting with the wedding planning for her uncle to the Dowager Countess of Blackbourne, indicating the young woman had a most orderly mind.

Still, he wished he'd had enough notice prior to the lady's arrival to remove himself from the premises. Taken a long walk and avoided the temptation of her.

"I said our return on investment in Booth's Liverpool and Manchester Railway will prove most lucrative over time and should help immensely with rebuilding the Glenmor coffers." Marcus, never one to mince words where business matters were concerned, crossed the room to stand at the window and peer outside. "What are you looking at? I swear your mind is elsewhere today."

Benedict turned away from the window to face the interior of the room. "Nothing in particular."

He tried to shake off the idea of Miss Sutherland, of the fact that she was only at the other end of the long hallway. If he kept this up, Marcus would no doubt figure out what had him so addle-brained. The man had an acute sense of observation that could be unnerving at times.

Miss Sutherland had proven to have the oddest effect on Benedict. Disturbing, really, and for the life of him, he could not pinpoint exactly why. She was not beautiful, at least not in the conventional sense. She dressed plainly and kept to a rather sedate palate of colors. In fact, she still wore her mourning garb of dark grays and pale mauves, though over six months had passed since her father had died. Nor did she arrange her thick, chestnut brown hair in an attractive coif. Instead, she pulled it back into a tidy bun at the nape of her slender neck. She did not wear baubles or such fripperies that most ladies of his acquaintance seemed to prefer. She did none of the usual things that brought one's attention to a lady, and yet...

He sighed. Yet she possessed the most expressive eyes he had ever seen. Deep and dark and steeped in mystery, as if she hid a secret she did not wish to tell.

Which was ridiculous. She'd spent the past two years playing nursemaid to her dying father. Before that, she'd had but one Season in London that, according to his sister, had been most uneventful. What possible secrets could she have locked away so tightly?

Marcus glanced out the window one last time, then back at Benedict, arching one dark eyebrow upward as if reading his thoughts. Most disconcerting.

Benedict left the window and crossed the room to his desk —or rather Blackbourne's desk that he had borrowed for his visit—and picked up the papers Marcus had brought with him. The numbers were indeed favorable and he breathed a small sigh of relief. The improvements to Maple Glen's manor house were costing more than he had intended, but the work was necessary.

Attracting a wealthy bride to help alleviate the chokehold on the family finances had proven far more difficult than he'd expected. Apparently, the title of Countess to an impoverished and scandal-ridden title was not considered a fair exchange. A true pity, as without a bride in possession of an ample dowry, he had little hope of refilling the Glenmor coffers his uncle had decimated before his untimely death.

What he did not need, most decidedly, were thoughts of Miss Sutherland infiltrating his mind and muddying his thinking. He understood his duty and she, sadly, was not it. While the Sutherlands had a comfortable income, Benedict needed something far more substantial than *comfortable* if he hoped to repair the damage Uncle Henry had levied.

"I was thinking we should consider increasing our number of shares in the railway," Marcus said. He'd stayed at the window, sitting against the protruding sill with his legs outstretched.

Benedict nodded, forcing himself to pay attention. Marcus's keen business sense had been the one saving grace that had allowed him to slowly start rebuilding the family fortunes. Unfortunately, he had no more money to invest. He'd tapped out his resources with his other investments, using their returns to pay off the last of the debt his late uncle had incurred.

"I can loan you the—"

Benedict gave a sharp shake of his head. "No," he said, harsher than he'd intended.

"Are you certain?"

Despite his lack of title, Marcus Bowen likely had more money than most titled gentlemen filling the House of Lords, but the idea of taking charity from even his dearest friend galled. He would do this on his own. He would not fail. Not again. He owed his family that much.

Benedict softened his tone. "No, thank you. I appreciate the offer, but I have no wish to be further indebted."

He would not incur another debt. He'd stopped the bleeding and repaid the outstanding debts, but with the ongoing repairs to Maple Glen, one misstep could easily send them teetering back on the edge of ruin. A possibility that kept him up at night.

Marcus didn't press. Of all the friendships he had acquired upon his sister Abigail's marriage to Lord Blackbourne, Marcus, a self-made man, understood best of all the need to make it on one's own.

"Well, there is still time if you change your mind. Are you still considering selling your interest in Western Trading Company?"

The Western Trading Company had been Uncle Henry's pet project when he was alive. He had invested heavily, convinced the promised returns would be the answer to their financial woes. Perhaps they would have been, had Uncle Henry not insisted on using up the early profits in a vain attempt to win back his mistress, the infamous Madame St. Augustine. In the end, both enterprises failed, one more miserably than the other. But Benedict did not share his uncle's faith in Western Trading. There was little alternative but to cut ties completely and sell back his interest.

Unfortunately, Uncle Henry's former partner in the venture was not only silent, but also unnamed, making tracking him down to discuss the matter an impossible task. Benedict's only contact with the mystery investor was through his agent, Mr. Francis Crowley, a blustery little man with a tendency to talk around any issue without ever providing a firm answer. Over the past year, as their profits had dwindled, Mr. Crowley had assured him they were on the brink of a financial boon that would see the company's shares soar. Desperation drove Benedict to invest further, an action he immediately regretted. The more he insisted on meeting his silent partner, the more excuses Crowley had until Benedict no longer believed a word out of Crowley's mouth.

"Yes," Benedict said. "I have determined to cut all ties with Western Trading Company. When I return to London, I will insist Crowley set up a meeting with this silent partner of mine, to put an end to the matter once and for all."

Marcus nodded and pushed away from the window to cross the room, clapping Benedict on the shoulder. "Perhaps you will find that rich bride you seek and all of this will be a moot point, hmm?"

"Perhaps." Though at this rate, he wouldn't hold his breath. The Season wouldn't get underway again until spring and he'd spent the past month holed up at Sheridan Park. While he loved spending time with his new nephew, not to mention his mother and sister, he could not stay here forever.

Though the House of Lords was not in session and many families had left the city for their countryseats, London still offered smaller parties and festivities. He needed to return and take part. To do his duty. Perhaps without the competition of more wealthy lords, he might stand a better chance at finding a suitably dowered bride before the New Year. Then he could increase his investment in the railroad and rebuild the family fortunes.

If only the idea of such a marriage came with even the smallest rush of excitement, instead of the constant dread pooling in the pit of his stomach. Choosing one's life mate in such a mercenary fashion left him cold. Oh, he understood that was the way of things, and perhaps if he had grown up in society, the idea would be more palatable to him. But his father's estrangement from his family had allowed them to live outside of such constraints. His parents had married for love, as had his sister. As had his friends, Huntsleigh and Marcus. Even the Dowager Countess of Blackbourne, whose wedding planning had brought the lovely Miss Sutherland to Sheridan Park this day, would in the end, marry for love.

Was it so selfish of him to have hoped to do the same?

"Tell you what," Marcus said, stopping at the door of the study, his fingers drumming absently against the oak frame. "Peruse the report at your leisure, preferably after you've had a sound sleep, and then you can get back to me, tell me how brilliant I am, and that you are forever in my debt for sharing with you my superb financial acumen."

Benedict smiled. "I promise I will give your suggestions my most rapt attention."

"Very good." Marcus said and gave a rare smile. "Now come. Let us go interrupt the ladies and their wedding planning."

Benedict's smile faltered. "Interrupt them?"

"Of course. They would be insulted if we did not."

Benedict hesitated. He did not want to see Miss Sutherland. Or he did, but he did not *want* to want to. It was all very confusing.

Marcus called back over his shoulder. "Or you could simply stare out the window at her carriage, if you'd prefer."

God save him from over-observant friends. With a low groan, he followed Marcus from the study.

J udith had serious doubts whether the Earl of Glenmor even remembered her name, despite the fact they had waltzed together only last month, and were on the verge of sharing family ties, once her Uncle Arran married the Dowager Countess of Blackbourne.

Granted, she was not necessarily the memorable sort. She had worked hard to enhance her natural plainness, a fact that had served her well to keep suitors at bay, and she saw no reason to change the way she looked. Still, it would have been nice to see a spark of recollection in the handsome earl's gaze when he entered the salon where she, her cousin, Patience, the Dowager Countess, and Lady Rebecca were planning the wedding between the dowager and Judith's uncle.

Oh, but pride was a tricky thing. A seductive entity that had led her down the road to perdition once before and needed to be nipped in the bud now, before she did something imprudent. Still, she would not lie to herself and say the apparently lackluster impression their dance had made on Lord Glenmor didn't hurt. It had been a waltz after all, and one would think holding a woman in one's arms would solidify a remembrance in one's mind. Somewhere. Even vaguely.

But when he entered the salon, his gaze slid over her without the slightest hint of recognition. If anything, it practically bounced off her to land elsewhere with all due haste. Oh, he had offered up a polite smile, but she suspected he did the same to every lady that crossed his path. A smile that, if translated into words, would have sounded something along the lines of, '*Ah, yes, lovely to meet you, Miss...*' followed by a blank stare and a pair of raised eyebrows as he tried to pull her name out of whatever dusty corner he'd stored it in. Obviously, the impression she'd made on him had been far less memorable for him than for her.

This was not the first time she'd been overlooked by a gentleman and no doubt, would not be the last. She wasn't the type of woman that men clamored to. Why she should be bothered that Lord Glenmor took no notice of her baffled the mind. Yet it did bother her. Not that she had spent a copious amount of time thinking about him since their dance.

Because she hadn't.

Fine. Perhaps she had, but only a little.

More than a little. But not a lot. Not quite.

But could she be faulted if her thoughts occasionally drifted in that direction? He was, after all, exceedingly handsome, with sky-blue eyes and strong, direct features. His hair was a thick, dark, burnished gold, threaded through with shards of light blond where the sunshine had reached down and kissed it. None of that would signify however, had he not been in possession of a pleasing manner, equal parts warmth and charm. In addition, he had held her in his strong arms and whisked her about the ballroom as if pixie dust had given her feet wings. An effect nothing short of magical, and thoroughly unexpected.

At least it had been for her.

"I trust the day is finding you well, Lord Glenmor." She offered a smile despite the hurt his indifference created.

He nodded. "It does." A brief hesitation, as if he would prefer to leave the conversation at that, but politeness forced his hand. "And you?"

"Indeed. Very much."

"Good. That is...good."

They smiled politely at one another, but his gaze continued to skid away, to land upon the drapery behind her, then the clock on the mantel of the fireplace. Likely counting the seconds before he could leave her presence. If not for the other three chatting away amicably, the room would have descended into an awkward silence. He did not engage her in further conversation, despite being forced to take the seat next to her, as it was the only one available.

Was she so far beneath his notice? But then again, that was the way of men of his stature, was it not? They may be polite when in public and such things were called for, but ultimately, they let you know where you stood.

Had she not learned her lesson in that regard?

She twisted her fingers around each other and tried to wrestle such thoughts from her mind. Hard to do when the object of said thoughts sat only an arm's length away. Despite the distance, however, she could feel him, as if his presence reached out and caressed the length of her. Scandalous thinking, but she could not help herself.

Lady Rebecca turned her silvery eyes on Lord Glenmor. "Your sister tells me you are planning to return to London before the Season begins, Benedict. Is this true?"

"Yes," he answered and Judith savored the sound of his given name. Benedict. She let the name echo in her mind, knowing that later she would whisper it aloud and hating herself for such weakness in advance.

"Why ever would you make such a journey at this time of year? What if the weather turns and you cannot return in time for the wedding?" Lady Rebecca asked.

"I promise to do my best to ensure a speedy return. But I must go. There is...business I must attend to."

"Business meaning bride-hunting," Mr. Bowen informed

them. Lord Glenmor scowled at his friend, but the expression did little to silence him. If anything, it egged him on. "He is making a preemptive strike before the rest of the lords return to town for the Season. If his hunt proves successful, perhaps you will all be planning another wedding soon."

Judith's cousin, Patience, clapped her hands. The young woman, currently suffering in forced exile from London, consistently looked for any excuse that ended in a party. "Wouldn't that be lovely?"

Judith's heart lurched. She did not find the idea lovely at all, much to her chagrin. Who the earl married was none of her affair. Clearly, whatever spark she'd imagined had occurred during their waltz had been in her mind only. A spark she must extinguish immediately lest she make a total fool of herself.

She refused to be made the fool by yet another titled lord.

"And you, Miss Sutherland," Lord Glenmor said, turning the attention onto her. "Will you be returning for another Season come spring?"

"Oh. Oh, no." Her face flushed, an embarrassing reaction to his unexpected notice, which made her flush all the more. Curses. "I am quite content to leave that to the younger miss-es." At three and twenty, she had put herself on the shelf and planned to stay there. She had other plans for her future. That those plans were a far cry from the silly dreams she once held, did not signify.

"Nonsense," the Dowager Countess said. "You had but one Season before your father's illness. I am certain he would not want you to give up on the idea of marriage so soon."

Judith forced a smile and tried to ignore Lord Glenmor's gaze. As much as she had longed for his notice earlier, she now wished it away with equal fervor. This was not a topic she cared to discuss with him present. To be true, it was not a topic she cared to discuss at all, with anyone.

"Well," Patience said, as if sensing Judith's discomfort. "We should be off. We promised Mother we would not tarry too long. I think she fears I will get over-excited at the idea of such celebrations to come."

The Dowager Countess laughed and Judith breathed a sigh of relief as the attention swung away from her. But for a brief moment, while the rest of them moved on to another topic, Lord Glenmor's gaze lingered, stirring an unbridled heat within her.

Chapter Two

"If you continue to sigh in such a manner, I will think you do not wish Uncle Arran to marry the Dowager Countess of Blackbourne, and for the life of me I cannot imagine why," Patience said, as the carriage bumped along the rutted road that led them back to Havelock Manor.

Judith forced her attention away from the window. "Forgive me, Patience. I suppose I am feeling a little out of sorts today."

"Why? You should be thrilled. We are marrying into one of the most prominent families in all of England! Even Mother is excited about what this will mean for our prospects on the marriage mart next Season." Patience's eyes gleamed. After having her first Season cut short due to a rather embarrassing debacle, her cousin was eager to return to London and throw her cap in the ring once more. The idea that their new affiliation with the Sheridan family would widen the pool of titled gentlemen showing an interest only excited her even more.

Judith, on the other hand, did not share Patience's enthusiasm. Once had been enough and she had made plans of her own in the hope of avoiding a repeat performance.

"I am extremely delighted for Uncle," she said, leaning back against the lush squabs of the carriage seats. "I cannot think of anyone who deserves happiness more."

The carriage had been an early wedding present from Lord Blackbourne to their uncle, who rarely used it, as he much preferred to simply ride his horse in the fresh air. Judith shared such a preference, but Aunt Beatris insisted it would not be ladylike to show up at Sheridan Park on horseback.

"Then what has your attention in such a tangle?" Patience tilted her head to one side with a curious expression.

Judith opened her mouth, wishing to confide in someone, but closed it just as quickly. As much as she loved her cousin, Patience had yet to master when to keep a confidence. She often blurted things out at the worst possible moments. It was never with malicious intent, only that her cousin's mouth usually ran at a faster rate than her good sense.

"I did not sleep well, last night. That is all." She forced a smile with some effort. Coming to Sheridan Park, knowing Lord Glenmor was in residence had indeed made sleep elusive.

The explanation proved enough to divert Patience's chatter back to the upcoming wedding, her excitement at taking part in such an event palpable. For Judith, she only hoped the event remained a small affair. She had no desire to mix and mingle with members of the ton, certain members in particular.

When they arrived home, Edger met them at the front door. "Ah, Miss Judith, a letter arrived for you while you were out."

Judith handed her coat off to the footman, the new staff a concession Uncle Arran had made on the behest of his sister. She had insisted that if he was marrying into society, he must have the proper staff so as not to embarrass himself. Her uncle cared little about such things, but as it was often easier to go along with Aunt Beatris on smaller matters, rather than get into a protracted battle of wills one was only likely to lose anyway, he'd acquiesced and raided the stables for a young man looking to move up.

"Promote from within, I always say," he'd told her with a sly smile, humor sparkling in his dark blue eyes. It did her heart good to see both Uncle Arran and her young cousin, Callum, happy once more.

Judith took the letter from Edger and flipped it over. Her hands trembled as her thumb rubbed over the hardened edges of the wax seal of the Marquess of Ridgemont. She had not expected to hear back so soon. In truth, she'd feared she would not hear from him at all.

"Thank you, Edger."

"Who is it from?" Patience peered over Judith's shoulder at the letter.

Judith pressed the envelope against her chest, causing the thick vellum paper to crinkle. "No one of consequence. A distant relative. We are still getting letters from those only hearing of Father's passing now."

"But it's been over six months."

Judith shrugged. "Some live in rather remote areas of Scotland. I suspect it takes a while for the post to reach them and be returned in kind. Either way, I shall read it in my room and respond." She turned to the butler, seeing in his gaze that he knew she lied, but thankfully, he kept his own counsel in that regard. "Would you send some tea up to my room, Edger?"

"Of course, miss. Straight away."

Judith made her way upstairs to her bedchamber and closed the door behind her, leaning her back against the solid wood as she stared down at the envelope. Likely, they were only writing to inform her she did not suit. She took a deep breath and broke the seal, unfolding the letter and reading the neat penmanship contained within.

· · ·

D ear Miss Sutherland,
It is with great anticipation that I respond to your inquiry of employment with respect to the position of companion as advertised. Your letter quite intrigued me and I believe you would be a more than suitable candidate.

H er heart pounded as she read on, lodging itself into her throat. They had considered her. More than that, they were offering her the position with enthusiasm, hopeful she would accept and come to London with all due haste.

She was to be a paid companion.

Judith swallowed, forcing her heart to return to her chest. This was what she wanted. What she had planned. She would be her own woman. Independent. She would no longer need to rely on Uncle Arran or Aunt Beatris to support her. Nor would she have to suffer through being trotted out before the titled gentlemen of the ton for another Season, expected to find a husband somewhere amongst the lot of them.

It was better this way. For everyone, really.

A paid companion. Such an odd idea to pay one for something most gave willingly and without cost. Still, the position that ensured her future was, at least for the time being, secure, and meant she would not have to rely on the largesse of others. Especially when others' plans for her future varied greatly from her own.

She pressed a hand against her stomach where a heady mix of fear and anticipation competed for supremacy. Applying for the position had been a bold move, and not one she'd expected would lead to success. Now that it had...

She swallowed and glanced around the room that had

been hers for the entirety of her life. She had always known one day she would leave this place, but she had never expected her departure to be under these circumstances. Yet hope and expectation were not things written in stone. They were subject to the whims of fate, and fate, as it turned out, had not been on her side.

She pushed away from the door and stared down at her shaking hands.

"We're Scots, lassie," Father had often told her, especially when his end grew near and he knew she feared for her future and what it would look like without him. *"It means we be stronger than most, ye ken? You'll be fine, my dear. You're made from brave stock."*

"I'm trying to be brave, Da," she whispered. She pulled in a deep breath and straightened her shoulders. If fate and luck had deserted her, then she would make her own destiny. What other choice did she have?

All that was left was to convince Uncle Arran and Aunt Beatris.

"Y ou're returning to London? Whatever for?"

Benedict winced. His younger sister's gaze brimmed with a potent mixture of surprise and betrayal, as if he were running away from home and leaving her behind. She'd given him the same look as a little girl when he'd left home to attend Eton after their Uncle Henry went against the rest of the family and offered to pay for his schooling. Regret bled its way through his veins and brought as its companion the same fear he always had at leaving his family. Foolish really. Abigail, now married to the Earl of Blackbourne, could not be in safer hands and Mother would accompany him back to London. But old fears died slow deaths. He could not help but feel, whenever he said good-bye to his family, it would be the last time he ever saw them. Or they would need him and he would be too far away to help as he had been with Father and little Roddy.

He crossed the room to the window. The view outside proved an easier landscape to look at than the disappointment in his sister's eyes and the guilt it induced. "I need to find a wife, Abby. I cannot do that while hiding out in the countryside."

She followed him, refusing to let the matter rest. "You don't need to find a wife that badly, do you? If you're worried over the finances, Nicholas would be more than happy to give you—"

"No!" He turned to face her. Bloody hell, why did everyone think he required charity? "I do not need Blackbourne or Marcus or anyone else for that matter, giving me hand-outs. Restoring the Glenmor estates and its finances are my responsibility and I do not need help in doing so."

Abigail lifted one blonde eyebrow and her mouth quirked to the side. "Save for that of your bride and her very large dowry?"

Benedict sighed, hating the truth in her words. "You make it sound so mercenary."

"Isn't it?" She reached out and took his hands. "Wouldn't you prefer to marry for love, Ben?"

The idea appealed greatly, but it was not to be. "I do not have that luxury."

"That's the same thing I told you when I faced the dire prospect of marrying Lord Tarrington for all the same reasons you now claim as your own. Was it not you who said I didn't have to do it? That no amount of money was worth a lifetime of unhappiness?"

He cleared his throat. His sister's long and accurate memory of past conversations had to be her most annoying trait. "I may have said something to that effect, but only because it was not your responsibility to save us. As earl, it *is* my responsibility and I must do whatever I can to see it done."

She squeezed his hands and made a sound somewhere between a short growl and an angry huff. "Benedict, you will regret this. Mark my words. A loveless marriage will yield an empty life wrought with discontent. I know you! You have a warm and generous heart. You don't deserve to be cast into a lifetime of misery! Please, reconsider this course."

He smiled down at his sister and pulled her into his arms, hugging her close as he had done all those years ago when he'd left for school. He'd promised her then that everything would be fine. He'd made the same promise when Uncle Henry had lost his mind over his obsession for Madame St. Augustine. He'd been wrong on both accounts. Horribly, disastrously wrong. It was that knowledge, and his inability to prevent the heartbreaking losses that followed, that stayed his tongue from making such a promise again.

"Abby, I am the last male heir in the Laytham line. This is our family legacy. *Father's* legacy. I will not fail him. Not again. Do not ask me to."

"Father walked away from his family to marry for love. He would want you to do the same," she countered. "And Father was the one who demanded you stay away when we fell ill. He would never blame you for obeying his wishes."

He hugged her tighter. Whether Father would have blamed him or not did not absolve him of the guilt that dogged him. He had done as Father asked and remained safely out of reach of the fever that ravaged his family and cost Father and Roddy their lives. But obeying Father's wishes remained, to this day, his biggest regret. Mother and Abigail may not hold him accountable, but he did. His family had needed him, and he had not been there.

"I love you, Abby, and I would do anything for you, but

not this. If I am lucky, perhaps I will find a nice girl with a large dowry. We will marry and eventually, over time, form an attachment." Though he wouldn't hold his breath. So far, most of the ladies who met his strict criteria had proven dull or shallow or a sad combination of both. The others had simply not been interested in an impoverished earl more captivated by her dowry than the woman attached to it. He couldn't say he blamed them.

Abigail pulled away, her shoulders slumped and unhappiness pulling the corners of her mouth down. "Mother will not like it."

Benedict nodded. "I know. She has already insisted she return with me under the guise of shopping for the upcoming wedding. I think she hopes to steer me around to your way of thinking."

"Then I wish her every success and hope she has better luck than I. When will you leave?"

"By week's end." There was no point in putting off the unavoidable any longer than necessary. The inevitability of what he must do had become a weight hanging about his neck, coloring everything he did. "I promise I shall return in time for the wedding." The newly engaged couple had no wish for a lengthy engagement and planned to marry two days before Christmas. Surely, he could have things settled by then.

"Fine. But I want it duly noted that I am not the least bit happy about this."

Nor was he, but he kept such sentiments to himself. To voice them would spell his doom, and destroy any hope he had of resurrecting his family name and returning the Glenmor title back to its former glory.

Uncle Arran stared at Judith as if her proclamation regarding her future was the most absurd thing she had ever said, and he must have heard her incorrectly. "You did what?"

She sat up straighter. She had sent her response to Lord Ridgemont two days ago, though she had waited until her letter was well on its way before confronting her aunt and uncle. "I have accepted a position with the Marquess of Ridgemont as paid companion to his sister, Lady Henrietta. I plan to leave for London as soon as I can make arrangements."

But even upon repeating her claim, her uncle continued to shake his head. "No. Absolutely not. I forbid it."

"You—" It was her turn to be stupefied. Over the months since her uncle had returned to Havelock Manor, they had grown close, but this was the first time she had witnessed this side of him. The totalitarian who told her what she could and could not do. "I beg your pardon? Forbid it?"

"Yes. Completely." If he continued to shake his head in such a manner, the poor man was going to give himself a beast of a headache. "You can't. There is no reason for you to...to—"

"Work." Aunt Beatris spat the word out as if it left a bad taste in her mouth. This was the first thing her aunt had managed to say since Judith delivered her news. "It would be unseemly!"

"Indeed." Uncle Arran echoed his sister's opinion and gave up shaking his head in exchange for a firm nod.

While Judith had not anticipated either of them would take the news well, their strict opposition to her employment left her flummoxed. She took a fortifying breath and forged ahead. "There is nothing unseemly about honest work and I'm surprised to hear such a sentiment from either of you. How many times have I heard stories of how Grandfather

Douglas ensured each of his children understood the benefits of hard work? That it was the Scottish way?" She leaned forward. "That it builds character?"

"Yes, well." Uncle Arran cleared his throat, avoiding her direct gaze. "That was then. And we have come a long way since. You are a lady, Judith. And you should focus your efforts on more ladylike pursuits such as..." His voice trailed off and he looked over to his older sister for assistance.

Aunt Beatris took up the charge with gusto. "Like marriage and having a family of your own. A new Season will soon be upon us and I am hopeful we can secure a proper husband for you."

Judith's shoulders drooped. Of course. There it was. Her one and only purpose in life. To tie herself to a man—an aristocrat at that—who viewed her as nothing more than a means to an end.

"You have good breeding hips, I'll give you that."

She shoved the words and the ugly memory from her head. Not now. She would not think of that now.

"I am not certain marriage is for me." A bold statement to be sure and not one that would garner any goodwill from her current audience. "And until I deem otherwise, I do not wish to spend my days idle, a burden to my family."

Aunt Beatris fell into shocked silence once again.

"You are not a burden," Uncle Arran stated. "I certainly hope we have not done anything to make you think so."

The wounded look on her uncle's face made her regret her choice of words. "No, of course not. But, I too, had a father who instilled in me an admiration for hard work and—"

Aunt Beatris recovered her tongue before Judith could finish. "Marriage is hard work, I assure you, my dear. Motherhood even more so!"

Judith sighed. This was not going as she had planned

"I do not mean to say otherwise, Auntie. But truth be

told, I have no interest in another Season. Even less in titled gentlemen who act as if proper manners and true character were things they put on and took off whenever it suited them!" The words shot out hard and harsh.

Uncle Arran leaned forward, concern etched into his handsome features. "Judith—"

She cleared her throat and pressed on. Some things she did not wish to address with her uncle. "I understand your reticence in letting me go, but you both misunderstand. I am not asking permission. I am simply informing you of my plans. I am three and twenty and perfectly capable of making my own decisions with respect to my life. I will be leaving following the dinner party."

If she put departing off any longer, the fear and uncertainty of what she was doing might creep back. She stood and strode from the room, before either of them could change her mind.

Benedict did his best to hide the smile that threatened as Sir Arran paced the length of the billiards table, forcing the Earl of Huntsleigh to move out of his way lest he bump against him and ruin his shot. A pointless exercise, however, as Marcus Bowen's skill at the game had improved greatly of late and was now far superior to Huntsleigh's. The earl really didn't have a hope of winning.

"What is she thinking," Sir Arran said, throwing his arms out wide as if he could corral the answer from the air around him. Blackbourne dodged and weaved to avoid being hit. "And what is this business about not marrying? What woman does not want to marry?"

"More than we think, I would hazard," Marcus said, leaning over the table and lining up his shot. With one swift, efficient movement, he sank the last two balls and the game ended. "Not all women take well to the idea of having their lives and futures controlled by others."

"True enough," Huntsleigh echoed. "I know my wife was not particularly fond of it."

Blackbourne leaned against the edge of the billiards table. "Nor mine."

Sir Arran stopped and faced his son. "Really?"

Blackbourne shrugged in response as if the idea did not faze him in the least. "Would it appeal to you?"

"Well, no but—"

"But you've never had to think about it," Huntsleigh said.

"Then you think I should let her go?"

Benedict set down the cue stick he'd been holding since his earlier trouncing by Marcus. Having Miss Sutherland in London left him unsettled. And excited. Which unsettled him even more.

He refocused his attention on Sir Arran's concerns. He could not afford such thoughts where Miss Sutherland was concerned. "Do you have a choice? She is of age and short of locking her in her room until she is a doddering old woman, I see little you can do about it."

He liked Sir Arran and considered him a truly honorable man in both word and deed, but when it came to the women in his family—a family only newly reformed after the death of Sir Arran's brother forced his return to Havelock Manor—he could be a bit shortsighted and overprotective. Benedict, for his part, came from a family of strong-minded women and had spent his formative years being raised in a home where both his parents had equal say. He hadn't realized until Uncle Henry took them in just how rare a situation that was.

"How am I supposed to sleep at night knowing she is alone and unprotected in London? London! The city is a cesspool of depravity!"

Blackbourne chuckled. "It is hardly that. Not all of it, at least. And I am confidant Miss Sutherland will have no interest in the parts that are. Lord Ridgemont is a good man. I'm certain he will not allow any harm to come to her."

Though the words were meant to pacify Sir Arran, they did little to settle the disquiet in Benedict's stomach. Ridgemont was indeed a good enough chap, but he was also a very unmarried chap.

Not that he should care one way or the other.

Except that he did.

"His great-aunt, Lady Dalridge, resides with him," Blackbourne continued. "I am certain she will ensure all propriety is maintained."

Sir Arran refused to be placated. "If she is hell bent on working, why could she at least not choose to become the companion to a doddering old widow in some remote country estate?"

Blackbourne clapped his father on the shoulder. "I am of the strong opinion that women were not put on this earth to make our lives easier, only more enjoyable."

"And interesting," Huntsleigh added.

Marcus nodded. "And happy."

Sir Arran arched one eyebrow. "I am not happy."

"If it will ease your pain any," Blackbourne said. "Glenmor and his mother will be leaving for London in two days. I am certain he will not mind escorting Miss Sutherland safely to Lord Ridgemont's home, will you, Ben?"

The tension eased from Sir Arran's brow as he looked over at Benedict. "Would you?"

He swallowed. He could think of nothing he wanted less. He needed to put this silly fascination with Miss Sutherland behind him and focus on the task of finding a proper wife. But he could hardly say no. It would be ungentlemanly. And, if in

Sir Arran's place, he'd want someone he trusted to afford him the same courtesy. Blast it.

"We would be happy to see her safely to her destination." Where he would leave her and that would be that.

"And," Huntsleigh chimed in, "As he is staying in London, he will be there to check in on her periodically to ensure she is safe, happy, and well. Will you not, Glenmor?"

Benedict gritted his teeth. When Abigail married Blackbourne, she'd gained not only a husband, but also her husband's dearest friends and, as her brother, Benedict was quickly ensconced as one of them. He'd never had close friends growing up, men who treated each other like brothers. At the time, he'd considered this a wonderful boon.

Obviously, he had been out of his mind.

He forced a smile. "Not at all. It would be my pleasure." Too much so.

And that, in a nutshell, was the problem.

Chapter Three

J udith sat quietly in the Glenmor carriage, the well-cushioned seat protecting her back and bottom from the worst of the bumps on the rutted road as Havelock Manor became a distant speck before eventually disappearing entirely from view. A half-day's ride ahead of them was another conveyance carrying their luggage, Mrs. Laytham's maid, and Lord Glenmor's valet.

Judith had seen little reason to employ a lady's maid herself, though Aunt Beatris had tried to change her mind to that effect. It had seemed a bit much to have someone in her employ, while another employed her. In the end, she'd brought little with her; only the items she deemed necessary for her newly acquired position. Serviceable dresses and undergarments, several books Lady Henrietta might enjoy discussing, a few gowns—albeit a little out of fashion now—in the event she was requested to provide companionship at certain events. A possibility she dreaded and refused to dwell on.

"Had you met Lord Ridgemont previously during your

Season in London, Miss Sutherland?" Mrs. Laytham asked with a smile. The lady was a favorite of Judith's. A tiny wisp of a thing with the same strong bone structure as her son, though while she often held a smile upon her countenance, Lord Glenmor seemed less prone to do so. Perhaps the tragedies Uncle Arran revealed that had befallen the Laythams had left their mark in different ways.

"I did not." Judith squeezed her hands together in her lap. She did not care to discuss her previous time in London, not even with Mrs. Laytham. It had not been a pleasant experience and revisiting those memories only served to heighten her apprehension at returning.

Her gaze flicked to Lord Glenmor who had said little beyond initial pleasantries since the beginning of their journey, allowing his mother to carry the bulk of the conversation. Had he heard of her humiliation in London? Did they still snicker behind her back at what good fun they'd had at her expense?

Heat burned in the apple of her cheeks at the thought he might be privy to her shame.

"Benedict has indicated he is a good sort, and Gloria told me only yesterday that his great-aunt, Lady Dalridge, is quite formidable. I think you should find yourself in good company. I'm afraid to say I know little of Lady Henrietta, however. Do you know of her Ben, dear?"

Lord Glenmor's gaze landed on Judith then slid away to peer out the window. The motion felt very much like a dismissal, as if she were of little consequence, or not worth looking at. It rankled, much as it had when others treated her similarly during her last stay in London. Did he, like the other members of the ton, believe her so far beneath him that she did not warrant his time or attention? As if the situation of his birth automatically made him a better person?

Oh, how she despised these horrible insecurities that crept

in when she let her guard down even a little. They had never existed before London. Then again, before London she had not come face to face with such duplicity. Before London, she'd believed everyone had good inside of them. But Lord Pengrin and Lady Susan had set her straight on that account, hadn't they? She forced the unwanted memory away. Given her new position, the chance of encountering either of them seemed unlikely. A fact that pleased her quite well.

"I'm afraid my knowledge of Lady Henrietta is limited," Lord Glenmor said. "Only that she is Lord Ridgemont's half-sister from his late father's second marriage. I believe she is of age, but has yet to be presented."

His mother sat back in her seat. "How odd. One would think as the sister to a marquess, she would be out in society by now and in high demand."

Lord Glenmor shrugged. "Perhaps they will present her to court this Season."

The idea, and what it meant for her, made Judith's stomach roll over. She pressed a hand against her belly in an effort to stop the sickening motion. Would she be expected to participate?

"If so, perhaps you should arrange an introduction and add her to your bride list." Mrs. Laytham's tone soured somewhat.

Lord Glenmor's gaze returned to Judith and she had the uncomfortable sensation of falling down a rabbit hole. There was something in his expression, lurking just behind the soft blue of his eyes. A familiar pain she recognized, having seen it in her own reflection each time she glanced in the mirror. It spoke of loss and survival, deeply imbedded, as if it had resided there for quite some time.

She clenched her hands more tightly together. She did not want to think of him in pain. She did not want to think of him at all. As much as his dismissal of a moment ago chafed, perhaps his lack of interest was for the best. At least when he stared at the landscape, the nest of butterflies in her belly remained dormant, instead of flitting their tiny wings against her insides. But this time he did not look away, nor did he speak, leaving her to break the strange silence that locked their gazes.

"Are you on a bride hunt, my lord?" She need not have asked the question, as Mr. Bowen had already inferred such in their last meeting at Sheridan Park. Nor should she have been so impertinent as to bring the matter up now in such a direct way, but it was the only thing she could think of to break the spell he wound around her.

He cleared his throat and hesitated before answering. "It is time."

And that was all. No elaboration on the why of it. Nothing that invited further conversation on the subject. Or any subject for that matter. He could not have made his disinterest in carrying on a conversation with her more apparent if he had straight out requested she stop speaking to him.

"I see." What else was left to say? His short answer lingered in the air between them, doing little to soften the awkward silence. She did not recall it being so difficult to converse with him when she'd attended the Dowager Countess's birthday party. Perhaps the gaiety of the event had loosened his tongue but now that they had returned to the every day, he cared little about carrying on a conversation with her.

Mrs. Laytham released a long sigh, though whether that was over Lord Glenmor's plans or his inability to carry on a pleasant exchange, Judith could not say. Regardless, the silence remained until Mrs. Laytham re-inserted herself into the conversation, bringing up the impending nuptials between the Dowager Countess of Blackbourne and Judith's Uncle Arran.

A safe topic and a happy one at that, to see the two reunited after decades apart.

But eventually, even that topic of conversation waned. Judith had not realized she'd nodded off until a sudden bump jolted her awake and the driver's urgent voice from above called for the horses to stop. She threw her hand outward in an attempt to steady herself, but grasped only air as the carriage came to an abrupt stop, pitching her forward in her seat.

Instead of landing on the floor of the carriage in a disorderly heap, Lord Glenmor leaned forward and caught her in his arms, pressing her against his chest. Once the surprise of her new circumstances receded, she became aware of the merest hint of stubble where his chin brushed her cheek, and the warm scent of sandalwood teased her senses. An unwanted thrill skipped up her spine when his lips grazed against her skin far too briefly before he pushed her back into her seat. She sat dazed, more so by the unexpected physicality of him than by the fact the carriage now listed to one side.

"Are you injured?"

She shook her head, unable to speak.

"Mother?"

Mrs. Laytham reached out her hand and patted Lord Glenmor on the arm. "Fine, dear. Though I daresay the carriage is not."

The door opened and the driver poked his head in, fear written across his features. "Yer lordship—"

"Everyone is fine, Cutler. The horses?"

"Fine, my lord. But the axel has broke. I can truss it up to get us to the nearest inn, but we'll have to wait there for proper repairs."

Lord Glenmor nodded, taking the news in stride. Judith held her breath and waited for him to give the driver a severe dressing-down as if he was somehow responsible for the sudden interruption of his master's plans. In her experience, most lords treated even the most minor of inconveniences as if the world stood on the verge of ending. But the flare-up never came. Lord Glenmor remained unruffled.

"How close is the nearest inn, Cutler?"

"Not far. Boar's Head is an hour's ride due north."

Lord Glenmor nodded. "Very good. Do you require assistance to implement the repairs?"

Judith raised her eyebrows. Since when did lords ask their servants if they required help in their duties?

"No need, my lord. It was a clean break. Like it'd been sawed straight in half. Odd to see such a thing, but I should be able to make it safe enough until we reach the inn."

Lord Glenmor nodded and stepped out of the carriage. "Very well. Do what you must, Cutler. The sooner we get on our way, the sooner the ladies can warm themselves in front of a fire. The air grows colder."

Judith's skin still tingled, but it had little to do with the cooling temperatures and everything to do with the heat generated where the ghost of his touch on her skin remained. Her heart beat hard against her breast.

Mrs. Laytham smiled, her own calm manner echoing her son's. "Perhaps we should consider this an adventure in order to keep our spirits up, don't you think?"

The woman's ability to stay positive despite the circumstances was a testament to her upbringing, no doubt. Mrs. Laytham had not been raised in society. She was a vicar's daughter who had run off and married the youngest son of the Earl of Glenmor against the wishes of both families, leaving the couple ostracized and without financial support. The current Lady Blackbourne, Mrs. Laytham's only daughter, claimed theirs had been a home filled with love and laughter, at least until tragedy came to knock on their door. What strength it must have taken to survive the heartbreak of losing one's husband and youngest son, and having her world turned upside down in the process.

Was that catastrophic loss the root of the pain she saw reflected in Lord Glenmor's eyes? Had he been a different man before the tragedy? Lady Blackbourne claimed he had once been full of smiles, as if he had an endless supply and never had to worry about running out.

But he had run out, it seemed. Any smile Judith witnessed from him now never reached his eyes and often appeared strained, as if great effort was required to conjure it up. She would have liked to have known him before, when he was simply Mr. Laytham and not the lofty Earl of Glenmor.

The two women stepped out of the carriage to allow Cutler to do his work. Lord Glenmor removed the two trunks from above for Judith and Mrs. Laytham to sit upon while they waited. They huddled together beneath fur blankets to ward off the growing chill. Judith didn't mind it overly much. She often spent much time out-of-doors and found the fresh air exhilarating, though her bottom soon grew numb from the hard surface of the trunk.

"It feels as if winter shall arrive early this season. I think I will greatly appreciate a roaring fire and warm cup of chocolate upon our arrival at the inn," Mrs. Laytham mused, pulling the blanket up farther.

"That sounds lovely." Judith leaned forward in her seat and stared closer at Lord Glenmor. He stood a distance away from them, silhouetted by the bright blue sky above, a pipe clenched between his teeth as he hunched against the cold. "Does Lord Glenmor know his pipe is not lit?"

Mrs. Laytham followed Judith's gaze to her son and gave a light laugh. "Oh, yes. He never lights it. It belonged to his father. Ben kept it after he passed away. During times of stress or upset he often takes it out. I think the idea of having a piece of his father still with him helps calm him."

"And which is he now—stressed or upset?" From her viewpoint, she could detect neither emotion from where he stood staring out into the horizon.

"I suspect a little of both. He carries much on his shoulders. Likely more than he needs to, but he will not listen to my counsel in that regard."

"Do you mean his bride hunt? Does he worry he will be unsuccessful?" She couldn't imagine how. He was an earl, after all, and an extremely handsome one at that. Not that she put much stock in either.

"Partly. The Glenmor title is still in a state of repair in many ways, and as such, he is determined to marry for monetary means. Not unusual amongst the ton, I know, but not the reasons he had originally hoped for."

Judith turned her attention back to Lord Glenmor in the distance. "What had he originally hoped for?"

Mrs. Laytham looked at her, surprise in her bright blue eyes. "Why love, my dear. What other reason is there?"

T he early November cold bit through Benedict's wool coat and the clothing beneath to nip at his skin. He should return to Mother and Miss Sutherland and make use of the fur blankets they had buried themselves beneath, but the idea of doing so left him rattled.

Instead, he braved the cold air, waiting for it to cool the heat that had burned through him when he'd caught Miss Sutherland in his arms. Perhaps the bitter air would freeze out the tantalizing memory of his mouth brushing against her soft skin. He'd released her quickly, like a hot coal caught in his hands, though every fiber in his body wished to pull her back. She smelled of spring flowers newly bloomed, filling the air with promise and possibility.

He clamped down on the pipe in his mouth. Madness. That's what this was. Sheer, utter madness! How was it she had enchanted him so? There were far more beautiful women out there. Why, he could name of any number of them. And yet, as he stood there in the cold, wishing Cutler would complete the repairs with all due haste, no names of ladies more enticing than Miss Sutherland came to mind.

How was that possible? She was a narrowly built, slip of a woman, a bit taller than average, who did nothing to enhance any of her features, dress to her best advantage, or even behave in a coy or flirtatious way.

No, Miss Sutherland did none of that. She spoke directly, dressed plainly and laughed...well, to think of it, he didn't recall ever hearing her laugh. Surely, he would remember if she had, as it appeared he remembered every other bloody detail about her.

Benedict pulled his father's pipe from his mouth and closed his eyes, letting his head hang back as a long sigh escaped him. This would not do. When he reopened his eyes, he stared down at the pipe's smooth contours and wondered what his father would have done in his situation. The answer caused him to smile, but proved little help at all.

When faced with the choice of marrying for love, or marrying according to expectation and obligation, Father had said the devil with it all. He'd whisked Mother from her home in the middle of the night and together they escaped to Gretna Green. He braved society's disapproval and being ostracized from his family. He turned his back on the fortune due him and struck out on his own. And in the end, he'd died far too young. An eventuality that likely would not have happened, had he done what was expected of him.

Benedict squeezed his hand around the pipe as the wave of pain and helplessness that came over him whenever the memory of losing Father and Roddy bled through him all over again.

"Was it worth it, Father?"

"Are you talking to yourself, my lord?"

Benedict spun on his heel and nearly dropped the pipe from his hand, catching it in time but not before looking like a juggling fool. "Has no one ever told you it is impolite to sneak up on people?"

She lifted one dark eyebrow. "Has no one ever told you it is impolite to point out a lady's follies?"

He clamped his mouth shut and glared at her, though, in truth, he was angrier with himself for barking at her than at her interruption. He usually had better control of his emotions than that, but something about her set his control teetering on edge. "Forgive me."

She acknowledged his apology with a small nod. "To whom were you speaking?"

He'd rather that she let the matter drop. He had no wish to explain his penchant for conversing with ghosts, and even less that he spoke to them about her in particular.

"I was talking to myself." And that was no better. If he kept this up, she'd think he was a lunatic, ready for the asylum. Maybe she was right.

"Ah." A hint of a smile played about her lips, drawing his attention. "That must have been a sparkling conversation."

He furrowed his brow. Had she just insulted him? "Forgive me if my conversational skills are not up to snuff. I have much on my mind."

"Bride-hunting and such."

"Yes. No. I mean, that is to say..." Had he always been such a bumbling idiot? He took a deep breath and tried to collect his wits. "Is there something I can do for you, Miss Sutherland?"

She waved her hand to the carriage behind her. "Your

mother suggested I fetch you before you freeze to death in the frigid cold. Come keep warm beneath the furs."

"It is hardly frigid." Though, it had grown colder and he could not claim the idea of slipping beneath the furs with her did not appeal to him greatly. Unfortunately, the image in his mind looked drastically different than the situation she suggested. For one, in his scenario, Miss Sutherland had far less clothing on than she did now, and his mother was nowhere in the picture.

Hell and damnation!

"My lord?"

"No. I am perfectly fine where I am." Fine being a relative term, of course.

"Is the idea of spending even a few moments in my company more than you can stand, my lord?"

Something in her voice caught him before he could answer in the affirmative. She believed he disliked her. The realization hit him like a strong, sudden wind. There could be nothing further from the truth. Just the opposite, in fact. The more time he spent in her company, the longer he wished to remain there. Her intelligence and wit made her stand out from the other unmarried ladies of his acquaintance, but it was more than that. Some indefinable thing he could not put his finger on, for whenever he thought he had it pinned, it shifted and became something else.

Maybe it wasn't even one thing. Maybe it was simply the totality of everything she was, and the longing to uncover all that still waited in the wings, yet to be revealed.

But she was not his to discover, nor would she ever be. His future lay elsewhere, and as such, he could never speak the truth to her. Never set the disquieting feelings he held for her free.

"I assure you I have not given the matter any consideration one way or the other, Miss Sutherland. As I stated, I have other things on my mind. Forgive me if I have not been the best of traveling companions."

She stared at him a long, quiet moment and within that moment he became caught in her gaze as if an invisible thread tied them together and he could not pull away. He wanted to say something else, to soften the claim he'd just made, but his voice deserted him. All that rested between them were the white puffs of air from their breaths.

He clasped his hands behind his back. If he didn't, he might reach out and touch her. Let his fingers run along the strong line of her jaw, the sweep of her cheekbone painted a soft rose from the cold air surrounding them. Despite her attempt at plainness, he saw beyond that and in that moment realized her true beauty. Not the simpering, coiffed type of many of the ladies populating his list of potential brides, but something more profound. Something that would grow over time and deepen. Something that would continue to take his breath away each time he saw her.

He could not afford this.

And yet, he could not release himself from it.

"Miss Sutherland—"

"Yer lordship!"

Cutler's voice startled Benedict, snapping the peculiar miasma his brain had entered into like a twig made brittle from the cold. He blinked, expecting the world around him to look different than it had a few moments earlier, before Miss Sutherland arrived to torment him.

He looked over her shoulder toward the carriage where his driver stood. "Yes, Cutler?"

"Repairs are made, m'lord. We can set out for the inn."

Benedict nodded and motioned toward the carriage, indicating she should go ahead of him. "It appears we will both be out of the cold and in front of a warm hearth soon enough."

She gave him no answer, but simply turned and headed

back toward the repaired carriage. He kept his gaze focused at some point in the distance, away from her, for fear if he looked any closer she might recapture his attention and leave him standing there, stupefied once more.

To hold such power must be a frightening thing.

To be at its mercy, even more so.

Chapter Four

J udith walked to the window and stared down into the courtyard below. The inn was comfortable, the room tidy, clean and warm. However, the delay of one night while the carriage was more thoroughly repaired proved most vexing. The more time she spent in the presence of Lord Glenmor, the more conflicted her feelings surrounding him became.

When she had approached him to suggest he come share the warmth of the furs with her and his mother, something had passed between them. And though she could not define it, it had left her exhilarated. An unexpected current had rushed through her, wrapped around her, and heated her from the inside out until she had no need of furs or fires or warm chocolate and comfortable inns.

Had he felt it too?

In the silence that fell between them, before Cutler interrupted, they had shared a special moment. He had started to say something—something important, she was certain. Though what she based such certainty on, she had thus far failed to identify. Certainly not facts. For the fact was, he'd clearly stated not a moment before that he did not think of her. That other things—not her—occupied his mind. To hear him tell the tale, he was barely aware of her existence even when she sat in a carriage not more than two feet away from him.

And yet...

She gave her head a sharp shake.

Her nervousness over her impending arrival at Lord Ridgemont's had obviously muddled her brain. What other explanation was there? No one in their right mind would even consider such silly things. Lord Glenmor was an earl, a Peer of the Realm. Men of his station did not fraternize with ladies of no consequence, and by the measuring stick of London society, that was where she fit.

To think otherwise was sheer madness.

To return to London after what had happened in the past, even more so.

The doubts she fought so hard to keep at bay crept in. What was she doing? What did she know about being a paid companion? And what if she was horrible at it and they let her go? She'd be no further ahead and likely her chance of gaining a reference would be void. Then what? A governess? She had little experience with children, save for her young cousin, Callum. She was educated, so she could apply to teach somewhere, but the idea did not appeal. A nursemaid? Illness only served to remind her of her father and his suffering, a pain she did not wish to revisit.

She pressed her forehead against the cold glass of the window and stared down into the courtyard. Night had encroached and moonlight reflected off the snow-covered ground, creating a natural light that illuminated the outbuildings closest to the inn. Quiet had settled about them as if everyone had already sought their beds for the night, but the oblivion of sleep eluded her. She needed to clear her mind of its doubts and thoughts of Lord Glenmor and the moment they had shared. The kind of sharp relief only found by filling her lungs with fresh air and allowing the peaceful quiet of the night to surround her.

Judith left the window and reached for her wool cape, wrapping it around her shoulders as she left the room. Venturing out was ill advised, but being outside always served to calm her mind, and if she had any hopes of sleeping this night and arriving at Lord Ridgemont's home well-rested and ready to tackle her new position, she needed to do something.

Lifting the cape's hood over her head, she took the back staircase to avoid the impropriety of being seen by other guests still in the taproom. The young girls working in the kitchen looked up in surprise as she passed through. She offered a smile, as if there was nothing odd about a young lady traipsing through their cook space at such a late hour.

The cold air hit her exposed skin as she stepped outside to stand beneath a lantern hanging from its hook, the only light beyond what the moon provided. She hugged the wool cloak closer to her body. She had left her fur muff upstairs and regretted her forgetfulness. As pretty as the night looked from her upstairs window, the actuality of the cold took her breath away. Still, she gulped it in.

She wasn't out long before the unexpected sound of footsteps crunching in the snow interrupted her peace. She whirled about. Stepping from the shadows, like an apparition conjured by her own imaginings, Lord Glenmor appeared, the unlit pipe gripped once again in his gloved hand as if it were a permanent part of his anatomy.

He stopped short when he spotted her, then quickly stepped closer. "Miss Sutherland? Is something wrong? Are you quite all right?"

"Lord Glenmor." His sudden appearance startled her and for a moment, anything beyond his name eluded her. The small pool of light cast by the lantern stretched out and illuminated the concern etched into his face. It struck her, as it always seemed to, how distractingly handsome he was. Why he didn't have a bevy of young women vying to become the Countess of Glenmor, she could not say. Most ladies of the ton she'd had the misfortune to associate with seemed interested in only a few narrow attributes when choosing a husband—how handsome he was, how large his coffers were, and how lofty his title. Given Lord Glenmor possessed two of the three; one would think he would be much sought after.

Provided the lady in question could provide the third—a large dowry.

Which left her completely out of the running. Not that she was vying for the position. "Are you not well?"

"I am quite well," she said, wresting thoughts of Lord Glenmor's bride choices from her mind. His marriageability was none of her concern. "I only wished to partake of some fresh air before turning in for the night."

His concern turned to censure. "It is not safe for you to be out here alone. You should return to your room with all due haste."

She looked about them, her gaze scanning the empty space of the courtyard between the inn and the outer buildings. She was alone, save for Lord Glenmor, and she hardly considered him a threat. At least not to her physical well-being.

"I assure you, I am quite capable of taking care of myself, my lord. Besides, you are here now. What possible danger could I be in?"

He took a step back at her answer. "We cannot stay here together—alone. It would be improper."

She pursed her lips, needled by how horrified he was at the possibility of any kind of impropriety between them. Not that she cared to court such scandal, but that was neither here nor there.

She sighed and her breath crystalized in the air, a white puffy cloud of frustration. The closer they drew to the city, the more rules and restrictions began to apply. Giving up the freedom of going where she wanted, when she wanted, without the constant need for a chaperone or someone else's approval chafed. As did the implication that Lord Glenmor had any right to order her about in this regard.

"If you are concerned as to what your presence here will do to my reputation, please feel free to remove yourself."

His shoulders stiffened. "I cannot leave you here alone."

"And yet you cannot stay for fear you'll compromise me and, heaven forbid, be forced to make reparations for such. That is quite the conundrum you find yourself in, my lord."

"One that would be easily rectified if you would simply return to your room like a proper young lady."

She laughed. Such a stuffy claim from such a young and handsome lord seemed so out of place she couldn't help herself. "Oh dear, you are quite the fusty sort, aren't you?"

Surprise registered on his features and he took a step back as if to avoid the label she'd pinned on him. "Fusty? I am nothing of the sort. I am trying to be a gentleman and save you from yourself."

"I don't require saving, my lord, certainly not from the likes of you. I am perfectly capable of taking care of myself." Had she not been doing just that for the past few years? Granted, she had learned a harsh lesson along the way, but that only served to increase her knowledge of what to expect from Lord Glenmor's ilk. His type played at being chivalrous, but the act was nothing more than smoke and mirrors used to lure in the unsuspecting.

His lips, full and generous and rather mesmerizing, pulled into a thin line and the lamplight caught the hint of stubble along his jaw. The warm, sky blue of his eyes hardened. "Is this what you consider capable? Flitting about in the middle of the night without a chaperon? Is this the type of behavior you plan to exhibit as Lady Henrietta's companion? I daresay you will not be long employed if such is the case."

His words cut, scraping against her fears and doubts. She sucked in a swift breath. But before she could answer with a sharp rebuke, Lord Glenmor let out a short huff and closed his eyes. His long lashes created crescent shadows against his cheeks and diverted her attention.

Her weakness irked her. His handsomeness was a distraction she did not care for. In truth, this unwanted draw toward him left her mortified. Was it still so easy for her to be fooled by an attractive face? Did the scars from her past imprudence not stand as warning against such a thing?

"Forgive me. I should not have spoken so harshly," he said. His words were soft, brushing against her skin as if the cloak and dress she wore did not exist. "It is only that I promised your uncle I would ensure your safety. I take such a responsibility very seriously. It would give me great relief, Miss Sutherland, if you would return to your room."

Her strong reaction to his tone, this weakness she could not seem to overcome, angered her. "It is not my responsibility to give you relief, my lord."

He raised one eyebrow and Judith's cheeks burned at the inadvertent double meaning of her words.

"What I meant to say, is that—"

Lord Glenmor held up a hand, cutting her off. "Please, Miss Sutherland. May we end this verbal sparring and simply return to our rooms? It is late, the night is cold, and we have an early morning and long day of travel ahead of us. We should both seek out our respective beds and get some sleep."

His weariness prodded her and pushed against her need to enjoy the last night of true freedom she would have for a long time. "As you wish."

"I assume you came downstairs through the servants'

entrance?" He motioned to the door behind her with the hand holding the pipe.

"I did."

"Then I shall wait here for a few moments to allow you time to reach your room before I enter through the main entrance."

Another precaution meant to protect her reputation, no doubt. "Very well."

He nodded at her acquiescence. "Sleep well, Miss Sutherland."

An impossible hope. Seeing him had only served to agitate her further, and bring thoughts of lost chances to the forefront of her mind where they danced and whirled and tormented.

Sleep would not come this night; of that she was certain.

B enedict let out a long breath and slumped against the wall of the inn once the door to the servants' entrance shut behind Miss Sutherland. Lord have mercy, but that woman had the uncanny ability to rile and unnerve him all at once. They could not reach London soon enough.

The last thing he had expected when he rounded the corner of the inn on his way to check in with Cutler was to find Miss Sutherland standing under the lantern by the servant's entrance. Her usually staid appearance gone, wiped away by the moonlight.

The rich navy of her cape made the ivory cast of her skin translucent, her brown eyes even darker. And her hair, freed from the tidy bun he'd become accustomed to associating with her, hung over her shoulder in thick, mahogany waves. His body stiffened. How he had longed to reach out and sink his hands into those soft waves to discover if they were as luxurious as they appeared beneath the lamplight.

What had she been doing outside alone? He had promised Sir Arran he would ensure her safety, yet the moment he left her, she had ventured out where anything could have happened to her. And what if it had? What if he hadn't been just around the corner, able to protect her? What if he had failed in his duty, as he had failed to protect Father and Roddy from the fever that took them? Or the way he had failed to save Uncle Henry from the madness that had ruined him.

Benedict cursed and softly banged the back of his head against the rough stone of the inn. The rational part of his brain realized he was comparing apples to oranges. Miss Sutherland was not ill—mentally or physically. She was a capable young woman with all her faculties about her. No one had been about to harass her, and had someone shown up, the door to the kitchens had been within reach. All of these factors were obvious—now—but in that moment as he witnessed her standing alone in the dark, the familiar fear of losing someone else because he had failed to protect them, rippled through him.

As a result, he'd been sharp with her. Heavy handed. If he'd had any hope of a friendship between them, her response to him this night put a swift end to that.

What had she meant, she did not require saving from *the likes of him*? As if she had lumped him into a group of individuals whose character she called into question. The comment irked.

"Bloody hell," he muttered, tilting his head to stare up at the midnight sky. "You're likely enjoying this, aren't you, Father?"

The stars winked back at him as if they were in on the joke. Benedict let out a soft chuckle. "Never mind. We both know you are. You're probably up there right now thinking I should run off with the girl and be done with it. Love above all else, isn't that what you always said?"

Not that he loved her. A ridiculous notion. She was a mystery, nothing more. A tantalizing, captivating riddle that once solved would no longer tempt him. No longer torment him with the idea of exploring her hidden depths. He did not have the freedom of indulging in such exploration. Duty ruled his future, not love.

He let out a long breath. How he longed for the bucolic days of his childhood where such choices did not exist. When he lived in a home with parents who did nothing to hide their affection for one another. How easily he could recall the way they slid each other sly looks, the way they always touched when they passed, stole kisses whenever possible. How many times had he walked into a room to find them locked in an embrace? Yes, theirs had been a home filled with warmth, love, and laughter.

Until it wasn't. Until death came to call and decimated the happiness they had once known, forcing those left behind to pick up the tattered pieces of their lives and leave everything they had known for a world of privilege they never quite fit into. Even now.

He kicked the cold earth with the toe of his boot. How many years did it take for the agony of loss to ebb? When would the pain scab over and no longer fester within him like a raw, open wound? How he missed his father's wisdom, his unending support and guidance. His strength. And Roddy. What had he done to deserve death before he'd truly lived?

How long before all the *what ifs* no longer plagued him? What if he had been there? Could he have prevented the illness, stopped it before it came into their household? Provided care that would have saved them? But he hadn't been there. He'd been away, safely shielded within the walls of his fancy school—safe, while the rest of his family had suffered.

Abigail especially. She had been the first to fall ill, though she'd recovered quickly, but not before the fever had spread to the others. What his sister must have gone through, so young as she tried to care for their family alone, still tormented him. How terrified she must have been, watching them die with no one there to comfort her. Even now, all these years later, he would catch remnants of that time in her gaze, especially when she looked at her own son who bore their father and brother's name as tribute.

He had failed her in his absence. He had failed them all and the guilt of that burrowed deep into the marrow of his bones, mingling with the culpability over his inability to stop Uncle Henry's self-destruction years later.

Now, he was expected to ensure Miss Sutherland's well-being.

He pushed away from the cold, stone wall of the inn and headed to the main entrance. They would leave early in the morning and he would place Miss Sutherland in Lord Ridgemont's care, ridding him of a responsibility history dictated he was ill equipped to handle.

And the sooner, the better.

Chapter Five

L ord Ridgemont's townhouse, set in the fashionable Grosvenor Square, gave the outward appearance of a warm and welcoming abode, with its cream-colored exterior reflecting the sun's rays and glinting off the windows four stories high. Judith's neck craned as she counted the levels, knowing her place would likely be on the stifling top floor with the other servants.

Servant.

She hadn't quite considered her position in that way. In her mind, she had steered clear of the label, telling herself she was simply being compensated for providing friendship to a young lady who apparently was in need of such a thing. Providing a service, rather than being *in service*. After all, it wasn't as if she would be scrubbing floors or acting as lady's maid. The most onerous of her duties would be providing conversation and company, perhaps offering guidance if requested.

Yet, when boiled down to the bare bones, the fact remained she was still, indeed, in service. And she would be living amongst the servants, clearly delineating her position in the household. She would not be supping with the family at meals, nor treated as their equal.

She had convinced herself she was fine with this, but as the carriage door opened and Lord Glenmor stepped down to assist Mrs. Laytham and her out, it struck her that, in truth, she was not completely fine with it. For years, she had been the lady of the house at Havelock Manor, her mother having died when she was too small to have a memory of her. Her father had counted on her and she had performed her duties well. When he had fallen ill, her responsibilities had extended beyond the running of the house and soon encompassed the entire estate, forcing her to learn an entirely new skill set as best she could.

She had loved the challenge of it. It gave her a purpose, something to focus on beyond Father's illness. She had understood it would not last forever. Father would either get well and reinstate himself, or he would not, and Uncle Arran would inherit the manor and the land. She'd assumed then, she would continue as mistress of Havelock, but with Uncle Arran's impending marriage to the Dowager Countess of Blackbourne, that position would fall to his new wife. And while she was very fond of the countess, she was unsure she could simply stand aside and relinquish all the duties that had once been hers, relegated to little more than a poor relation in her own home. Pride was a funny thing in that regard.

Her family wanted her to marry. They'd made no bones about that. Father had left a decent dowry. Nothing to send men running to her doorstep, but it was enough to keep her from being embarrassed during any marital negotiations. Not that there were any. Though at one time, she had thought there would be. Not that he had proposed, but that he would was an unspoken promise between them. Or so she had believed. Instead, it turned out, the only thing he had for her was the worst kind of betrayal.

She pushed the memory away. Some things were best left forgotten.

No, marriage was not for her. It required a level of trust she no longer possessed.

She had chosen her path. Independence. A life of her own. Though looking at it now, staring up at the top floor of Lord Ridgemont's home, her impulsive actions mocked her.

Oh dear, she really had not thought this through, had she?

The doubts that had needled her since she'd accepted the position rushed forward like an oncoming steam engine and she could not seem to get out of their way.

"Miss Sutherland? We are here."

Lord Glenmor's deep, even tone broke through her fears and she glanced at him where he stood outside of the carriage. He extended a hand toward her, a questioning look rampant in his raised eyebrows.

"Yes." But she could not move. Her limbs refused and her mind had gone numb. Likely, he believed her daft. A correct assumption, given all she wanted to do was crawl back into the furthest corner of the carriage and hide beneath the fur-lined blanket.

Lord Glenmor's brows dipped and two deep furrows appeared above the bridge of his nose. "Have you changed your mind?"

Yes. Yes, she had. But the horrible thing was, she had nowhere else to go. There was no place left for her at Havelock. No going back. She had set her course and now was stuck upon it.

She needed to buck up and face it. To use her stubborn Scottish pride to her advantage for once.

"No," she whispered. She slid her hand into his outstretched one and his fingers wrapped around her and held her firm. She embraced his strength, hoping it would seep into her and give her courage.

As her feet touched the cobbled walkway in front of Lord Ridgemont's home, Lord Glenmor tilted his head to one side and studied her. He had yet to release her hand and despite the protection of the gloves they both wore, she swore she could feel the heat of his skin burning into hers.

"If you are hesitant, we can take you to Glenmor House. You may stay with us until you make a final decision."

"Of course," Mrs. Laytham echoed. "My dear, if you have indeed changed your mind, you need not worry. We shall ensure you have a place to stay and return you to Havelock Manor once Benedict's business in London is complete."

Except that Lord Glenmor's business was to find a wife, and, if she were honest with herself, she did not want a front row seat to that event. Nor did she care to be indebted to him.

She straightened her shoulders and reluctantly pulled her hand away. "No, I am fine. It is normal to have a certain amount of nerves when embarking on a new adventure, is it not?"

"One would expect," Lord Glenmor said.

Did he experience the same type of nerves over choosing a bride? She wanted to ask, but she wasn't sure she cared to hear the answer.

"I thank you both for conveying me to Lord Ridgemont's. It was kind of you."

Mrs. Laytham slipped her arm through Judith's and turned toward the door. "Think nothing of it, my dear. Now, come, I should like to meet this Lord Ridgemont."

"Oh, no. That is unnecessary. And likely I should go in through the servant's entrance." A fact that had not even occurred to her until this moment, and one that did nothing to bolster her belief that she had made the right choice.

"Nonsense!" Mrs. Laytham straightened to her full height, which still only left the top of her head beneath Judith's nose. Still, the steely bent of her blue eyes and militant tilt of her chin did not brook argument. "You are a Sutherland, my dear. You will walk through the front door like the lady you are. It is best to set the tone from the start that you are a woman of quality and will be treated as such."

Lord Glenmor stepped forward and lifted the brass knocker on the door, a lion's head with a rather fierce expression. Her stomach flipped over and her knees shook as she followed behind him.

The door swung open and a tall, stately butler stood across the threshold and looked down his sharp nose at them. He said nothing, simply raised his eyebrows in question, giving the impression their arrival upon the doorstep was of great inconvenience to his day.

Lord Glenmor handed over his card, seemingly unaffected by the butler's demeanor. "You may tell the marquess Lord Glenomor have arrived with Miss Sutherland, whom I believe he is expecting."

The butler's gaze slid past Lord Glenmor and bounced between Judith and Mrs. Laytham, as if he couldn't quite determine which of them bore the title. She opened her mouth to speak, but only a small puff of air came out, so she closed it and concentrated on calming her nerves instead.

The butler stepped aside and allowed them to enter. "This way, please." The first words he had spoken since he'd appeared. His voice, a deep baritone, reminded Judith of dark places you encountered in the dead of night.

He led them to a well-appointed receiving room. The room, decorated in white with pale rose and green accents, held a warmth to it Judith had not expected after their less than cordial welcome. Windows lined the length of two walls, filling the room with light and allowing a generous view of the street below. It was quite pretty and her nerves eased a little. Perhaps this would not be so bad after all.

"I shall inform his Lordship of your arrival."

"Well, we may as well sit, yes?" Mrs. Laytham lowered herself to the sofa. Judith followed her, thankful to no longer have to stand on shaky legs.

A moment later, tea arrived; served by a maid who did not look at them, but simply came and went, quiet as a mouse. Would she have to move about in a similar fashion? Become so unobtrusive that she virtually blended with her surroundings?

Before she had a chance to give the matter more reflection, a well-dressed gentleman stepped into the room and she stood. His dark hair, crisp cut of his jacket and handsome visage took her by surprise and her nerves raged once again to the forefront. She had been expecting someone older, but Lord Ridgemont appeared on par with Lord Glenmor, though physically they were as opposite as night and day. The only similarity was their striking blue eyes, though Lord Glenmor's reminded her of a summer sky while Lord Ridgemont's were more reminiscent of an impending storm.

"Glenmor!"

Lord Glenmor turned and smiled, extending his hand toward the gentleman who had entered the room. "Ridgemont, old chap. You're looking well."

The words sounded strange to her ears, as if the earl had slipped into a role and become an actor on stage. The two men exchanged brief pleasantries before turning to address the ladies.

"Lord Ridgemont, may I present my mother, Mrs. Laytham, and the young lady is Miss Judith Sutherland, whom I understand you've already had correspondence with."

"I have indeed." Lord Ridgemont stepped forward and inclined his head toward Judith and Mrs. Laytham. "It is a great pleasure to meet you both. Lady Henrietta has been anxiously awaiting your arrival. Forgive my great-aunt, Lady Dalridge. She had wished to be here to greet Miss Sutherland when she arrived, but she has not returned from her travels as yet. Though, I suspect she will be very disappointed to have missed meeting Miss Sutherland's esteemed escorts. How is it you know each other?"

Judith cleared her throat and forced her voice, which had deserted her on the doorstep, to return. "Lord Glenmor is brother to Lady Blackbourne, whose mother-in-law is to marry my uncle, Sir Arran Sutherland."

"Ah. So family, almost." Lord Ridgemont swept them with an easy smile and turned toward Lord Glenmor. "Then I suspect you have stern warnings for me, have you not?"

"I have." The words were issued quite seriously, taking Judith by surprise. When had he become her protector? He, who had given every indication he wished to be well rid of her.

"Indeed. Then let's have it." Lord Ridgemont appeared to take the matter with a sense of humor. His informal manner should have relaxed Judith, but it did not. She knew too well the folly of trusting an easy smile, and while Lord Ridgemont gave no sign he was anything more than he appeared to be—a nice gentleman with no ill-conceived notions or plans—she had fallen for such a trap before and therefore could no longer find solace in such things as simple appearance.

"We expect that Miss Sutherland be treated with all due respect given to one closely associated with both the Glenmor and Blackbourne titles. She is a well-bred young lady with an intelligent mind and a welcome addition to any household. These are not traits that should be taken for granted or over-looked as unimportant. Should they be—should she be mistreated in any way, shape or form—I assure you it will bring down the wrath of both families."

Lord Glenmor's words left Judith at a loss. He disliked her and yet had praised her in such a way it shocked her into silence. So much so, that she lacked the ability to inform him his protection was not necessary. And, as it turned out, she wished he would say more. Something about the idea that he watched over her made her insides stop shivering, only to start up again, but for entirely different reasons than before.

"Oh dear. Well. I shall be on my best behavior and ensure Miss Sutherland is treated with every respect." He turned toward her and his smile increased a notch. "I am certain you will find nothing to complain about and I have every confidence you will come to think of this as your home."

Mrs. Laytham reached over and patted Judith's arm. "Splendid. And I do hope it will not be remiss if I come by to visit upon her and Lady Henrietta from time to time? I have become quite fond of Miss Sutherland's company and would hate to give it up altogether."

"You are welcome in my home at any time, Mrs. Laytham. As are you, Glenmor. Don't feel you need to be a stranger. In fact, I am hosting a small dinner party in a week's time. I would love it if you could both attend."

"How splendid." Mrs. Laytham smiled warmly.

"Yes, splendid," Lord Glenmor echoed with far less enthusiasm than his mother. The current Lady Blackbourne had indicated to Judith that her brother was not fond of social gatherings, preferring the quiet solitude of country life. She could not fault him there, though this preference would not serve him well if he wished to find himself a bride in London. Not that such a thing was any of her concern.

"Well, we should leave you then, Lord Ridgemont, and allow Miss Sutherland to get settled." Mrs. Laytham turned to Judith and enveloped her in a generous hug that ended all too soon. Part of her wanted to cling to the other woman and beg her not to leave, like a child to a mother, but that was foolishness. She had never experienced the love of a mother, not that she remembered at least.

"Certainly." Lord Glenmor left Lord Ridgemont's side to stand in front of her. "If you need anything—anything at all— you will contact us immediately?"

His gaze bore into hers. A hint of anxiety glinted in his blue eyes, as if he was actually worried about her, or cared about her happiness. Foolishness. Likely it was all for show. Gentlemanly bravado. Yet she found herself nodding and promising to do just that if for no other reason than to ease the furrow of his brow and bring him comfort.

As Lord Ridgemont escorted the earl and his mother from the receiving room, a part of her wanted to call Lord Glenmor back. To burrow into the safety of his arms and beg him to return her home to Havelock, to the world she knew instead of this upside down world she had thrust herself into.

Silly, the notion of turning to him for comfort. No doubt he would spin her around and send her back to Lord Ridgemont, happy to be rid of the burden of her.

A moment later, Lord Ridgemont returned and stood in the doorway. "Well then, I shall call Mrs. Pierce and she will get you settled. I expect you are weary from your travels, yes?"

"Yes. I am, a little. Thank you."

He nodded once and disappeared, leaving Judith alone in the lovely, well-lit room. But the warmth she had experienced when she first entered was no longer in evidence. Perhaps it hadn't been the room, after all. Perhaps it had been the company she shared.

Company that was now on its way to Glenmor House, leaving her behind to fend for herself.

An unwanted loneliness crept up on her and sank deep into her bones.

Chapter Six

"I don't like it." Benedict stared back at Lord Ridgemont's house as it grew smaller with each turn of the carriage wheels. "I don't like it at all."

His mother gave a small laugh. "What don't you like?"

"Leaving her there. With him. It is improper. Sir Arran can not be pleased with this arrangement." He certainly wasn't and he wasn't even her kin. Though he supposed in a round-about way they would be loosely connected once his sister's mother-in-law married Judith's uncle, but it was a tenuous connection at best. Regardless, she was not his concern and it irked him that her situation suddenly made her so. He needed to put her out of his mind.

"I'm certain there is nothing to worry about. Lord Ridge-mont seems a lovely gentleman and has promised to treat her with all due respect. And, given that you all but threatened to have the man drawn and quartered should he not comply, I am confident he will do just that."

Benedict scowled. "I hardly threatened him to that degree."

"It was implied when you stood there glaring holes

straight through the man." Before he could argue further, Mother continued. "I must say, I am surprised by your vehemence. I had the sense you did not much care for Miss Sutherland. Though why, I cannot imagine. I don't know that I have met a lovelier young lady."

"I have never said she was not lovely."

"You behaved rather rudely toward her."

"I did nothing of the sort." Had it been that noticeable? He had not meant to be rude, just...distant. It was better that way. She captivated him and he could not afford to be captivated. At least not by a lady without a sizable dowry.

Mother gave him a curious look. "It is unlike you to be so unpleasant toward someone, Benedict. What is the matter? Is it this marriage business that has you so riled up? You need not go through with it, you know. You are doing a fine job at rebuilding the finances. Resorting to such drastic measures as marrying for money just seems so..." She rolled her hand through the air as if she could pluck the right word from the ether.

But Benedict already knew the right word. Had he not thought it a hundred times? "Mercenary?"

"Yes. That. Would you not prefer to marry for love?" Mother smiled, but her eyes grew misty. "I highly recommend it."

A pain shot through his chest, striking close to his heart. "I cannot afford such an indulgence, Mother. The finances are improving, but we've a long way to go. The journey to solvency is a lengthy one and not without its challenges. Uncle Henry left us with some questionable investments that continue to bleed. Marrying well will ensure a strong influx of income that will allow us some buoyancy until I can untangle us from certain business arrangements and set us on the right path."

Mother gave him a stern look. "Marrying rich and

marrying well is not the same thing, Benedict. I rue the day when you realize this, only to discover it is too late to do anything about it."

He did not bother telling her he had already discovered it. He was well aware the course he'd set for himself was not a recipe for a happy life, at least not the kind of happy his mother and sister had found in theirs. But the dye for his life had been cast. It was his responsibility to ensure the stain on the family name was repaired and the coffers rebuilt for future generations. As the last male heir in the Laytham line, he was all they had left. He'd failed to save Father, who would have been far more equipped for the job, and he had failed to save Uncle Henry from himself, but he would not fail in this regard. He could not. No matter the cost.

Perhaps, if he were lucky, the woman he married would possess enough of the qualities he wished for to make their union palatable. It was the best he could hope for.

Benedict slumped back against the cushioned seat for the short ride home. Glenmor House was only two streets over from Ridgemont's. Still, he dreaded arriving. What awaited him there was nothing pleasant.

He must contact Mr. Crowley and insist he reveal the name of his silent partner so that he could inform the man he would be severing his association with the Western Trading Company and, in fact, selling his shares back to the company as per the contract Uncle Henry had signed, that allowed him to exercise this option. Unfortunately, before such severance could be instituted, the silent and unknown partner must sign off on the agreement. A difficult task given he had no idea who the man was and Crowley had been decidedly cagey about the matter whenever he brought it up. The conversation would doubtless not go well.

The carriage stopped in front of Glenmor House and he stepped out. He could have walked the distance in the same amount of time. It was part of what he disliked about London, aside from the crowds and lack of fresh, unsullied air. One could grow inert and slovenly if they were not careful, between carriage rides and rich meals at dinner parties and the general ennui from doing the same thing day in and day out. At least Hyde Park was not too far away. It offered a pleasant respite from the monotony of city life and he often escaped to it during its less popular hours. His shoulders drooped. He supposed if his goal was to find himself a bride he would have to change that.

Would Miss Sutherland be at the park, or would her newly acquired position keep her vaulted inside the walls of Ridgemont's townhouse? Little was known of Lady Henrietta, other than that she was the half-sister of Ridgemont, the result of the late marquess's second marriage. If memory served, Ridgemont's father and stepmother had perished in a fire years earlier, though he recalled little of the story. He rarely paid attention to gossip and avoided parties where such information was rampant.

"You know," his mother said, as he assisted her from the carriage. "You may want to consider Lady Henrietta as a possibility. It does not sound as if she has been out in society much, and as the sister of a wealthy marquess, I'm certain she would be in possession of a considerable dowry. She may be a hidden gem waiting to be discovered. If you act quickly, perhaps you will be the one to do so before the other gentlemen of the ton return for the new Season and beat you to it."

Benedict watched his mother curiously as she walked to the steps of the townhouse, Titus already standing with the door open ready to greet them. "Did you not moments ago voice your displeasure at my plan to marry?"

She glanced over her shoulder and shrugged, a small smile playing about her lips. "Perhaps Lady Henrietta will be a pleasant surprise. I expect Lord Ridgemont would be pleased to have you consider her. It would eliminate him weeding through those gentlemen simply looking to marry her for her fortune."

Benedict shrugged out of his coat and handed it off to Titus. "But am I not one of those fortune hunters, Mother?"

She shrugged and smiled. "Convince him otherwise. You are a good man, Ben, and you will treat her well. She will never need worry where you're concerned. You are as steady and constant as the sunrise."

He scowled and picked up the mail Titus held out to him on a silver salver. Steady. Constant. The words landed upon him with the weight of responsibility, pushing him down as if trying to root him to the ground when all he really wanted to do was take flight. Run. Put all this business about finding a wealthy wife aside and instead pick a woman he actually wished to marry.

Miss Sutherland.

No! He shoved the disobedient notion away. *No*. Not her. Even if he was at liberty to make such a choice, she had intimated she had no interest in his *type*. Whatever that meant. He should have asked, but likely prying into her private affairs would not have assisted in winning her friendship.

His mother interrupted his thoughts. "Perhaps Miss Sutherland may be able to help you where Lady Henrietta is concerned, if you can manage to be pleasant to her."

Doubtful. She had made her feelings about him clear and he'd been happy to let the matter stand, for both their sakes.

Well, perhaps happy wasn't the correct word.

How quickly he could recall the image of her luxurious, dark hair cascading over her shoulder, begging for his touch, tantalized him. How he'd longed to bury his hand in its softness and pull her to him. Taste the fullness of her lips and breathe in her sweet scent once again.

Damnation!

No. He would not request Miss Sutherland's assistance with Lady Henrietta.

He would find another way.

***

"Has his Lordship told you much about Lady Henrietta, Miss Sutherland?"

There was something about the way Mrs. Pierce asked the question that put Judith on alert. What was there to tell? She was a young woman in need of a companion, at least in the opinion of her brother, Lord Ridgemont. Yet the way the housekeeper phrased her inquiry and the sideways glance she gave when she spoke made the hair on the back of Judith's neck prickle.

"No, he has not."

"I see." Mrs. Pierce's mouth tightened into a firm line and did little to ease Judith's growing apprehension that she had walked into something blind.

"Will I be meeting Lady Henrietta this morning?"

Once she had settled into her room last night, she had been brought a hearty supper and instructed her services would not be required until the following day and that she should rest for the evening. Her room—not in the attic as she had expected—was, in fact, a comfortably sized room attached to Lady Henrietta's bedchamber. For easier access, should Lady Henrietta need her in a hurry, Mrs. Pierce had indicated. Although, what that urgent need would be had not been disclosed and Judith, too pleased at not being stuck under the rafters, had paid the matter little heed. Until now.

"I believe so," Mrs. Pierce said as she led the way down the servant's staircase to the kitchens below. The scents reached Judith first and her stomach rumbled. "For today, you will eat here with us. Going forward, it will be up to Lady Henrietta as to whether you will sup with her or continue to take your meals with the other servants."

The other servants. The reference grated far more than she'd expected it to. It wasn't as if she didn't have a choice, after all. She had taken this position on willingly, determined to claim her independence despite her family's wishes. But the idea of independence quickly went the way of the wind as the reality sank in. Her time no longer belonged to her. Where she went, what she did, would now be at the whim of someone else. Someone she had not yet even met.

The long kitchen table was sparsely filled with young gentlemen and a few women. Some her age, one much older, and two who were barely more than girls. All of them fell silent as she entered the room.

"Everyone, this is Miss Sutherland. She is her Ladyship's new companion."

Judith took a deep breath and forced her nerves to settle. She offered a smile and nod at the servants gathered around the table. "Good morning."

A murmur echoed her greeting and while no one seemed overly enthused at having a newcomer in their midst, none turned their noses up at her.

One of the young ladies close to her own age spoke first, though her comment was directed at Mrs. Pierce. "I wasn't aware Lady Dalridge had hired a companion."

"She hasn't," the housekeeper said. "Miss Sutherland will be companion to Lady Henrietta."

Silence and wide eyes met Mrs. Pierce's statement. How odd. What was it about Lady Henrietta that turned everyone suddenly mute?

"Lord Ridgemont is hoping to present Lady Henrietta to society this Season," Mrs. Pierce continued. "It is his hope Miss Sutherland might ease her transition."

The statement took her aback. Lord Ridgemont had mentioned nothing to her about helping Lady Henrietta enter society. She had taken this position partly because she wished to have nothing to do with society or husband hunting or the falseness of the people who inhabited that world.

Frustration filled her. According to Lord Ridgemont, Lady Henrietta was one and twenty years of age. She should have been presented well before now. What had she not been told? "I was not aware Lady Henrietta had not been presented as yet. Why is that?"

One of the younger girls with frizzy red hair escaping from a tight knot at the top of her head spoke up. "It'd be on account of the scars, I imagine—"

"Magda!" Mrs. Pierce's sharp rebuke muzzled the young girl. "Do we gossip about the lord and ladies who employ us?"

"No, mum." Magda's face turned a hardy shade of red. She stared down at her porridge and did not look up again.

Mrs. Pierce turned her hard glance to Judith. "I will come for you once your services are required. Until then, you may wait here."

She nodded, her mind reeling from what little information Magda had let slip before being quickly silenced. She was to re-enter a world she reviled, something she was ill-prepared for. What had she gotten herself into?

"Come, 'ave a seat, miss. You'll want to fill your belly before you start a long day." The older woman with the ruddy complexion nudged the chair beside her out from the table. "Porridge is on the sideboard, along with some bacon and biscuits."

Judith went through the motions of filling her plate, but the appetite that had greeted her as she descended the servants' staircase had fled, leaving her stomach a roiling mass of nerves.

The woman who had thought she'd been hired as

companion to Lady Dalridge offered a smile. "I'm Elise, lady's maid to Lady Dalridge."

"It's lovely to meet you." Judith had never been one to make friends quickly. Her insular nature made it difficult to reach out to other women and when she did, it was often to discover she had little in common with them. While she had been busy running a household and nursing her father, reading books on philosophy and animal husbandry, they had been busy learning needlepoint, what was and wasn't fashionable, and the fine art of being a lady.

Elise leaned forward, her spoon poised over her bowl. "Did I see you arrive in the Glenmor carriage yesterday evening?"

"Oh—uh, yes." It amazed her how well versed servants were on the goings-on of those who employed them, as well as the rest of the aristocracy. "There is a thin family connection and when they heard I was coming to London, Mrs. Laytham and Lord Glenmor offered to escort me."

"Then Lord Glenmor was in the carriage with you?" Elise sat back in her chair, her spoon dropping to her bowl and her hand fluttering to her chest. "Oh, what a wonderful trip that must have been. I have seen him only twice, but heavens, he is the most handsome of lords, is he not?"

Judith's answer arrested in her throat, but it mattered not. Elise continued on without her, peppering her with more questions.

"Was he very gallant? He looks like he would be a very gallant sort. Were you nervous being with him the whole way? Oh, that glorious golden hair of his. Honestly, I think I would have swooned within the first hour and might never have recovered."

"Heavens, Elise," the older woman scoffed. "You might as well not waste your time on such foolishness. It ain't as if some lord is going to come sweep you off your feet and take you away from all of this, especially no' the likes of Lord Glenmor. Everyone knows 'e needs to marry for money, and unless you 'ave a stash of gold coins somewhere, you might as well put that silly dream away."

Elise made a face. "Just because a dream has no hope of coming true, doesn't mean you can't dream it all the same, Agnes." She turned to Judith. "Tell me it was wonderful riding in the carriage with him like a bona fide lady. Is he as handsome up close as he is from afar?"

Judith didn't want to crush Elise's dream and inform her the journey had been uncomfortable and unsettling. Besides, she could not find the proper words to describe Lord Glenmor's handsomeness, which increased the longer she spent in his company. A rather disturbing fact she did not care to acknowledge aloud. "Lord Glenmor is every bit the gentleman, and his mother, Mrs. Laytham, is a very lovely woman. The journey was quite pleasant."

If one considered being tormented with wayward thoughts and unwanted desires pleasant. She most certainly did not. Yet, she was powerless to keep Lord Glenmor from filling every corner of her mind and dogging her dreams. Worst of all, she could not forget the pain that lingered in his eyes. A pain that called out to her as if she alone could soothe it. Ridiculous. What did she know of his pain? Or if he even suffered any? More likely, her imagination had concocted a fairy tale around the man and now demanded she read on to discover how it would end.

But she already knew the ending to that type of tale Heartbreak and humiliation.

Yet even that knowledge was not enough to force away the memory of being held in his arms, whether it was twirling her around the dance floor at Sheridan Park or catching her when the carriage came to an abrupt stop, throwing her out of her seat. If she did not know better, she would think her memory and her imagination were in cahoots to bring about her downfall.

She took a large spoonful of her porridge, hoping to end the conversation, but the thick concoction lodged in her throat and it took several swallows of tea before it finally worked its way down.

Chapter Seven

B enedict wound his way around the gaming tables at The Devil's Lair toward the back room. The doors of the hell had yet to open to the public for the evening and the strange quiet cast an eeriness about the place.

The man he had come to see, Hawksmoor, spent the majority of his time here, having long ago given up the normal pursuits of a gentleman in favor of the seedier side of London's underworld. He held a majority ownership in The Devil's Lair, one of the more upscale hells in the city. Hardly a respectable pursuit for a gentleman, but given Hawksmoor's disinclination toward respectability, the hell made for a perfect fit.

Benedict didn't normally associate with such fellows, but Marcus Bowen had suggested he meet with Hawksmoor in the hopes of discovering the identity of his silent partner in the Western Trading Company. The man had contacts the average gentleman did not, though whether he would be willing to share his knowledge remained to be seen. Hawksmoor was not in the habit of going out of his way to help others unless there was something in it for him.

And unfortunately, Benedict had little to offer in that regard.

A mountain of a man guarded the door to the backroom, his nose appearing as if it had been broken more times than Benedict had fingers on one hand.

He handed the man his card. "He's expecting me."

One did not simply drop in on Hawksmoor. He was a notoriously solitary sort and, while he had a few acquaintances he consorted with, he didn't care for visitors to simply come by unannounced. One sent word they were coming and waited to hear back as to whether that was acceptable. It all seemed perfectly cloak and dagger.

The mountain opened the door and Benedict walked in. The lighting of the room was dim; furthering Benedict's impression of Hawksmoor's life lived in shadows.

"Glenmor." The man in question stood near the room's only window that looked out into the alley below. The building next to it blocked most of the natural light that would have otherwise seeped in. The outer edge of the window was adorned with stained glass, the design filled with jagged edges and anger, as if the artist who'd designed it had been having a particularly bad day.

"Good afternoon, Hawksmoor." Benedict nodded.

"I understand our friend, Mr. Bowen, believes I can help you with a particular matter." Hawksmoor smiled and stepped away from the window, turning up the wick of a nearby lamp and spilling its light over the shadows.

"I hope so." To his left a painting caught his eye. It was a large mural depicting a scene that Benedict could only assume was an orgy of some sort. He turned away from the mass of naked, tangled limbs. It conjured too many images of being tangled in a similar fashion with a woman who had taken up residence in his dreams and refused to leave.

"And what is it you require my help with, in particular?"

Benedict hesitated. He did not care to speak of his problems or share them with others, but Crowley had ignored his pleas for a meeting and every avenue he'd tried to discover the identity of his silent partner on his own came up empty. Whether he liked it or not, he needed help. "I am rather heavily invested in a particular company with a silent partner who prefers to remain anonymous."

Hawksmoor leaned against the high back of a chair that faced the hearth where a low-burning fire spit out little in the way of heat. "And you wish this partner to be a little less anonymous, I assume."

"Yes. I wish to end my association with this particular company, but my repeated requests to meet with the man get no further than his agent."

"And who might that be?"

"A Mr. Crowley."

"Francis Crowley?"

Hope soared in his chest. "You're familiar with him?"

Hawksmoor made a face and pushed away from the chair. He walked past Benedict to the bar behind him and poured a drink without asking him if he cared to partake. "Somewhat. Little weasel of a man. Always looks in need of a proper bath."

"Yes, that would be he."

"Hm." Hawksmoor took a long pull on the brandy.

"Can you help?"

"Doubtful." Hawksmoor shrugged as if he cared little one way or the other. "It's been my experience that men who wish to remain anonymous often stay so, as they go out of their way to ensure such. It sounds, to me, as if your partner is one of those men."

Benedict slumped, his shoulders weighed down by disappointment.

"Very well, then. I thank you for your time."

Hawksmoor nodded and remained silent, a clear indication their meeting was at an end.

"If you do discover anything, will you let me know?"

For a moment the viscount said nothing, as if he mulled over whether the idea appealed to him or not before lifting his drink slightly. "Certainly." But the word held no commitment.

Benedict left the gaming hell to meet his friend, Charles Elmsley, at White's, holding out little hope that Hawksmoor would make good on his claim.

"It can't be as bad as all that." Charles Elmsley slid into the seat across the table from Benedict, his usually affable smile firmly in place. Charlie was a recent acquaintance, the eldest nephew of Sir Arran and cousin to Miss Sutherland. Yet despite their short association, Benedict could not recall the man ever being in possession of a bad mood. It made him agreeable company and a stark contrast to Hawksmoor.

"It is on the verge of being as bad as all that," Benedict answered as he took another drink and leaned back in his chair.

"Ah, well then." Charlie motioned with a nod of his head for more drinks to be brought to their table.

Benedict didn't stop him, despite his need to keep a clear head to focus on the problem at hand. Unfortunately, the more he focused on the problem, the more swiftly he kept coming back to the same solution.

Marriage.

"Ah, it must be a woman then. Only such a creature could bring a man so low." Charlie nudged the glass of brandy set upon their table toward Benedict.

"You might say that. I must marry—sooner, as opposed to later."

Charlie made a face, as if the brandy had soured in his mouth, leaving a bad taste. "A fate worse than death. My deepest sympathies. And who have you chosen for your countess?"

"I haven't. Not yet. I want..." Well, what he *wanted* did not signify. "Rather, I need a lady who meets certain criteria."

"Pretty?"

"No. Not necessarily." It would be nice if she at least possessed a pleasant face, but at this point, he could not be choosy.

"Buxom?" Charlie held his hands up to his chest and juggled them up and down.

"No. And put your hands down, man."

"Money, then." Benedict did not answer, but apparently his expression said enough. "Well, that is a bit of a conundrum, given your family's recent circumstances."

"Yes, thank you for the reminder." The one thing he liked about Charlie was his ability to leave his words unfiltered. At least, he usually liked it. Today, perhaps not so much.

The future Baron Elmsley leaned across the table and grinned, his green eyes practically dancing in their sockets. "Then, I have just the lady for you."

Benedict raised one eyebrow. "Is that so?"

"Lady Susan."

His shoulders drooped. "The Duke of Franklyn's daughter?"

"The very one. Mother and Father tried to convince me to cultivate an association with her in the hopes of forming a match, but sweet heaven, there is not a dowry large enough to convince me to spend a lifetime with a woman so unpalatable."

"Is that your attempt to convince me I should take her

on?" Lady Susan was not a favorite amongst his family and for good reason. Both her mother, the Duchess of Franklyn, and Lady Susan herself, tried to bring ruin and distress to members of his close and extended family.

"You did say your bride needed to be wealthy. You will not find a larger dowry than the one the Duke is offering for whoever is brave enough to take his daughter's hand in marriage. The man must be desperate if he was considering marrying her off to a lowly baron's son."

Despite the less than stellar depiction of what Benedict could expect from a life with Lady Susan, Charlie had said the key word.

"How large a dowry, exactly?"

Charlie shrugged and sat back in his chair. "Things did not progress that far, thankfully, however, word is, it is quite significant. It will need to be if they have any hope of finding her a titled husband. Her odious nature precedes her and most gentlemen of my acquaintance refuse to even consider a match with her."

Should he pursue the idea, his family would be less than pleased by his choice. But his current circumstances did not allow him to be too choosy. He must do what he could to save his family's fortunes, even if it meant considering a harpy like Lady Susan as a potential bride.

He tried to picture what a life with her would be like, facing her from across a table or sitting by the fire with her in the evening, sharing a bed with her at night. The image wouldn't come.

Or it would, only the lady lying next to him in his bed had long, dark hair and matching eyes that drew him in and refused to let him go, filling him with sweet torment.

Hell and damn.

He reached for his drink and downed it in one swallow, then motioned for another.

J udith entered Lady Henrietta's bedchamber and found her sitting near the window. The heavy brocade curtains were drawn closed despite it being mid-afternoon, casting the room in shadows. Only the lamplight from a nearby table cast a warm light on a lovely young woman, with fine bone structure and long, flowing hair the color of sand streaked with sunlight. The scars Magda had alluded to were nowhere in evidence.

Judith closed the door behind her, but came no farther into the room. The silence that hung in the air between them became oppressive and she longed to speak up. Did companions speak freely? Or were they like the other servants, meant to be unobtrusive, barely seen, and never heard? Though, how one would act as companion if that were the case, she could not say.

After a long, quiet moment, Lady Henrietta spoke, her voice barely more than a quiet whisper. "I understand my brother has hired you as my companion."

The realization that Lady Henrietta had not had a part in the decision struck Judith as odd and brought with it the uncertainty of whether she would be accepted. "He did, my lady."

"I see." She pulled the lace shawl more tightly around her shoulders.

Lady Henrietta turned toward the window. She possessed a strong profile, despite her delicate features. Her mouth was a bit wide, her lips full. Her nose straight, yet small. Her eyes, framed with arched brows, appeared to be a light blue though it was difficult to say without proper light. But it was her hair that captivated one's attention. Unlike most ladies, who wore their hair up, Lady Henrietta's cascaded over her shoulder and down her breast in thick waves.

Judith took a breath, unsure of what to do, but unable to remain silent. "I take it his Lordship did not consult you on the matter."

"He did not." The young woman's narrow shoulders lifted before sagging downward. She was a little slip of a thing and a sense of fragility lingered about her like brittle air.

"And you are displeased with the situation."

Lady Henrietta turned and looked at her. "You are rather forward." It was a simple statement and Judith detected no sense of judgment placed around it. Curious. Often her plain-spoken manner took reserved ladies by surprise.

"Forgive me. I should tell you this position is new to me. I am unsure of the boundaries and those which I should not breach."

The merest hint of a smile curled the corners of her mouth before disappearing. "Then we find ourselves in a similar circumstance. As I have never had a companion before, and do not know what it is I am supposed to do with you. Though I am certain my dear brother wishes you to convince me to enter society and find myself a husband. I believe he wishes the burden of me to be taken from him and placed upon someone else."

Judith reflected back upon the correspondence she had shared with Lord Ridgemont. "I detected nothing of the sort in his letters. His words implied a true concern for your happiness. Do you not wish to enter society or marry?"

A sharp laugh escaped Lady Henrietta. Judith jerked her head back, surprised at the hint of bitterness within it. "What have you heard about me?"

"Nothing beyond what your brother's letters contained, indicating he wished you to have a companion."

Lady Henrietta lifted one eyebrow. "And what did you learn of me from below stairs?"

Judith suppressed a smile. The lady may give the appearance of a reserved little thing, but she possessed a backbone hidden within her slight frame. "One of the servants indicated something about scars before Mrs. Pierce silenced her." She hoped Lady Henrietta did not ask which servant let the comment slip. It would not get their relationship off on the right foot when she refused to answer the inquiry.

Lady Henrietta inclined her head toward the window. "Open the drapery."

Judith crossed the room and complied with her request, pushing the heavy fabric back and catching it in the hook at the side of the window. As she turned, Lady Henrietta let the shawl fall away, revealing her bare arms. The sunlight caught the right one and gave Judith her first view of Lady Henrietta's scars. Mottled red and white marks twisted together down the outside of her upper arm, stopping at the elbow. She reached up and lifted the heavy veil of hair, pushing it behind her to fall down her back. The same scars that marked her arm continued up the side of her neck to just beneath her ear, leaving it, and the rest of her face miraculously untouched.

What had happened to her to result in such a violent display?

"I was burned in a fire," Lady Henrietta explained, as if reading Judith's mind. "The scars carry on down one side of my rib cage and curl around my hip." She pulled her hair forward once again to protect the scars on her neck from view and shrugged her shawl back onto her shoulders. In the blink of an eye, she returned to the very picture of a demure young lady. But the challenge in her eyes, the fear as she awaited Judith's response, was anything but demure.

"Hence your reticence at entering society."

"What man is going to want to marry a monster?" The moniker was delivered harshly, as if she had heard it before. "I have no desire to walk about like some animal on display while the lords and ladies of the ton whisper behind their hands at my...disfigurement."

Judith left the curtain opened, as if she could chase away the darkness around Lady Henrietta by doing so, though as she sat on the window seat facing the young lady, she realized the darkness did not come from outside but from the inside. Still, a little light burned through. Despite the wariness in Lady Henrietta's gaze, Judith detected a sliver of hope that she would not turn away in disgust or horror.

"It has been my experience," Judith said, picking her words carefully. "That it is not one's outsides that make them a monster, but rather what lives inside. I have known men more handsome than you can imagine, and ladies whose outward beauty appeared completely flawless. Yet in the end, what lived inside of them spoiled whatever beauty their outsides held."

"A lovely sentiment," Lady Henrietta said, her smile turning sad. "Unfortunately, it does not stop them from ridiculing me, or viewing me as something worthy of their scorn, or worse—pity. My brother has approached several gentlemen in the hopes of making a match and not one has been willing to make an offer, regardless of how large a dowry James offers."

Lord Glenmor flitted unwanted into Judith's mind at Lady Henrietta's mention of a large dowry. Would he consider her? Judith's insides turned cold for reasons that had nothing to do with Lady Henrietta's scars.

"Perhaps it is a matter of letting people get to know you, allowing them to see beyond the surface."

"And is the ton in the habit of looking beneath the surface? It seems the people I have met are more prone to making snap judgments and leaving things at that."

Judith wished she could argue Lady Henrietta's point, or

offer a different view, but it appeared they were two peas in the same pod when it came to their opinions on society.

"I'm afraid I have little to offer in that regard. I had but one Season before my father fell ill." Before she returned to Havelock Manor with her tail tucked between her legs and her heart bleeding heavily from the grievous wounds inflicted.

"And did you enjoy your Season?"

"No. Not particularly."

"And yet you are to prepare me for mine and send me out into the fray upon my brother's request."

"So it would seem."

"He plans on throwing a dinner party, did he tell you? In one week's time. A small gathering meant to allow me to wet my feet before I plunge in head-first."

"No, he did not tell me of his plans." Judith swallowed "Do you know who will be attending?" Her heartbeat fluttered in her chest and she held her breath.

"He mentioned a few names. Particular friends mostly, people he trusts. Lord and Lady Alderset have accepted. Lord Glenmor and his mother, Mrs. Laytham, with whom I understand you have an acquaintance."

Butterflies flitted about inside of her at the prospect of seeing Lord Glenmor again so soon.

"The Duke and Duchess of Franklyn, as well as their daughter, Lady Susan. Also Viscount Pengrin, I believe."

Judith's heart slammed against her rib cage. A sharp, sudden assault of such force it made her wonder how her bones did not shatter from the impact. The humiliation she had gone to great lengths to put behind her rushed through her all over again, and it was all she could do not to run from the room to avoid it. Perhaps she would have, if only her limbs would comply, but instead they turned numb. Useless.

"You appear as thrilled with the prospect as I." Lady Henrietta smiled and this time the gesture struck Judith as genuine, but she remained too rattled to take more notice of it than that. "Perhaps we are well suited after all."

"Perhaps so." The words came out strangled while she mentally calculated how quickly she could pack her bags and hire a conveyance to take her back to Havelock Manor. She had taken this position thinking she could leave her past behind her, only to discover it lurked just around the corner, waiting to pounce when she least expected it.

"I don't suppose we can convince my brother to halt this madness, much as I wish we could. He is determined, and when James makes up his mind on something, it would be easier to move a mountain than change his course. Perhaps if we attend the dinner party together, it will not seem so daunting. Or frightening."

And there was that hope again, lighting Lady Henrietta's gaze and lifting her voice up at the end. A question directed at Judith, a challenge for her to accept.

Though she wanted to run—oh, how desperately she wanted to!—looking at the young lady before her, scarred and fearful and feeling like a monster when she was clearly anything but, was more than Judith could stand. She could not abandon her. She could not be that much of a coward.

But how would she ever get through an evening with Lord Pengrin and Lady Susan, knowing what they had done to her?

"**M**y lord?"

Benedict glanced up from his desk and blinked, his eyes blurry from perusing the accounts for the Glenmor estates and the costs accruing for the necessary renovations at Maple Glen. Despite keeping a tight control on expenses, the numbers added up until they came perilously close to shifting into the red column.

"Yes, Titus? What is it?"

Titus stepped into the study holding a silver salver where a lone vellum envelope sat in the middle. "A letter has come for you. It is marked urgent."

Benedict's stomach dropped into his boots. Nothing good came marked as urgent. A fact quickly discovered over the past two years while he dodged Uncle Henry's creditors, stealing from Peter to pay Paul while still maintaining a suitable roof over everyone's head. He was certain he'd paid off the last of them. Had another crawled out of the woodwork? With trepidation, he picked up the envelope and turned it over in his hand. It bore a "C" on the seal.

Crowley. Finally! Benedict had sent several letters to the man requesting a meeting with no response.

"Thank you, Titus."

He waited for the butler to leave and the doors to close solidly behind him before he broke the seal and unfolded the vellum. The note was short, but far from sweet.

Crowley had refused his request for a meeting. Refused him! Was such a thing even possible? The man was his agent in this godforsaken enterprise. The go-between. If he refused to meet, how was Benedict to converse with his partner? How was he to discuss the matter of selling his shares back to the company and getting his signature on the papers that would severe their business arrangement and allow him to move on? All the monies invested into the Western Trading Company had been given to and managed by Crowley, to the best of Benedict's knowledge, and now the man had simply disappeared? Unconscionable.

He read on, but what came next offered him little comfort.

The light lunch Benedict had eaten an hour earlier at the insistence of his mother turned over in his stomach as the words swam before his eyes.

It could not be.

He re-read the letter once more. And then a third time. Nothing changed.

According to Crowley, the Western Trading Company's profits, which he had previously promised were on the upswing had, in fact, plummeted. There would be no payout on the investment this quarter.

Benedict closed his eyes and took long, slow breaths to steady his rapid heartbeat. "It's not the end of the world," he whispered to the empty room. The words rang false. He had been counting on the promised payout from the last quarter to cover the majority of the renovation expenses now due. Without such a return on his investment, he was left with...nothing.

"Ben, dear?"

His eyes snapped open and he turned to the door to find his mother standing there. He hadn't heard her come in. "Mother." He swallowed and steadied his voice, but the tone didn't sound natural as it echoed in his head. "Do you need something?"

"I just wanted to let you know I was leaving to pay a few calls. Are you all right?"

"Yes. Yes, of course." He forced a smile, but felt like the worst kind of fraud the longer he held it. "Everything is fine." If one considered teetering on the edge of ruin, *fine*.

"You look a little pale. You need to get out-of-doors, dear. Why don't you go for one of your walks? The fresh air will do you a world of good, I'm certain."

"Thank you, Mother. I will."

He bid her good-bye, waiting until the door closed behind her before he crumpled the letter in his hand, destroying it, as much as the words within now threatened to destroy him.

Chapter Eight

"Should I feel insulted, Glenmor? It has been less than a week."

Benedict glanced over the rim of his glass to Lord Ridgemont. Though the man smiled, there was a question in his gaze that indicated he did not appreciate having someone check up on the well-being of his employees. Benedict didn't particularly care about Ridgemont's injured pride, however. He needed to see her.

Further proof he'd lost what was left of his mind.

Likely, Miss Sutherland did not appreciate being checked up on. She'd made her wish to be independent quite clear in her actions, but fool that he was, as his world was crashing down around him, the only thing he could think to do to improve the situation was to see her. To let her outward calm and straightforward manner soothe him. And, in a sense, to say good-bye.

He'd admitted to himself on the walk over from Glenmor House that a part of him had been holding onto the ridiculous hope that if he was able to sell his shares in the Western Trading Company and invest the monies into the railway, that maybe—just maybe—he would not have to marry for money. That he could marry a woman of his choosing based on nothing more than the fact that he enjoyed her company and wished to spend the rest of his days in it.

But that had been nothing more than a foolish dream. He saw that now.

"I assure you, there is no insult intended," Benedict said. "I am certain Miss Sutherland is in the best of care. However, I have promised her uncle, Sir Arran, I would ensure such with my own eyes."

Ridgemont crossed his arms over his chest. "It is highly improper. I am not in the habit of leaving young ladies in the company of men without a proper chaperone."

"Feel free to leave the door wide open with a maid sitting in the room. I have no interest in incurring her uncle's wrath or injuring her reputation with any impropriety."

Ridgemont stared at him a moment then scowled. "Very well. I will see if she is amenable to it. But I will have a maid stationed outside the door, and the door will remain fully open. I will give you ten minutes to visit with her. Not a second more. Are we in agreement?"

"Of course."

Ridgemont gave him a hard look, issued a curt nod, and turned on his heel. His footsteps echoed down the hallway until they disappeared altogether. Benedict dropped to the sofa and let his head fall into his hands. His world spiraled around him until hope faded to nothing more than a distant memory. How had this become his life?

"Lord Glenmor?"

He looked up and pushed to his feet, the sight of her rocking him back on his heels. She wore a plain dress of deep forest green, void of any ruffle or bows or other such adornments. But something was different. His gaze roamed over her.

"Your hair?"

She reached up and touched the thick curls draped over her shoulder self-consciously, her gaze dropping to the floor. "Oh, yes. Lady Henrietta's idea."

"It's beautiful." The words rushed out of him before he could stop them.

A pretty pink hue tinged the apple of her cheeks, but she said nothing in response to his compliment, leaving an awkward silence developing between them. Finally, he cleared his throat. "I thought to drop by to see how you fare."

"I am quite well, thank you. But you really needn't—"

"I know." And he did. If anyone was capable of looking after herself, it was Miss Judith Sutherland. Did everyone in her family not press on about how capable she was? What a steady mind she possessed?

"And yet here you are."

He smiled and some of the worry he'd carried with him into Ridgemont House receded. "Here I am." He waved to the chair next to where he sat on the corner of the sofa. "Will you not sit?"

She glanced at the open door. He could see the skirt of the maid just at the edge of it, sitting sentinel. "For a moment, I suppose."

He waited until she was seated before retaking his seat.

"How is Mrs. Laytham?" she asked.

"Quite well, thank you. I have received word from your cousin Charles that your aunt, Lady Elmsley, will be arriving in town shortly. You will be most pleased to see her, I'm sure."

"If time permits." She gave him a steady look. "I am not at my leisure here, after all."

A subtle reminder of her position in the household. It struck a chord with him. He did not care for the idea that she served anyone. She deserved a better life than that. A life it would have been nice to share with her. Something he could freely admit to himself, now that any possibility of that lovely dream had been dashed.

"Of course. Though I'm certain Lord Ridgemont will not begrudge you a visit from your family. He allowed you to see me, after all and I am not family at all."

She smiled, but the motion did not reach her dark eyes. God help him, but he loved her eyes. So deep and dark a man could get lost in them and wish never to be found. The idea appealed to him immensely. There was nothing he would like more than to escape his life and become lost in her.

She interrupted his reverie. "Forgive my saying so, but you do not look well, my lord. Have you been under the weather?"

"Oh—no. Not exactly."

"And what does that mean...exactly?"

A small laugh escaped him. "I received a little bad news about an investment I made." And by little, he meant completely catastrophic.

"Nothing too serious, I hope."

"Nothing I cannot overcome." By marrying the likes of Lady Susan or one of her ilk and being miserable for the rest of his days.

"I am happy to hear. I understand you and Mrs. Laytham will be attending Lord Ridgemont's dinner party."

He had intended on passing on the invitation. In light of Crowley's news, he was in no mood for merriment or parties or smiling and being charming while he desperately held the tattered pieces of his world together. But looking at Miss Sutherland as she sat with her back straight and her hands folded in her lap, a hopeful expression on her pretty face, he found himself nodding. "Yes, we will."

If his world was to fall to pieces around him, he at least wanted a pleasing view and the balm of being near Miss Sutherland for as long as possible. Soon enough, she would be torn away from him. He wanted to soak up whatever time he had left, even if each moment was all for naught.

She leaned forward in her chair. "May I ask you for a favor?"

"Anything."

She smiled again and this time the soft gesture warmed her eyes until it reminded him of dark chocolate. Sweet and enticing, though he doubted she had any idea the power of the gentle curve of her lips. "Should you not like to know what it is first before you agree?"

A light laugh escaped him and the tension pounding in his head eased a little. "I am certain you will not ask anything that would overtax me."

She had such a lovely light in her eyes. Funny, given how dark they were, but it was there, shining brilliantly out at him. How lovely she was. Coming here to see her had been the right thing.

"When you come to the party, could you perhaps seek out Lady Henrietta?"

"Seek her out?"

Miss Sutherland nodded and leaned forward in her seat. "She is likely to hide in a corner, I'm afraid. You see..." Her voice trailed off and she glanced toward the open door before adjusting her seat to bring her closer to him. The scent of daisies filled his senses and he had to force himself to concentrate on what she said next.

"As you may know, Lady Henrietta suffered a great loss when her mother and father were killed in a fire."

Benedict nodded. He remembered hearing of the ghastly event a handful of years ago, though the details had always been sketchy. "Yes, I recall."

"What only a few know, however, is that while Lady Henrietta survived, she did not do so without suffering injury. Injuries she is quite self-conscious about, hence her reticence at entering society. She fears everyone will look upon her and think her a monster and nothing could be farther from the truth. She is a sweet young woman. Perhaps if you spoke to her and treated her as if her injuries did not exist, it might ease her anxiety."

"I think that could be easily accomplished. I will be my most charming self." She lifted an eyebrow and he laughed again. "Fair enough. I suppose I have not been overly charming of late. But I will do better."

Miss Sutherland smiled at him and in that moment, she could have asked him for the moon and he would have gladly climbed up into the sky and grabbed it for her. Ah, such power her smile wielded.

"You are very kind, Lord Glenmor. I'm sorry if I have been harsh with you. I suppose my past experiences with titled gentlemen have left me a bit sour."

Her comment caught him and he started to inquire further as to what she meant, but a commotion at the entrance to the receiving room drowned out his words.

"Good heavens! What is this rumpus occurring without my knowledge? Ridgemont!"

Benedict stood and spun on his heel at the commanding voice punctuated by a loud bang—the result, he realized, of a walking stick striking the gleaming hardwood. An older woman, splendidly attired in a plum traveling dress and plumed hat, stood inside the doorway of the receiving room glaring at them.

Within seconds, Ridgemont joined her, slightly out of breath. He brought himself up short as he entered the room, giving the woman a brilliant smile that looked more painted on than heartfelt. Benedict couldn't blame him. The stern set of the lady's mouth and the flash in her eye was enough to make grown men quiver in their boots.

"Lady Dalridge. I was not aware you had returned."

"Obviously." The statement came without so much as a glance in the marquess's direction. Instead, her gaze landed directly on Benedict. "And might I inquire as to who you are and why you are in my receiving room with this young lady?"

"Aunt, may I present Benedict Laytham, Earl of Glenmor, and Miss Sutherland. You'll remember I mentioned her in my last letter. Lord Glenmor, Miss Sutherland, it is my great pleasure of introducing you to my great-aunt, the Viscountess of Dalridge." When his great-aunt did not respond to their murmured greetings, Ridgemont continued. "Lord Glenmor is well acquainted with Miss Sutherland's family and came by to see to her well-being."

The older lady's ice-blue gaze did not relent. "Was there a concern for it?"

"Not at all," Benedict said, hoping to quell the lady's ire as she walked farther into the room, each step punctuated by her walking stick.

"And yet, here you are."

"I was in the neighborhood," he offered with what he hoped was a charming smile.

For a brief heartbeat, Lady Dalridge hesitated then arched one silver eyebrow. Benedict's smile faltered, dying a slow death.

"I knew your uncle. Lovely man until he lost his mind."

"Thank you," he said, though he was unsure whether it had been meant as a compliment.

The viscountess turned toward Miss Sutherland. "And might I assume then, that you are the companion Ridgemont has hired for my great-niece?"

Miss Sutherland's hands tightened where they clasped in front of her. "I am." Despite the nervous edge to her expression, her voice remained calm. She released her hands and offered a curtsey. "It is a pleasure to meet you, my lady."

"Hrmph." She turned back to Ridgemont. "And what,

pray tell, are you doing leaving this young lady alone in here with the likes of him?"

Benedict opened his mouth to take offense to her depiction of his character but Miss Sutherland nudged him and gave a small shake of her head. He closed his mouth and held his tongue.

"The door was left open and Magda sat just outside. There was nothing improper about the situation, I assure you," Ridgemont said.

Her gaze slithered over her great-nephew then back to Benedict. "Then it appears I have arrived just in time. Your views on propriety need improvement, my boy." Benedict wasn't sure whether the comment was meant for him or Ridgemont. Nor did she clarify before moving onto her next issue. "And have I heard correctly that you intend on throwing a dinner party a few days hence?"

Ridgemont straightened. "Yes, that is my intention."

"And you think that is wise?"

"She cannot hide in her room forever, Aunt."

The viscountess's expression softened slightly but she said no more on the subject, turning her attention to Miss Sutherland. "My dear, I shall assume Lord Glenmor is satisfied over your well-being and therefore I see no need to tarry here any longer. Come. Take me to my great-niece. If Ridgemont is determined to throw her to the wolves, we have much to prepare."

Miss Sutherland gave Benedict one last look and mouthed a silent thank-you before trailing behind Lady Dalridge and disappearing down the hallway. How odd that her removal from the room could take with it all the warmth, leaving him cold and weary.

Ridgemont turned to him. "Well. That went well, I think."

Chapter Nine

"It is an improvement, I will grant you that," Lady Dalridge said as her gaze slid over Judith's attire for the dinner party. The two gowns she had brought with her had been deemed unsuitable for the dinner party and therefore hasty arrangements had been made, altering one of Lady Henrietta's gowns to make due. "But I still think it inappropriate that she attends."

Despite Lady Dalridge's ongoing disagreement that Judith should not be attending such an event, citing her position within the house, the more she tried to draw a line, the more effort Lady Henrietta put into erasing it.

"Auntie—"

"Hen, my sweet, it is simply not done," Lady Dalridge stressed when Lady Henrietta first broached the request that Judith attend the dinner party with her. "While I mean no disrespect to you, Miss Sutherland, you are an employee. What will people think?"

Lady Henrietta held her ground, showing Judith that despite her fear of the whispers and ridicule she was likely to suffer, her internal fortitude had not wavered. "Miss Sutherland is the grand-daughter and niece of knights, Auntie. Both of who were great heroes and rewarded for such by the King. The Dowager Countess of Blackbourne is to become her aunt. She has had one Season out in society. She is hardly without consequence."

"Regardless, she is in our home as your paid companion."

"She is my friend." Lady Henrietta lifted her chin in a militant angle, reminding Judith a little of her cousin Patience when she got a particular idea in her head. "And I will not attend this ridiculous dinner party without her."

Part of Judith wished it would come to that. She would much rather stay in Lady Henrietta's room for the duration of the event and avoid the spectacle altogether. Especially since learning her cousin, Patience, would not be attending despite Lord Ridgemont issuing a last minute invitation. Unfortunately, last Season, Patience had a most unfortunate encounter with Lady Susan that resulted in her cousin giving the other woman a rather public dressing-down, followed by dumping a half-empty bowl of punch over her head. The debacle had sent Patience into strict exile in the country before the Season had ended.

Had it not been for the Dowager Countess of Blackbourne smoothing the matter over with Lady Susan's parents, the Duke and Duchess of Franklyn, likely her cousin would still be cooling her heels at Havelock Manor.

As much as Judith wished to see her cousin again, she was thankful for not having to deal with the added stress of what might occur should Lady Susan prove less forgiving than the Duke and Duchess. An occurrence, given Judith's knowledge of the young woman, that was quite likely.

"Besides," Lady Henrietta continued, turning her attention to Judith. "You look far too lovely to be hidden away, Miss Sutherland. You are a true beauty once we wrestle you out of those dreary dresses you insist on wearing."

Over the past couple of years, she had become accustomed to seeing herself in much dowdier attire, a look she'd adopted to keep others from taking notice of her. If they didn't notice her, they could not target her. She caught her reflection in the full-length mirror from across the room. Dressed in cream satin, with her hair piled atop her head, and pearls wrapped around the base of it to help hold it in place, she had no such hope of fading into the background tonight.

"It was kind of you to lend me the dress."

Lady Henrietta smiled, an uncommon event. "It is a selfish thing, I'm afraid. I am hoping you will shine so brightly you take all the attention away from me."

Judith's stomach curdled.

She had hoped beyond hope that both Lady Susan and Lord Pengrin would turn down the invitation to the dinner party, but such was not the case. On the rare occurrence that the Marquess of Ridgemont issued an invitation, one did not turn their nose up at it. Likely Lady Susan and Lord Pengrin were chomping at the bit to walk through the doors of Harrow House and get their first look at the reclusive Lady Henrietta. Judith's heart ached for the young woman. What agony she would suffer under the scrutiny of others, the pains she took to keep her scars hidden from prying eyes.

"I think I would like to go down to the drawing room early, Miss Sutherland, so I might stake out a quiet corner and remain there until the dinner bell is rung."

Lady Dalridge waved a hand as if to brush aside Lady Henrietta's plan. "No, no, no. You must make an entrance, my dear. People are expecting it. There is no reason for you to hide yourself—"

"There is every reason, Auntie." Lady Henrietta's words came sharp and unexpected. "I do not wish to be a spectacle. I am sure you can understand."

Lady Dalridge's face softened, no longer the indomitable

lady of the house, but a loving aunt who wanted the best for her great-niece. She stepped forward to where Lady Henrietta sat on the stool by her vanity and placed a gloved hand to her niece's cheek, just above where the scars hid beneath her hair. "If you are a spectacle, my dear, it will be due to your exceptional beauty and sweet nature and for no other reason. You have nothing to hide from."

But she did. Judith understood that more than most. Society could be cruel. And many of its constituents cared little about beauty and sweetness unless it was their own. Their stock and trade came in tearing others down, finding their weaknesses and exposing them for all to see. They thrived on humiliation and whatever entertainment they could derive from inflicting it upon the unsuspecting.

Judith braced herself for the night to come. She could not, in good conscience, allow Lady Henrietta to face that alone. "I am ready whenever you are, my lady."

Lady Dalridge sighed and her hand fell away. "Very well. Do as you see fit. But you cannot hide forever, my dear. Your brother is determined to find you a proper match by the end of the upcoming Season."

"Then my brother is to be sorely disappointed. No man of consequence is going to want to saddle himself with someone like me, no matter how much he tries to sweeten the pot with the size of my dowry. And I have no interest in marrying a man who can be bought so easily."

Judith smiled. Despite her quiet nature, Lady Henrietta had a mind of her own. Lord Ridgemont would have his work cut out for him if he thought to try and change it.

Lady Henrietta stood and slipped her arm through Judith's. "Come. Let us appease the masses with their gaping stares and get this torturous night over with."

I f he were to jab himself in the eye with the poker leaning against the stone hearth of the fireplace and well within his reach, would she notice? As Lady Susan continued to blather on—Benedict had lost track of the conversation, but assumed the main topic remained herself, as that seemed to be a particular favorite of hers—he guessed that no, in all likelihood, she would not notice.

Perhaps if he toppled over, having inflicted grievous injury to himself, and spilled his drink on her bright pink gown, she might take notice, but he was still not convinced it would be enough to stop her tongue from wagging incessantly.

Good Lord above, how would he ever survive marriage to this woman? She would talk him to death before they could ever procure an heir. It did not help matters that the very idea of such procurement left him cold. It wasn't that she was a hideous sort, but the more she spoke, the less attractive she became and the less the idea of marrying her, bedding her, and spending a lifetime with her, held even the smallest appeal.

To distract himself from the potentially unbearable future that awaited him, Benedict glanced across the room to the shadowed corner where Miss Sutherland sat with Lady Henrietta. Something about Miss Sutherland's posture and the way she had set her chair reminded him of a centurion guarding the gate. If anyone hoped to get to Lady Henrietta, they would first have to bypass Miss Sutherland, and she did not wear the most welcoming of expressions.

She was, however, wearing a lovely gown that enhanced the warm tones of her skin—skin that was much more on display than he had ever seen before. The cream color of her dress gave her an ethereal appearance. Her upswept hair showed off the graceful sweep of her neck and fine bones of her jaw. How his hand itched to touch her flawless skin, to run his fingertips along the angles, press his lips where her neck curved into her collarbone. Breathe in her scent.

Warmth spread through him, liquid and wonderful. He closed his eyes and savored the sensation, a respite from the constant gnawing of Lady Susan's nasally voice.

"Lord Glenmor, do I bore you?" Lady Susan's sharp tone snapped him back to reality and he opened his eyes to find her glaring at him, her mouth pinched, but for once not in motion. Small miracle.

"No, not at all. I, uh, was merely absorbing what you were saying. Much easier done with my eyes closed. Allows me to concentrate better." He gave his most charming smile but it withered and died before it reached full potency. Unlike Charlie, he could not turn the charm on at will. Where was Charlie for that matter? He scanned the room. The moment his friend had laid eyes on Lady Susan, he'd made himself scarce. Judas.

"Hmph. Well perhaps you can stop your concentration long enough to honor my request?"

Benedict's attention snapped back to Lady Susan. "Your request?"

"That you escort me over to Lady Henrietta and provide a proper introduction. I cannot believe Lord Ridgemont has not yet sought me out and done the honors. It is highly improper and I will be sure to let him know."

Of that, he had no doubt. Lady Susan appeared to hold the strong belief that the world revolved solely around her.

"You have been introduced to her, I assume?"

"Yes, upon my arrival," he said. Though their interaction had lasted only long enough to exchange a few pleasantries before Lady Dalridge pulled her grandniece away and presented her to the other gentlemen in the room. "Were you not?"

Lady Susan stuck her nose in the air. "No, but Mother and I arrived late. A lady likes to make an entrance, after all."

Lucky for Lady Henrietta. She'd been saved from the same fate Benedict had suffered for the past few hours, listening to Lady Susan drone on like a hive of buzzing bees. Very well, perhaps it hadn't been a few hours, but it had certainly felt like it.

He glanced around the room at the other guests. It was a safe grouping for the most part. Lord and Lady Alderset were both blind as bats and likely unable to see the scarring Lady Henrietta went to great pains to disguise. He had no fear his mother would do or say anything to make the young lady uncomfortable and Lord and Lady Phillipot were old friends of the family.

The only uncertainty in the guest list fell with Lord Pengrin and Lady Susan, along with Lady Susan's mother, the Duchess of Franklyn, though Mother had attached herself to the Duchess. In truth, the duchess's attitude appeared to have mellowed somewhat, according to Mother, ever since the incident at Sheridan Park several months earlier that left a man dead.

As for Lord Pengrin, Benedict knew very little about the man, save for his penchant for gambling. While not uncommon amongst their set, word was the man did not have a knack for the games and lost more at the tables than he gained. How much truth there was to the rumor, however, Benedict could not say. They shared few acquaintances and where Benedict had not spent much time attending the events of the past few Seasons, he'd had little contact with the man personally.

"Lord Glenmor!"

His attention shot back to Lady Susan who stood before him appearing more than a little peeved. Or was that her normal expression? "My apologies, Lady Susan. You were saying?"

"I was saying that you could make the introductions.

Come." Lady Susan slid her arm through his, leaving him no option but to comply. Not that it took much convincing. The short walk brought him closer to Miss Sutherland and, as much as he told himself he should avoid her for the sake of his own sanity, he could not help but want to be near her. The dichotomy was nothing short of torturous. Yet it was the sweetest kind of torture he had ever experienced.

"Lady Henrietta, Miss Sutherland." Benedict nodded at the ladies and gave a brief bow. "It is my great pleasure—" he managed not to choke on the word, "—to introduce you to Lady Susan, daughter of the Duke and Duchess of Franklyn. Lady Susan, may I present to you Lady Henrietta Harrow and Miss Judith Sutherland."

Lady Susan waved a dismissive hand in Miss Sutherland's direction. "Oh, I met Miss Sutherland during her first Season several years ago. I have not seen you since, however. Why is that?" Lady Susan's smile reminded Benedict of a snake about to strike. He half-expected her tongue to shoot out and test the air.

Miss Sutherland stiffened. "My father fell ill. I remained at Havelock to care for him."

"Do you not have nurses and servants to do such work? But oh," she said, continuing before Miss Sutherland could answer. "You are a servant, aren't you? Quite a downturn in your affairs, is it not?"

Miss Sutherland's cheeks bloomed with color at Lady Susan's cutting remark. Charlie had been right. The woman truly was a vile sort. Guilt filled him at having brought her over to meet them, only to have her spew such caustic remarks.

"It is lovely to see you again, Miss Sutherland," Benedict interrupted, saving her from the need to answer. For what answer could she give that Lady Susan wouldn't immediately jump upon and twist around? "I hope both of you are enjoying the evening thus far?"

"We were, up until recently," Miss Sutherland answered in her smooth, steady voice.

Lady Susan's shoulders shot back as if she'd been struck. Her sharp smile turned more acidic and in a blink, before Benedict could interfere, she switched targets. "Lady Henrietta, it is so lovely to finally meet you. I have heard so much about you. How odd we have never met before. I am most surprised you have not yet been presented at court."

"Are you?" Lady Henrietta's quiet tones filled the tight space around them. "Why is that?"

The pinched expression Lady Susan had worn only moments ago returned. The response left her nowhere to go, no answer to give without causing direct offense. Lady Henrietta had rendered her mute. It was a beautiful thing to behold. He would need to remember that in the future.

Benedict smiled. "I, for one, am simply pleased that you are both here with us now."

Lady Henrietta returned his smile and her hand lifted to pull her soft curls closer to her neck before her gaze slid away from him. "Thank you, Lord Glenmor. That is very kind."

No, he wanted to say. Kindness would have been never approaching you with this harpy in the first place. He sighed and glanced at Lady Susan as an uncomfortable silence settled around them. Was this what his future held? Is this what it would take to save the Glenmor fortunes in the wake of his new state of ruin?

And was it a price he was willing to pay?

Chapter Ten

If it was a sign Judith had been waiting upon to prove her return to London had been a foolhardy idea, likely this was it. She glanced down the length of the table at the guests. Unfortunately, she had been separated from Lady Henrietta, though she was pleased to see her cousin, Charlie, and Mrs. Laytham on either side of her. She would be safe with them. Regrettably, that left her bookended by Lord Glenmor and, far worse, Lord Pengrin.

She took a few mouthfuls of the oyster soup, but could manage no more. Close proximity to Lord Pengrin made the sumptuous food Cook had prepared curdle in her belly. Her hand trembled as she tried to navigate the spoon to her mouth and she feared spilling the contents down the front of her borrowed gown.

Oh, to be anywhere but here! Sitting outside in the cold without benefit of a shawl or boots on her feet would have been preferable to being at the same table as Lord Pengrin, let alone directly to his left. But she had not been given that option, and as such, must now endure his company, as well as his veiled jabs at her current situation.

"A lady's companion. And what, pray tell, led you to lower yourself to such a degree?" He kept his voice low; his easy smile on full display so that anyone looking their way would think they shared a most pleasant conversation. How had she ever fallen for such false charms? How had she not seen him for the snake in the grass he truly was?

"My choices are none of your concern, my lord."

He continued as if she had not spoken. "Of course, I suppose it isn't that much of a fall, is it? It isn't as if you are truly one of us, born to this world, as it were." He made a small motion with his hand, his fingers spreading to indicate the others sitting at the table around them. "Your grandfather was merely handed a knighthood after crawling out of the furrows of battle. Not a true aristocrat."

Her jaw ached from where she clenched her teeth. She set her spoon down and clasped her hands in her lap until the fine bones ached from the pressure. How much longer must she suffer this man's company?

"My grandfather was worth a hundred aristocrats and my father a hundred more on top of that. They were good men. Honorable men. Such character you know nothing about."

"My, my, such a barbed tongue. I do not recall tasting that upon you during our previous encounter." The words slid out of him like oil, clinging to her skin.

Bile burned in her throat and her heart battered the inside of her chest like a hummingbird stuck in a cage, desperate to escape. The same such need overwhelmed her. She could not do this. She could not sit here and suffer through this man's inference of their past for anyone to overhear. She needed to flee. Her feet pressed against the floor, but before she could push away from the table, a warm hand covered hers.

She froze. For a fleeting moment, she feared the touch was Lord Pengrin, but her body's swift reaction tempered just as quickly. Something in the touch soothed her, lifting the haze in her brain enough for her to realize she was safe. It was not Lord Pengrin.

Lord Glenmor's hand released hers. She missed his touch instantly, but forced herself not blindly grope to find it again.

"Are you quite all right, Miss Sutherland?" His voice whispered near her ear, though a sideways glance indicated he had barely turned his head in her direction. She wasn't even sure she saw his lips move. Had she imagined his inquiry? No, she couldn't have. The ghost of his touch remained upon her skin where it seeped through the thin material of her gloves.

"I am fine, my lord."

"Has he said something to upset you?"

His very existence upsets me. But no, it wasn't his existence that caused her such upset. It was the reminder of her foolishness to have fallen for his lies. To have let her guard down so far that she nearly ruined herself for him. Would be ruined, if he spoke aloud to anyone about it. But she held her tongue. What would Lord Glenmor think if he knew how far she had fallen? The idea he would look at her with derision, or worse —pity... She could not bear it.

She stared at her plate. "No, my lord. He did not."

"I hope you do not take offense when I tell you that I do not believe your claim."

She turned in time to see a warm smile crease the corners of his eyes, though not enough to remove the concern that lived in their blue depths. How strange to see such a thing directed toward her, from him of all people. She had been convinced he did not care for her, and yet since her arrival in London he had been nothing but kind. Her instincts told her she could trust him, but past mistakes counseled caution.

Lord Pengrin leaned forward to speak around her. His voice lifted enough for others within close proximity to hear. "Glenmor, I hear you have returned to London in search of a well heeled bride."

The muscle in Lord Glenmor's jaw jumped, but it remained the only hint the viscount's words had any effect. "As you will be too, I assume, given your lack of luck at the gaming tables."

The words slid out, quiet and deadly. Judith had not seen this side of Lord Glenmor before. In her interactions with him, he had been distant and polite, then warm and engaging. But this was something different altogether. This was a man who would brook no disrespect. Lord Glenmor was a man who stood up to the likes of Lord Pengrin without hesitation, effectively shutting him down until the dandy was left with no other choice but to offer a stiff smile and return to his own business.

"Forgive me, Miss Sutherland. That was likely not well done."

"On the contrary, my lord." She longed to reach out and touch his hand, to feel its warmth and strength. To lean into him and the sense of safety he had effectively cocooned her in. Wanted to, but didn't. Trust was a hard thing to come by in her world. "I believe it was quite well done, indeed."

He smiled at her again and a warm tingling spread through her. She trod on thin ice. Ice that, experience had taught her, could crack and plunge her into the frigid waters below without warning.

"Try to eat some soup," he suggested, returning his attention to his own meal, though the aftereffect of his gaze lingered. "I would hate to see you waste away due to the likes of Lord Pengrin. He is hardly worth a ruined appetite."

She lifted her spoon and complied, though her appetite was no longer affected by Lord Pengrin, but rather by the nest of butterflies flitting about in her stomach. She pressed a hand against her belly, but the little creatures refused to settle.

· · ·

Once the gentlemen had finished their brandy and cigars, they rejoined the ladies, much to Benedict's relief. He found he had little in common with the other lords present, whose gravest concerns revolved around recently purchased horseflesh, the difficulty in keeping good help, and the current state of politics. They blustered on for the most part on the first two and came to no real consensus on the last one. Was it any wonder nothing seemed to get done in the House of Lords?

No matter how long Benedict spent apart from the world he'd grown up in, he had yet to acclimate to the point where he placed the same level of importance on matters of frivolity. After all, did it really matter who had what tailored where and by whom? In the end, a jacket was just a jacket. If it kept you warm, was that not the most important thing?

Not that rejoining the ladies altered the conversation much. Many of them partook in the most recent gossip. Who had been seen with whom and which young lady was rumored to be considering which fortunate, or unfortunate, gentleman. Who wore what and whether they approved of it or considered it ghastly.

But at least in mixed company he could rest his gaze upon Miss Sutherland and remind himself there was at least one sensible person in the room who understood that the important things had little to do with gowns and jackets and tailors and pompous politicians, and everything to do with more immediate concerns. Putting food on a table, a roof over your head. Family.

"Would you sing for us, Lady Henrietta?" Lady Susan asked, clapping her hands to garner everyone's attention. "I'm certain a lady of your skill and disposition sings like an angel."

Lord Pengrin stepped forward and placed a hand upon his heart. Or where his heart would be. Benedict remained on the fence as to whether the man actually possessed one. There was something rather cold lingering about his roguish demeanor. "What a splendid idea. Certainly a lady with such external beauty has a voice to match."

Benedict cringed at the over-the-top compliment and the slithering way it was delivered. He had never quite mastered the skill, if one could call it such. He preferred a more straightforward approach. What his method lacked in romanticism it made up for in truth.

Lady Henrietta, for her part, appeared like a deer caught in the sights of a huntsman's rifle. Miss Sutherland, who remained at the young woman's side, reached over and took her hand. Sympathy filled him. What were they thinking, drawing such direct attention to her? Had they not caught on yet that she did not care for it? The fact that she spent most of the meal with her head bowed, speaking little, and most of the time before that sitting in the shadows, should have been indication enough.

Miss Sutherland caught his gaze and shot him a pleading look. *Fix this!*

Unable to resist her, he offered the first thing that came to mind. "Miss Sutherland, I hear, has a very clear voice that is a joy to behold. Would you join me at the pianoforte? I play a little and should not make too much of a mash of it."

In truth, he had no idea if Miss Sutherland could carry a tune in a bucket and likely she had no wish to be made the center of attention any more than Lady Henrietta did, but his choices on helpmates in this regard was limited.

"You flatter me, my lord," Miss Sutherland said and he was quite certain she gritted her teeth. This did not bode well, but she stood regardless, giving Lady Henrietta's hand a squeeze before she let go. "My skills are middling at best, but perhaps your abilities on the pianoforte will make up for where I am lacking."

Benedict offered her his arm to escort her to the splendid instrument that took up a corner of the room. He leaned down, breathing in the scent of daisies and loveliness that he had come to associate with Miss Sutherland and no other.

"Do you sing then?"

"Somewhat." Hardly encouraging. "Do you play?"

"Somewhat less."

She set her shoulders back and slid him a glance as they reached the instrument of their doom. "Well this should be quite the spectacle then, shouldn't it?"

Once Miss Sutherland was seated, Benedict flipped the tails of his dinner jacket out and sat down on the bench next to her, grinning like a fool. He really shouldn't be so thrilled about the prospect of what they were about to do, but he couldn't help himself. It felt like a bit of mischief and he could not recall the last time his life allowed for such a thing. "Indeed."

They leafed through the music sheets available to choose a simple tune they could pull off without massacring it completely. Though it proved dreadfully difficult to concentrate on choices when Miss Sutherland sat so close he could feel the warmth of her. She had a way of leaving him in a rather impassioned state.

He pulled out a sheet from the middle of the pack. "Will this do?"

"As well as any other." And then she stiffened. Benedict glanced up sharply, just in time to see Lord Pengrin sit next to Lady Henrietta. What was it between Pengrin and Miss Sutherland that agitated her so? He wanted desperately to ask, but did not imagine she would divulge the answer. Their relationship had improved to the point where she had looked to him for assistance, but he doubted it had reached such capacity that she would reveal her secrets to him.

Just as well. Such closeness would only serve to increase

this strange need he had for her. A need that would never be fulfilled. No point in taunting himself with something he could never have.

Benedict plunked out a few notes and soon enough Miss Sutherland joined in. Her voice surprised him, filling the room with its smooth, clear tone. Much like her, it was strong and without unnecessary embellishment. His playing, unfortunately, was far less so. It was a sad and true fact that none of the Laytham children had inherited their father's musical ability. Only Roddy had shown signs of promise, but he had not lived long enough for it to come to fruition.

His fingers slipped onto the wrong keys, his concentration subjugated by memories of Roddy, as often happened when his little brother infiltrated his thoughts, bringing with him the burden of guilt and failure. Miss Sutherland's voice grew stronger, drowning out his errors until he could get himself back on track. A pang of regret filled him once it ended. The chances of such an event reoccurring were slim to none.

"Brava!" Lord Pengrin said, standing up and cheering over the sound of the other guests' polite clapping. "Another, please!"

As much as he would have preferred to spend the rest of the evening sitting next to her, the cost of making herself the center of attention was written across Miss Sutherland's lovely face, pulling her mouth into a tight smile. Yet she had willingly done so to protect Lady Henrietta from the same fate. His opinion of her rose another notch, as did his interest. She was an intriguing and complicated woman. Full of goodness and hidden depths he only wished he had the opportunity to plumb further.

But he would not. Could not. Reality robbed him of the joy he'd experienced only a moment ago.

"I think you have all been subjected to my lack of skill on the pianoforte long enough," he suggested with a smile, stepping away from the instrument and offering Miss Sutherland a hand. He walked her back to Lady Henrietta, forcing Lord Pengrin to give up the seat to her and effectively ending his bid to win over the affections of Ridgemont's sister.

At least he hoped it ended his efforts. Something about Pengrin rubbed him the wrong way. It would be a shame if Ridgemont considered Pengrin as a suitable match for Lady Henrietta's hand in marriage. Benedict did not doubt that was the viscount's ultimate goal. If his gambling debts were as rumored, likely he could use the dowry Ridgemont offered.

Benedict let out a slow breath. Perhaps he should consider Lady Henrietta after all, as Mother suggested. She was a pretty thing, though a bit shyer than he would have liked. But perhaps if they grew comfortable with one another that would ease. And certainly a little timidity would be a vast improvement over Lady Susan's penchant for narcissism and spiteful cruelty.

He offered Ridgemont's sister a warm smile. "Are you enjoying yourself this evening, Lady Henrietta?"

She looked up at him—only briefly—but returned his smile as she pulled her blonde hair closer to her neck. He could see the burn scars where a few threaded over the edge of her jawline, a soft pink and white. "More than I had expected to, my lord. And you?"

Benedict nodded. "I find I share your feelings in that regard."

But as he said the words, his gaze slid to her companion and once again, the wish for a different kind of life pulled at him. What would happen if he followed this desire? If he allowed such a dream to lead him where it wished? He looked away.

No. He mustn't entertain such impossible ideas. It would only make what he must do all the harder.

Chapter Eleven

"Lord Pengrin seems quite the charming sort," Lady Henrietta said as Judith entered her bedchamber the following morning with a tray of all her favorites for breakfast, having met Mrs. Pierce in the hallway and taken over the chore.

Lady Henrietta was still abed, though wide-awake and smiling in such a way Judith wished she could share her joy. Instead, her words stabbed into Judith's chest like jagged shards of ice.

After her duet with Lord Glenmor—had she really done that?—Lady Dalridge had all but dragged her away from Lady Henrietta, claiming she hovered like a vulture over her great-niece, giving the appearance she would swoop down and peck the eyes out of anyone who approached. It wasn't true of course, unless the person was either Lord Pengrin or Lady Susan.

Besides, Judith could tell from the way Lady Henrietta played with her hair, pulling it more tightly toward her neck, that the attention made her uncomfortable. She waited until Lady Dalridge became occupied in another conversation before rejoining Lady Henrietta, but by then a good hour had passed. An hour that gave Lord Pengrin free rein to work his charms upon the young woman, with great success it appeared.

The very idea made Judith sick to her stomach.

"My lady, Lord Pengrin is—"

"Quite surprising," she finished, though Lady Henrietta's claim was a far sight different than the warning Judith had planned to issue. "Why, he did not comment on my scars even once, nor did he stare like some of the others, such as Lady Susan. Did you know she came right out and asked me if I was in pain while waving her fan at my neck? Imagine such forwardness! It was awful. I was very thankful when Lord Pengrin stepped in and redirected the conversation so I did not have to answer her."

Judith swallowed. "How thoughtful of him."

"Do you know much about him, Miss Sutherland? You have had one Season, after all. Likely you have met many of the people in attendance last night." Lady Henrietta sat up in bed.

Judith set the tray across Lady Henrietta's lap then concentrated on removing the coverings from the dishes. What did she say? To divulge the truth would mean revealing her own behavior and, as much as she wanted to protect the young woman, she could not say the words. They stuck in her throat and refused to come out.

"I have a brief acquaintance with some of them, but nothing beyond that."

Lady Henrietta glanced up, the forkful of scrambled eggs hovering in her hand. "Save for Lord Glenmor."

She swallowed. "Yes, I suppose."

"It was very gallant of him to rescue me from performing. I would have been mortified. You must thank him for me when you see him next."

"Oh, I don't expect to see him again any time soon." He had a bride hunt to put in motion after all. And she had already instructed him that he did not need to check up on her, though his visits had been the highlight of her employment thus far. Not that she minded being companion to Lady Henrietta. The young woman was lovely and kind, but the restriction of not being able to come and go as she pleased, and to be at someone else's disposal, still left her out of sorts. She longed for her freedom, something she had not expected when she'd sought out the position.

"Do you think Lord Pengrin will call on me?"

The question caught Judith off guard. She had only known Lady Henrietta for less than a fortnight, but in that time, her reticence at being seen by others outside her family, or attending public events had seemed well ingrained. Yet one evening in Lord Pengrin's company and she was ready to cast her fears of being made a spectacle of aside for the hope of being in his company.

Her loathing of the man only increased. What was he planning to do? Humiliate Lady Henrietta the way he had her? Likely not. Lord Ridgemont would have his head on a spike if he tried. Perhaps something even worse. Perhaps he meant to marry the young lady for her dowry and shackle her to a lifetime of unhappiness? Because that was what it would be. Once he had what he wanted, the true Lord Pengrin would show his face and it would not be charming or handsome. It would be ugly and riddled with deceit. Lady Henrietta deserved better than that.

She had deserved better than that.

But he had never intended to marry her, had he? He'd only made her think so to get what he wanted. To have a bit of fun. Then to blame any assumption he had created on Judith's wishful thinking.

"I made you no promises. Do you recall a time when I did?"

She couldn't. That was the worst of it. His promises were implied through his actions, for what else could they mean if he had been a true gentleman? Yet, in hindsight, he'd always been careful with his words. Leading her on without promising anything. Making her believe with a touch of his hand, a secret smile, a searing glance that she read as something other than what it was. Which had been his intention, and which she had fallen for all too easily. She had been the proverbial lamb who allowed herself to be led to the slaughter.

"Miss Sutherland?"

Judith gave herself a mental shake and turned her attention back to Lady Henrietta. "Forgive me. I suppose I am still a little fatigued from last night."

Lady Henrietta picked up her previous question. "Do you think he will call on me?"

"I cannot say."

But she could hope. And her hope was that Lord Pengrin would steer his attentions elsewhere. At the time he'd toyed with her, Judith had little in the way of male protection. Her father was far away, her cousin, Charlie, busy chasing whatever lady had caught his attention at the time, and Uncle Arran had still been living in Scotland, nothing more than a childhood memory. At least Lady Henrietta had her brother.

But if Lord Pengrin did not stay away from Lady Henrietta, what recourse did she have? She was but an employee. Would her warnings hold any weight? Would they believe the truth if she were bold enough to reveal it? No. It would be assumed, as Lord Pengrin had informed her afterward, that the fault had lain with her. That she had tried to jump above her station and trap him into a marriage she would not otherwise have been able to achieve.

He would tell his lies and Judith would be ruined. How could she save Lady Henrietta from him when she couldn't even save herself?

B enedict let his fingers run along the spines of the books lining the shelves of Marcus Bowen's library wall. The room, with its large oak desk, also doubled as his study in the townhouse three doors down from Glenmor House.

He found it an uncommon kind of comfort, having one's friends and family so close. He had not expected to experience such a thing again after Father and Roddy's death. After their passing, he had been left scrambling, wishing desperately to return home to Mother and Abigail, but being refused. Mother, who still convalesced, feared if he returned from school, he would contract the fever that had taken her husband and youngest son. She had forbidden his return and instead of being with them in their time of need, he'd remained safely abandoned at school, with only Abigail's regular letters to keep him connected.

They did not offer much comfort, nor had he yet cultivated the friendships he now had to help ease his pain. The other students, most of whom carried titles and family lineages far loftier than his, looked at him as some sort of anomaly. He'd been ignored for the most part, and looked down upon when ignorance no longer suited them. He'd learned how to defend himself, both verbally and physically when needed, though mostly he'd kept to himself. Father had insisted the education Uncle Henry offered would serve him well in his life and as such, Benedict had held on, learned how to shut himself off from others, to step outside of the situation and see it for what it was. Unimportant. A small speck of time that would eventually become a distant memory.

Or so he told himself. Reality proved a bit different.

"Glenmor, forgive me for keeping you waiting," Marcus said as he walked into the room and immediately filled it with his quiet, commanding presence. For a man with no title and a rather enigmatic background, he carried within himself an authority most titled gentlemen wished they possessed. And it was Marcus, far more than the other two friends Benedict had inherited through his sister, who understood his common background the most.

For his part, Benedict straddled two worlds—the working class world he'd grown up in, and the high society world of London he'd been thrust into shortly after Father's death. Even now, with the title of Earl of Glenmor weighing on him, he still felt like a pretender to the crown, wading deep into a world in which he didn't fully feel he belonged.

The two men shook hands and Marcus waved them over to the table near the window, where they sat down. "Did you have any luck with Hawksmoor?"

Benedict scowled. "No. None. He was familiar with Mr. Crowley, though beyond admitting to that, he proved no help at all. Still, I cannot shake the sense that he knows more than he is telling, but the man is cagey and hard to read."

Marcus rubbed at his chin. "Hm. Hawk always keeps more information than he gives away. And what he does give away usually comes with a price. It is simply a matter of discovering what he wants in exchange. In the meantime, have you managed to reach Crowley after his last letter to you?"

Benedict had filled Marcus in on where things stood with respect to Crowley's refusal to meet and indication no profits would be forthcoming. "No, he remains elusive. I have stopped by his office twice now, but he hasn't been there, which makes me both curious and concerned." His assistant, a nervous little man who suffered from excessive twitching, was of little help as to when Crowley would return. "I have a bad feeling about this."

Marcus nodded in agreement as the afternoon sunlight poured over his dark hair until it shone, reminding Benedict of a raven. "Perhaps we should pay Hawksmoor another visit? He is usually more amenable to divulging information when he is beating me on the billiards table."

Benedict raised his eyes brows. "There is someone who can beat you on the billiards table?"

"It is generally an even match, provided I have my wits about me, but he's usually a bit more amenable when he believes he has won fair and square." Marcus stood. "We shall pay him a visit this evening. But first, let us go to Crowley's apartments. Perhaps he is holed up there. If we press him hard enough, he may give up the identity of this mysterious silent partner. It is worth a try, at least."

The two men took the Glenmor carriage to Cheapside. Crowley did not answer his door and after a short search uncovered Crowley's landlord, they interrogated him after promising to make it worth his while.

"Ain't seen 'im in about a fortnight, but 'e said 'e was leaving after the Yuletide. Didn't say where, jus' somewhere more suited to a gentleman of 'is station." The older man made a face, but otherwise did not seem overly fussed whether his tenant came or went. The information Crowley planned on leaving left a raw feeling in the pit of Benedict's stomach. Something wasn't right.

After slipping the landlord a few more pounds, he unlocked the door and allowed them access to Crowley's apartments, but the rooms yielded more questions than answers. Nothing appeared out of place.

Benedict turned in a slow circle.

"What is it?" Marcus asked.

"It's just that...it is surprisingly neat."

"That strikes you as unusual?" Of course Marcus wouldn't think so. His friend's desk was much the same way, not a paper or quill out of place. Work neatly stacked in proper piles, likely all set out in numerical or alphabetical order. Benedict had actually seen the man stop whatever he was working on to straighten a pile of papers that had become ever so slightly askew.

"Yes. Very unusual. If you had seen the man's office, you would know." Though on his last visit, Crowley's assistant had refused him entry, practically barring the door with his small, twitchy body. "The man is a bit of a disaster in that regard. To find his living space so tidy is nothing short of...odd."

"As if someone came in and cleaned up, you mean?" Marcus cast a critical eye about the place.

Benedict nodded. What did it mean? "Perhaps he has simply tidied up in preparation to move to other lodgings."

Marcus reached for a bureau drawer and pulled it open. It revealed a mess of underclothes and other sundry items, all of which were in the state of disarray Benedict had expected to see in the rest of the rooms.

"Odd indeed," Marcus stated.

Benedict took his time, scanning each nook and cranny in the room. Something poking out from beneath the bed caught his eye. "What is this?" He bent to retrieve it.

"Anything?"

Benedict nodded and handed a slip of paper to Marcus. "A receipt for what appears to be several custom made suits from a proprietor on Bond Street. It's dated two days before I sent him my missive, insisting that we meet."

Marcus raised an eyebrow. "Bond Street seems a little high end for the likes of Crowley, is it not?"

"One would think." Any time he had met with Crowley, the man had appeared rather unkempt, his suits pieced together without thought or care. The material had been worn and the seams frayed in spots as if he could not afford to replace them.

"I think I'd best send a missive to Hawksmoor," Marcus

said. "Perhaps with the right cajoling he will give us the information we need."

"Such as allowing him to trounce you at billiards?"

Marcus put a hand to his chest. "The things I do for my friends. I shall indicate I wish to speak with him on an important matter. Hopefully this will get us an audience sooner, rather than later. In the meantime, perhaps we might find some entertainment for ourselves this evening."

"Charles Elmsley has invited me to attend the theatre this evening. Join us."

"Ah, the theatre. I have not been in quite some time. It sounds like a most pleasant way to spend an evening."

Benedict said nothing in response. He did not care to admit that his only reason for going was to further his acquaintance with Lady Henrietta. Though, in truth, it was Miss Sutherland he hoped to see.

I f Judith had known she'd be attending so many events, she would have packed much differently. Not that her wardrobe would be considered fashionable by most of the ladies of the ton. Looking at the selections her cousin Patience had brought from Havelock Manor for her, it was a wonder anyone had noticed her at all during her first Season. She had resisted all of Aunt Beatris's attempts to truss her up in frills and fripperies. The idea of making a spectacle of herself had always left her uncomfortable. Unfortunately, her reticence now left her awash in a wardrobe of browns and grays with an occasional navy and plum thrown in for good measure.

Then again, the only one who had noticed her had been Lord Pengrin. Had it been her rather subdued wardrobe that made her such an obvious target for his put-upon affections?

"Honestly, Judith. I cannot believe Mother allowed you anywhere near London with these," Patience said, waving her hand at the dresses spread out over the bed. "You cannot honestly be considering wearing any of these to the theatre tonight."

"What other choice do I have? I can hardly expect Lady Henrietta to alter another one of her gowns."

"What of mine?"

Judith smiled. "Patience, I am at least four inches taller than you. I cannot wear a dress that reaches well above my ankles. Your poor mother would have an apoplectic fit and likely Lady Dalridge would relieve me of my position as companion on the spot."

"That, I would not mind at all." Patience flopped on the bed with a pout. "I hate that I cannot have you all to myself or that we cannot go here and there of our own accord. Why do you insist upon doing this? You know mother and father would be only too pleased to have you stay with us."

"As a poor relation? No, thank you. I love you all, but I do not love the idea of being anyone's burden."

"Family is never a burden, Judith."

Patience's words caught her. For all of her flightiness, occasionally she surprised by uttering something so wise, there was no way for Judith to refute its truth.

"I simply want to make my own way in the world."

"Isn't that what a proper dowry is for?"

The mention of her dowry, such as it was, brought Lord Glenmor to mind. Not that it was a huge stretch. It seemed thoughts of him were always within reach, ready to taunt her at the slightest provocation.

"My dowry is hardly going to bring the gentlemen of the ton running to beat down my door. And even if they did, I would not be interested. I have had my fill of titled gentlemen, thank you." She failed at keeping the bitter edge out of her voice.

"One bad apple cannot possibly spoil the whole barrel."

"It is indicative of the species, I believe."

Patience laughed, the sound light and airy. "Good heavens, Judith! They are hardly a separate species. I grant you, they are nothing like our uncle in many regards, but they are not all bad. Take Lord Glenmor, for instance? Or Mr. Bowen. And what about Lords Blackbourne and Huntsleigh, for that matter? All wonderful gentlemen and nothing like the despicable Lord Pengrin."

"Hush!" Judith glanced over her shoulder at the door that adjoined her bedchamber to Lady Henrietta's.

"What is it?" Understanding slowly dawned across Patience's pretty features. "No! Oh, no, Judith. She cannot! Not him! You must warn her."

"How can I?" Judith played with the buttons of her high-necked dress. Speaking of the subject always agitated her, even after all these years. "There is no way I can tell her what I know of Lord Pengrin without telling her *how* I know it. I simply cannot—" She stopped short, biting off the rest of her words. Only Patience knew the truth, and even she had been spared the most sordid of the details. "I cannot, Patience. I don't think the words would come."

Patience stood and walked to Judith, encircling her in her arms. "I'm sorry. I understand. And of course you need not speak of it. Perhaps we can find another way. Is there someone who may be privy to whom he truly is? Someone who we could enlist to relay the information to her?"

The night of the dinner party flashed in Judith's mind, the way Lord Glenmor came to her defense when Lord Pengrin mocked her. And again, afterward, when they tried to draw Lady Henrietta out to sing. Bit by bit he had shown himself to be colored by a different palate than Lord Pengrin and much as Judith fought against being fooled again, somewhere deep inside, she had begun to trust him. After all, was it not Lord Glenmor she looked to the instant she needed a champion to save Lady Henrietta from being made a spectacle of? Instinct had made her do it. But could she trust it? Her instincts had let her down before, after all. Still, Lord Glenmor may be the only avenue she had.

"Perhaps there is someone."

"Wonderful." Patience clapped her hands and turned back toward the dresses. "Now, what are we to do about making you presentable for the theatre this evening? You cannot sit in Lord Ridgemont's box looking as dowdy as a housekeeper."

Judith perused her choices and determined that unless Patience had the ability to work miracles, she had little choice in the matter.

As it turned out, Patience was indeed a miracle worker. She had chosen the plum gown and disappeared with it, hurrying off to enlist Mr. Bowen's housekeeper, Miss Cosgrove. She had traveled ahead of her employer's arrival to set up the newly purchased townhouse and hire the proper staff.

The young woman was a wonder with a needle and thread and had recently altered the Dowager Countess of Blackbourne's gown for her birthday party only a short while before. Toiling away as housekeeper to Mr. Bowen and Lady Rebecca was a true waste of Miss Cosgrove's talent, according to Patience. After her cousin returned with the finished gown, Judith was of a mind to agree.

Tiny seed pearls had been stitched along the bodice in an intricate pattern. A bodice that, upon putting the dress on, Judith realized had been lowered and brought in, lifting her décolleté to a rather daring degree. The sleeves had also been shortened and expanded with a lovely cream satin inset, creating a striped appearance. The same striping was repeated in the hem, now a flounce, and a cream sash added as well. How the woman had accomplished all of this in one afternoon boggled the mind.

With her thick hair coiled atop her head and threaded through with matching pearls, Judith truly felt as if she stared at someone else's reflection in the full-length mirror.

"Absolute perfection!" Lady Henrietta clapped her hands, then reached out for Judith's. "You will be a shining star tonight, Miss Sutherland and most successful at keeping all eyes on you and off of me."

Judith tried to smile, but the edges of her mouth caught before the expression could take flight. Being the center of attention appealed to her about as much as it did to Lady Henrietta. The idea of playing the part of buffer for her made her insides flip and flop until she feared eating, in the event whatever went down came back up. She'd hardly be a vision then, would she?

"That is kind of you to say, my lady."

"Honestly, must we be so formal? You should call me Hen. All my friends do." Lady Henrietta's smile turned downward. "Or they used to. When I had them."

It struck Judith, as it often did in moments like these, how lonely Lady Henrietta must be. Locked away by the fears and insecurities her scars had created within her. And what courage it must take for her now to step outside into the world once again, after hiding in the shadows for too many years. Judith wished she could tell her that the ton would be accepting, but she could not make herself lie in such a way and send the poor girl out into society unarmed. She was right to be wary. Right to be fearful of what they might say or do.

If only someone had given her such warning, perhaps she wouldn't have made the mistakes she had in trusting so easily.

Mistakes that had landed her here, playing the part of lady's companion.

"Lady Dalridge would not like me using such familiarity with you, I'm sure."

"Nonsense." Lady Henrietta lifted her nose in the air. "It is my name and I say who shall uses it."

Judith allowed a small laugh. Had Lady Henrietta not suffered such devastating scars, what a force she would have become. Could still become, if she allowed herself.

In that moment, Judith made a promise to herself she would do everything in her power to help Lady Henrietta —*Hen*—become the woman she would have been, before the fire robbed her of it.

"Then Hen it shall be," she smiled. "And you must call me Judith."

A mist appeared in Hen's eyes. "It is nice to have a true friend. Now come, let us venture out. The theatre awaits and my dear brother has confirmed that Lord Pengrin will be joining us in our box. Is that not the most exciting news?"

Any joy Judith experienced a moment ago fizzled and died. "Lord Pengrin is joining us?"

"Indeed. He and James are quite good friends. I think my brother will be most amenable should Lord Pengrin have an interest." She smiled and clasped her hands beneath her chin, the mist that had shone in her eyes only a moment before now lit with a hopeful excitement. "Do you think he is interested? I fear getting my hopes up. I am, after all—" She waved her hand near her scars, craftily hidden as best they could be beneath a high, open collar and the fall of thick, blonde curls. Her smile dampened.

Judith grabbed her hands, hating the fear and insecurity that so easily found its way back to the young woman, no matter how often she beat it back.

"You are beautiful, Hen. Inside and out. Any man who

cannot see that is a fool and not worthy of your notice. You would not want to be married to a fool, now, would you?"

Hen's smile returned. "No, I don't suppose I would."

"Then come. Let us go downstairs and meet Lord Ridgemont and Lady Dalridge. They are likely wondering what is taking us so long."

They were halfway down the sweeping staircase when Hen asked her, "Is there any particular gentleman you are hoping to see this evening?"

The question took her by surprise and one name hovered on her lips, but she bit it back and avoided Hen's pointed gaze. "No. No one in particular."

When she sought out Lord Glenmor this evening, it would be to enlist his assistance in getting Hen to see Lord Pengrin for the charlatan that he was. Nothing more.

Chapter Twelve

G enerally, Benedict enjoyed the theatre. He loved the spectacle of it, of being taken away for a couple of hours and transported to the world that existed on the stage. If the play was particularly well done, he managed to forget his troubles and actually enjoy himself. Tonight, however, was not one of those nights, though through no fault of the play. Drury Lane's rendition of Shakespeare's *The Twelfth Night* was entertaining and the actors on stage more than talented, but Benedict could not stop glancing upward and to his left, where Lord Ridgemont's box resided.

Just two boxes to the right of that was the former Glenmor box. Benedict had let the family's box go, considering it an unnecessary expenditure during their leanest times. Times that were on the verge of returning, if he did not act fast. Lord and Lady Kemptville occupied the box now. He pushed the melancholy away and turned his attention back to Miss Sutherland.

She sat in the first seat of the back row, unobstructed by the row in front of her. Resplendent in a plum and cream gown that set off her ivory skin and dark hair, he marveled that anyone had ever considered her plain. Nothing could be farther from the truth. She was an absolute vision. She was also very distressed. Her rigid posture and the constant worrying of her hands where they were clasped in her lap gave away her inner workings.

He glanced to the next row down from her. Lady Henrietta sat flanked by the indomitable Lady Dalridge on one side and the pompous Lord Pengrin on the other.

"A shame Mr. Bowen had to send his regrets," Charles Elmsley said as he leaned closer and peered in the direction of where Benedict's attention had strayed. "Who is it you keep staring at? Lady Henrietta? Really, Glenmor? Are you considering her?"

Benedict straightened and shot his gaze forward to the stage, embarrassed at being caught, but thankful Charlie had missed the mark. He didn't care to explain to the future baron that he had been in the process of lusting after his cousin. Such confessions would likely bring their new friendship to an abrupt end, and he rather liked Charlie. The man was easygoing and lighthearted.

"Word is," he said, in the hopes of distracting his companion. "Ridgemont hopes to marry his sister off this coming Season and is supplying her with a dowry meant to entice. It is difficult not to consider it."

Charlie craned his neck to get a better view. "And the scars do not put you off? I think I would fear touching her, worried it would cause grievous pain. Do you think it would?"

Benedict shook his head. Sometimes the thoughts in Charlie's head flew out of his mouth before any filter of propriety or the company they were in could disseminate it. "I could not say, though I wouldn't think so."

"And what of children? What if she is too damaged to carry a child? You will need an heir, you know. You are the last of the Glenmor line, are you not?"

Benedict squirmed in his seat. "Yes. Thank you for that

reminder." As if he didn't have enough pressure weighing upon him without adding propagating a proper heir for the title and lands to the list.

Lady Scallywaite turned in her seat and shushed them. Charlie flashed her a charming smile, then continued the conversation, though he did manage to lower his voice a notch.

"Well, if you are considering Lady Henrietta, you may want to hurry. It looks like Pengrin has the jump on you there, and I hear ladies find him to be quite appealing."

"Your cousin doesn't."

Charlie scowled. "True enough. Though she did, once upon a time. I think she may have had a hope there early on."

"Truly? For Pengrin?"

Lady Scallywaite turned once more and glared. Benedict offered her an apologetic smile, but he could not stop now. His need to plumb the depths of Miss Sutherland had grown too strong to be silenced.

He leaned closer to Charlie and lowered his voice to a whisper. "I would not have suspected Pengrin to be her type." Although that did go a long way to explaining her distaste for sitting next to the man at Ridgemont's dinner party, and her discomfort as she watched the viscount court Lady Henrietta now. His heart stuttered. Did she still have tender feelings for the viscount?

"I guess even someone as level-headed as Judith can have their heart captured by a charming man." Charlie grinned and wiggled his eyebrows.

Charlie should know. His friend's ability when it came to enchanting the ladies was almost as legendary as Lord Huntsleigh's, at least before Huntsleigh had married Benedict's cousin, Caelie. Now she was the only one who received the full force of his charm.

Still, it seemed unlike Miss Sutherland to have her head

turned so easily. "Did Pengrin lead your cousin to believe she could expect a proposal?"

Charlie shrugged. "I am not certain. She was rather tight-lipped about the ordeal or what became of it. I can say he did pay her a certain amount of attention and courted her to some degree, but nothing that could be outwardly construed as having singled her out. Though what he may have said to her in private, I do not know. Regardless, near the end of the Season his interest in her appeared to have waned and she was reluctant to even leave the house, insisting she be returned to Havelock immediately. I assumed she was nursing a broken heart."

"And did she return to Havelock?"

"Yes. Never to return to London, until now."

Benedict leaned back in his chair and considered this new information. What had happened between Miss Sutherland and Pengrin that had put her in such a state? A state that, from all appearances, continued to this day. And why had Pengrin harassed her in such a manner at Ridgemont's dinner? Benedict had only caught snippets of what the man had said, but based on Miss Sutherland's reactions he had not misread their interpretation. It was almost as if Pengrin had purposely taunted her. His estimation of the man dipped even lower.

When the intermission came, Benedict glanced over at Ridgemont's seats. Miss Sutherland was the only one who remained.

"Excuse me," he said, tapping Charlie on the shoulder. "I believe I will take a walk about."

Benedict wound his way through the theatre, dodging anyone who appeared to want to make his or her conversation longer than a passing pleasantry. When he reached the Ridgemont box, none of the others had yet to return. He stood at the edge of where the curtains parted, separating the box from the hallway behind it.

"Miss Sutherland."

Her head turned swiftly and her breath caught. She was jumpy tonight. How unlike her. Benedict offered her his warmest smile and entered the box without invitation. He took the seat one over from her, leaving an empty one between them for propriety's sake.

She returned her gaze forward. "You should not be here."

"Really? Why is that?"

She opened her mouth. She had the most beautiful lips. Wider, perhaps, than was considered fashionable, but ruby red and curled upward at the corners so that no matter how stern or serious her manner, her mouth always appeared ready to smile at the smallest provocation. How had he not noticed that before? The sudden realization made him want to lean across the empty seat between them and kiss her soundly. Repeatedly.

Ah, what a scandal that would create. What a relief it would be to surrender to it nonetheless.

"What will people think? Seeing us here?"

"I suspect they will think I stopped by to say hello to a friend."

"We are not friends."

"Are we not?" Benedict leaned forward and stared at the seats that lined the center of the theatre. "I had thought we had turned a corner in that respect. After all, we did perform together and one cannot accomplish such a feat when there is acrimony or discord between them. It sours the performance."

"Does it?"

"Absolutely."

"I had not heard such a thing. And truly, I'm not sure we can qualify what you did to the pianoforte as performing."

Benedict glanced at her from the corner of his eye in time to see a bewitching smile tug at those lips he so desperately wanted to kiss. How lovely she was. And surprising. "What would you call what I did to the aforementioned pianoforte?"

"Brutalizing, perhaps?"

He placed a hand over his heart and groaned, but he could not help his own smile. Somehow, that they had such an experience to share made his day all the richer. "You wound me! I think I did quite well, under the circumstances."

Miss Sutherland finally relented and let the promise of a smile spread across her features, lighting them up. "Perhaps. I suppose I did coerce the situation by looking to you for assistance."

"Indeed. It is truly all your fault. I was merely doing my duty as a gentleman and assisting a damsel in distress."

"Such knightly behavior coming from a Peer of the Realm." Her smile faded.

Benedict itched to reach out and take her hand, bring her smile back, but he had the sense that it had disappeared for the evening and in its absence, a dark curtain had fallen behind her deep, brown eyes. He softened his voice. "We are not all a bad sort."

"No?"

He turned toward her. "No. But I suspect your experience has made you believe otherwise."

She stiffened immediately. "Whatever do you mean?"

Benedict chose his words carefully. If he probed too deeply, she would shut the door to him and likely not reopen it. "I have the sense you and Lord Pengrin have had a falling out and that now you base your view of all gentlemen on your experience with him."

Her cheeks burned, a slash of red across warm ivory. He had hit the nail on the head, yet still, he remained in the dark. What exactly had Pengrin done? Was it, as Charlie believed, nothing more than a bruised heart? Miss Sutherland was a proud woman and likely would not have taken to humiliation or rejection well. But she was also a sensible one and he found it odd she would carry such a grudge throughout the years. Or that Pengrin would taunt her as mercilessly as he did because of it. There must be more.

"I cannot imagine any scenario where my business with Lord Pengrin becomes yours, my lord."

"I hate it when you *my lord* me."

Her eyebrows dipped and two grooves appeared between them. "What is it you would have me call you?"

"My family calls me Ben."

The redness in her cheeks burned brighter, or was that just a trick of the gaslight flickering light and shadow over her? "I am not your family."

But I wish you to be.

Hell and damn. Where had that come from? Perhaps coming up here to unravel the mystery of Miss Sutherland had been a mistake. He'd acted rashly. Unusual for him. But when it came to Miss Sutherland, rationality did not appear to factor into his decisions. Instead, instinct took over.

"My close friends also call me Ben. Or Benedict. Even Glenmor if you prefer. But not *my lord*. I dislike the sound of it."

Her shoulders loosened their rigid hold a fraction and she turned to look at him. "Why do you dislike it so? You are a lord. A Peer of the Realm. I would think such a high rank in society would bring you joy and fulfillment."

"On the contrary," he said, losing himself in the depth of her gaze. How did she do that? Make everything around them disappear, as if they were the only two people left in the world? "It has brought me nothing but misery and anxiety."

"Why is that?"

"Because it came at too high of a price." The words slid out of him and he wondered how she did that too, because until this moment it had been a truth he had kept locked up inside with all the bad memories that led to it and all the ones that came after. He had pushed the memories deep to ensure they would not escape, afraid if they did and he spoke them aloud, he would fall into a dark abyss, never to return.

Such a fall could not be countenanced. People depended on him. Failure in his duties was not an option. Was it not his past failures to save Father and Uncle Henry that had landed him in this position in the first place? Had either of them lived, he would not be here now, fighting to keep the family fortunes afloat and making a dismal mash of it.

Yet there it was, the truth, laid bare for her to see even if she didn't know exactly what she was looking at.

Benedict held his breath. Waited. Stayed silent in the depth of her gaze and lingered there far longer than was right or proper. Finally, she spoke. "Is your bride hunt part of the price?"

He should deny it. "Yes."

"And once you have found your bride with her ample dowry and marry a woman you do not love, will that not make the cost even higher?"

"People in our circle generally marry for some type of gain, whether it be financial or social."

"Not in your family. Not from what I've seen. In your family they marry for love."

He smiled and glanced down where his hand rubbed at the knee of his breeches. At some point, he had turned even farther in his chair to face her completely. Funny, he did not recall doing so. "I suppose you have the right of it there. Unfortunately, I do not have the same luxury. I have responsibilities. It falls to me to restore the Glenmor name and fortunes."

"And what if you recover your family's fortunes, only to realize it was not the most important thing in the end?"

Her words prodded the fear that had lived inside of him

since Uncle Henry's premature death shackled him with the title and the responsibilities that went with it. What if the path he had chosen, the decision he believed to be the right one, was wrong? What then?

He had no answer.

"Have you always been this wise?" he asked her, an attempt to divert her question.

"It is not wisdom," she said, the intensity in her gaze easing a bit, as if she had read his intent and allowed him the reprieve he'd requested. "It is common sense. What is more important than love and happiness? Your family is well cared for. Your sister has married Lord Blackbourne and your mother wants for nothing, save your happiness. Would the true let down not be in achieving this to please her?"

"It is not as simple as you make it sound."

His concerns were not simply about the immediate future —although now, even that hung in the balance. It was about his family's legacy. The one that should have been his father's, had his family not rebuffed him and left him to live the life of a common man, and die in much the same way. But Roderick Laytham had been anything but common. Intelligent, resourceful, and strong-willed, it should have been he who inherited the title Earl of Glenmor from Uncle Henry. His father would have known what to do to remove the stigma left behind by his older brother. Likely, he would have been able to prevent Uncle Henry's downward spiral in the first place.

Uncle Henry had loved his youngest brother and, despite the family objections, had never fully cut off his ties with him. It was his uncle who had ensured Benedict was schooled like a proper lord, and his uncle who took them in after the death of Benedict's father and brother. It was only then he learned how Uncle Henry had looked up to his little brother. Roderick had escaped the life set out for him and forged his own, while

Uncle Henry had been left to marry a woman he thoroughly disliked and wear a title he did not want.

Benedict could commiserate as now the same mantel rested upon his shoulders. It was up to him to pick up the pieces following Uncle Henry's scandalous death and try to reinstate both the title and fortunes to their former glory. Then, when the time came, his own son would not inherit the disaster Benedict had and would be able to choose a life of happiness instead of necessity and duty.

But how did he tell Miss Sutherland that? How did he make her understand? And why did it even matter? He let out a quiet breath. Perhaps if he could make her understand, he could convince himself it was the right thing to do. Because as things stood now, being with any woman other than the one who had so captivated his attention from their first dance, seemed horribly wrong and he could not fathom going through with it.

"Miss Sutherland. I feel I must tell you—"

"Glenmor!" Ridgemont's voice filled the box and his hand clapped down on Benedict's shoulder, jolting him from the cocoon he'd been enveloped in and yanking him back to the real world. "Imagine finding you here. Checking up on Miss Sutherland's well-being again, are we?"

Benedict forced a smile and straightened in his seat. "I thought I would come pay my respects to Miss Sutherland and your family and thank you again for the wonderful dinner party. I hope my abysmal attempt at entertaining the guests has not ruined your reputation as a good host."

Ridgemont laughed and folded his long limbs into the chair he had vacated earlier. Despite the relaxed nature of the man, Benedict had the sense from the warning in the marquess's gaze that he missed little and saw much. "I expect my reputation as a good host will remain intact. Provided I do not allow you near the pianoforte any time in the near future."

"I believe I can accommodate you there."

"Now, Miss Sutherland on the other hand," Ridgemont said, leaning forward in his chair to better look at her. "You may sing to your heart's content. You have a lovely voice."

Miss Sutherland's gaze dropped to her hands. "Oh no. I believe that was my one and only performance."

"Ah, well then." Ridgemont sat back in his chair and slapped a hand on his thigh. "We shall just have to make do with Cleveland's incessant humming."

Benedict raised an eyebrow at the suggestion Ridgemont's haughty butler did anything musical. "Cleveland hums? I find that hard to imagine."

"It may be more of a growl," Ridgemont admitted. "It can be difficult to tell sometimes. Ah, there you are! I worried I had lost you in the crush."

Ridgemont stood and Benedict followed suit as Lady Henrietta, Lady Dalridge and Lord Pengrin entered the box.

Pengrin shot him a hard look that drifted briefly to Miss Sutherland before returning to him. "Glenmor. What brings you up here?"

"A brief visit." He turned to the ladies and executed a smart bow. "Lady Dalridge, Lady Henrietta. You both look absolutely lovely. I hope you are enjoying the play."

Lady Dalridge scowled. "I have never cared much for Shakespeare. This performance has not changed my mind in that regard."

"Nonsense, Auntie. It has been quite entertaining. Are you here alone, Lord Glenmor?" Lady Henrietta smiled and her hand toyed with the curls at her neck, pulling them inward. Benedict forced his gaze away from the scars, not wanting to make the young lady any more self-conscious than she already was.

"No, I have a seat below and am joined by Miss Sutherland's cousin, Mr. Elmsley."

"You do not have a box?" Pengrin pretended to look surprised, though it was naught but a ruse, a way of pointing out Benedict's rather unfortunate financial situation.

"I do not. I am afraid I do not get to the theatre often enough to warrant it."

"A thrifty mindset," Miss Sutherland said, her voice drifting up clear and strong next to him, coming to his defense. "We don't see enough of that these days."

"I suppose you are in a far better place to judge that than I, Miss Sutherland," Pengrin stated with a nod of his head and a gracious smile that did not fool Benedict for a moment.

"Would you care to join us?" Ridgemont asked. "There are plenty of seats and I'm sure Miss Sutherland would love to have the company of her cousin, would you not?"

He should say no. Spending time in Miss Sutherland's company only hindered his goals, yet even as this truth flitted through his head, what came out of his mouth was something entirely different.

"I would like that very much," he said. "Let me go below and fetch Mr. Elmsley."

As he made to leave in search of Charlie, he determined he would use the time with the Harrows to consider Lady Henrietta as a viable prospect for his bride hunt. A boldfaced lie if he'd ever told one. How would he ever be able to pay notice to Lady Henrietta when every fiber of his being was all too aware of Miss Sutherland?

It was a mission doomed to failure from the start.

Chapter Thirteen

Agony.

There was no other word for it. She was in complete and utter agony. And forget the play. Despite using every last ounce of her willpower to keep her gaze trained on the stage, the players could have stripped down and paraded about in their underclothes and Judith would not have noticed.

How could she? Trapped in a box at a theatre with the man she despised above all others positioned in front of her, and the man she wanted more than any other sitting next to her. And while she wished Lord Pengrin would burst into flames and be rendered to cinder and ash, it was her body that had been set afire from being so close to Lord Glenmor.

When the evening began, she'd believed nothing could be worse than being forced to endure an evening in Lord Pengrin's company, watching him use his false charms to draw Hen under his spell. She had been wrong. As it turned out, sitting like a mute statue while Lord Glenmor engaged Hen in conversation proved even more torturous.

Not that he ignored her. He was very inclusive in his

conversations and directed an equal number of comments her way. But it mattered little how much he spoke to her or what attentions he paid. She was not the one he was interested in. It was Hen. Or, more precisely, Hen's dowry.

To make matters worse, she had grown very fond of Hen over the weeks she'd spent as her companion, and despite Lord Glenmor's reasons for marrying, she could say unequivocally that he would be a far better choice as husband then Lord Pengrin. Yet, while she wanted the best for Hen, the idea of the two of them together soured in her belly and made her heart ache.

Foolish, foolish girl! How had she allowed this to happen? Had she not promised herself she would refrain from falling for a gentleman's charms? And a titled lord, at that! They had their own agendas, and they stuck to them.

Still, Lord Glenmor, despite his title and his plan to marry for money rather than love, was nothing like Lord Pengrin. He was not greedy. He was simply desperate. An emotion she understood all too well. His past actions in helping her prevent Hen from becoming a spectacle at the hands of Lady Susan proved he was not mean-spirited. In truth, he had an innate kindness within him, a gentleness that unnerved her, and a humor that made her smile in spite of herself.

When he had looked at her earlier, it was as if they were the only two people in the theatre. The world even. She had not wanted it to end. And earlier, she was certain Lord Glenmor had been about to say something. Something rather important. Revealing. Potentially monumental. But Lord Ridgemont's return had shattered the moment, scattering it like fine shards of glass on the floor at her feet.

What had he wanted to tell her?

The question plagued her for the rest of the evening making it impossible to concentrate on the play, or the conversation swirling around her. A haze had descended, pushing out the extraneous, leaving a distant whispering in her ear that was close enough to be heard, but too far away to be understood.

An eternity later, the play finally ended and Charlie and Lord Glenmor said their good-byes. She longed to go with them, to return home to the Elmsley's townhouse on Chesterfield Street and burrow into the bed she'd often shared with Patience when they were younger and her father would allow her the occasional trip to London. Back then, the city had seemed a magical place filled with all kinds of enchantments. Now, it was only a reminder of her downfall and humiliation.

She had been wrong to return, to take this position, but she could not turn back now. Not while Lord Pengrin had Hen in his sights. The despicable viscount may have the rest of them fooled, but Judith had seen how truly black his heart was. How could she abandon Hen, knowing if she fell under his spell, it would lead to pain and heartbreak? The young woman had suffered enough in her life. Judith would not allow her to suffer more if she was in a position to prevent it.

"Each time we are together, I am more and more certain he has feelings for me," Hen said as they returned home and made their way to her room. Judith had waved off Lady Henrietta's maid. She needed time alone with her in the hope of dissuading her infatuation with Lord Pengrin, but it appeared the viscount had already entrenched himself in her affections and the mountain Judith must scale proved far higher and rockier than she'd anticipated.

"Has he said as much?" She stood behind Hen and undid the long line of buttons along the back of her dress. It was easier to speak to her from this vantage point. Less of a chance she would realize her warnings came from first hand experience.

"Not in so many words, but he has made claims to my beauty on several occasions. Imagine that!"

As Judith worked the buttons free, the remnants of the burns Hen had suffered became visible, rippling over her skin until it appeared unnaturally smooth in some areas, as if stretched too tight, then covered with angry welts in others. She claimed the scars did not cause her much pain any longer, but Judith found it hard to believe.

"Why would he not make such claims?" she asked.

Hen glanced over her shoulder. "Forgive me, Judith, but you can't possibly understand. You have no scars marking your body, turning you into a monster."

"You are not a monster, Hen!" Her claim stoked Judith's anger. Despite the physical reminder of what she had suffered, Hen's beauty could not be denied. How long would it take for the young woman to realize this and not allow others to make the determination for her? "You are lovely both inside and out. These marks on your body are nothing more than part of your story. They are not the total sum of who you are and anyone who thinks so is not worthy of your attention."

A sad smile touched the corners of Hen's mouth. "It is the scars that keep me from getting the type of attention I want, and instead, make me a spectacle. Yet Lord Pengrin does not make me feel that way. He makes me feel like...a woman. He makes me feel like the scars are not there."

The ground Judith stood upon shifted. She was losing the battle in keeping Hen from being taken in by Lord Pengrin. If it were any other man, she would believe the sentiments he spouted to Hen, because they were true. She was beautiful. She was lovely. How could she argue otherwise? To do so would be to say Hen was everything she feared—ugly, not worthy of love, a monster.

Lord Pengrin played a cunning game and excelled at it. He gave Hen exactly what she longed for—someone who saw beyond the scars to what lay beneath. Was that not what he had done to Judith? Made her feel beautiful? She'd spent her life feeling plain in comparison to Patience, whose beauty and vivacious personality made her stand out in any crowd, big or small. While Judith, with her quiet, more reserved nature, had always faded into the background.

Lord Pengrin had seen past that, however. He had singled her out. Made her feel beautiful. Special. Loved. Then he'd betrayed her and left her humiliated, feeling as if her near ruin was all her fault. If he married Hen, what then? Likely, he would reap the rewards of her family connections and substantial dowry, then cast her aside like an afterthought, returning to his wicked ways. The probability did not paint a pretty picture of Hen's future.

Judith rested her hands on Hen's shoulders. "We all have scars. Some of us carry them on the outside, where they are more visible. Others of us carry them on the inside. But they are there nonetheless, and every bit as present as the ones you can see with the naked eye."

"And where are your scars, Judith?" Hen turned around and let the gown fall to her feet. The welts on her body traveled over her right shoulder, thin tendrils where the flame had licked her tender skin to leave its mark before crawling up the side of her neck. Hen had admitted the fire had burned most of her hair off until she'd looked like a boy for the better part of a two years while it grew back. Now, it reached down her back in soft, silky waves any woman would be thrilled to have, yet she used it as nothing more than a shield to hide the parts that she could not fix.

Judith did not answer Hen's inquiry. She couldn't. Giving voice to what Lord Pengrin had done, reliving those moments when her own actions brought her the greatest humiliation, were beyond her ability.

"Come now. I know you have them. You have seen mine." Hen waved her hand at her neck. "Something has brought you

here and I do not think it is your bid for freedom and independence as you claim."

"What is wrong with independence and freedom?"

Hen smiled. "Nothing at all. Except it is a false claim. You
live here in my brother's home, basically at my disposal. Is that
independence? Freedom? Yet you stay, and I cannot help but
feel you are hiding from something."

"Then I suppose you have your answer," Judith said. "My
scars are on the inside."

"And will you not tell me what they are? Can I not help
you overcome them as you have helped me?"

Tears hovered in the corners of Judith's eyes until Hen's
image blurred. She quickly blinked them away. "No. I'm afraid
what's done is done. The only thing I can do is learn from
them and move forward as best I can."

Except that she wasn't moving forward, was she? She *was*
hiding—from her humiliation. From the fear of being blind-
sided by her heart and falling into such a trap yet again. No
matter how much she tried to claim she wanted independence
and to strike out on her own, the truth of it was, she was not
brave enough to face the world again. To put herself out there.
To put her heart in danger.

"And what have you learned?"

That love could be feigned. That her heart was not to be
trusted. That certain kinds of hurt lingered far longer than the
event that created them.

"I have learned that being a lady's companion suits me
quite well," she said, smiling past the knots in her insides as the
memories of her humiliation assaulted her from every angle.

This was not a lesson she wanted Hen to learn if there was
way she could prevent it. And yet to prevent it, she may need
to do the one thing she feared most—expose her own
humiliation.

Hawksmoor raised his eyebrows at Marcus Bowen's rather firm and direct request that he divulge what information he possessed about Crowley's apparent disappearance and the silent partner Benedict had been saddled with.

"That sounds very much like an order, Mr. Bowen."

"Does it?" Marcus grinned and looked over at Benedict. The man's ease at dealing with the rather enigmatic and disreputable Hawksmoor surprised him. Then again, the more he got to know Marcus Bowen, the more Benedict realized the adage was true. Still waters did, indeed, run deep.

Marcus rested his billiards cue on the table, the game having ended with Hawksmoor the victor, though now that Benedict knew what to look for, he realized Marcus had directed the contest to the desired outcome the entire time. Had Hawksmoor seen it too? It seemed unlikely the man often referred to as *The Hawk* would have missed it.

"Yes, it does." Hawksmoor's gaze traveled to Benedict and settled there. "What is it about Crowley that interests you so? He is a mundane little creature better left in the dark crevices of society he prefers to frequent. As for this silent partner you refer to, I'm certain the same is true."

"Crowley is the gatekeeper of the investment my uncle entered into before his death, an investment I continued with and now wish to extricate myself from. A feat I cannot accomplish if I cannot find Crowley and discover the identity of my silent partner."

"I take it maintaining this partnership will leave you in rather desperate circumstances. Am I correct?"

Benedict shifted his stance while pride and humiliation reared within him. But this was not the time to put on a brave face and pretend all was well. Not if he wanted Hawksmoor's assistance. If he held back, the viscount would know and likely be insulted enough to refuse to help. After all, there was nothing in it for him and the Hawk was not known for his altruistic nature.

"It will," Benedict admitted. Somehow, the admission made the weight on his shoulders a shade lighter. Ridiculous, since nothing had changed and even with Hawksmoor's help, there was no guarantee anything would.

"And you haven't the smallest inkling of who this partner is? None?"

"I do not."

Hawksmoor walked to the bar and poured a generous helping of brandy into the tumbler. "That seems a rather strange way to enter into a partnership."

"Such was not my doing. My late uncle entered into the partnership before his death. I merely inherited the circumstances."

"Hm." Hawksmoor leaned against the solid, mahogany bar, its smooth surface shining where lamplight spilled across it. How the man lived in such murk defied logic. The room, though large and beautifully furnished, held little in the way of natural light and the constant flickering from the lamps lit about the room created dancing shadows that gave no relief. It was as if the man lived in a cave. To hear Marcus tell it, he rarely left the gaming hell to join society since his older brother's tragic death years earlier.

"As for Crowley," Hawksmoor said. "He is a shady character, often preying upon gentlemen who find themselves in dire situations. Much like yourself. Or, as the case was, your uncle. When the late Lord Glenmor had exhausted his coffers, he used what was left to invest in the Western Trading Company. My understanding was that whoever this mysterious silent partner of his was, he also required an influx of cash, and used your uncle's desperate desire to recapture his mistress's affections to lure him in with promises of swift and large returns."

Hawksmoor's understanding of Uncle Henry's decisions and the reasons behind them did nothing to improve Benedict's mood. He loathed being kept in the dark. If Uncle Henry had only come to him, he could have counseled prudence. "Then you know who this silent partner is?"

Hawksmoor took a slow draw on his brandy but refrained from answering.

"Hawk?" Marcus prodded.

"What is in this for me, exactly? You come here, drink my brandy, take up my time, ask me questions, then demand answers, and yet I fail to see what any of this has to do with me or why I should help you."

Benedict twisted his mouth to one side. This did not bode well. "I suppose suggesting you do so out of the goodness of your heart would be asking too much?"

Hawksmoor raised one dark eyebrow. "That would be insinuating I have one. As I'm sure you've heard, such is not the case."

"What do you want? Money?" If so, Benedict might as well cut his losses now and leave. He had nothing to offer in that regard and he doubted Hawksmoor would care much for being paid in gratitude.

"I have money," he said, confirming Benedict's suspicions. "But I might like a proper introduction."

The man spoke in riddles. "To whom?"

"Not from you," Hawksmoor said, turning back to where Marcus stood, arms folded across his chest. "From you."

Wariness invaded Marcus's expression, as was to be expected when one negotiated with a wolf such as Hawksmoor. "And who could I possibly introduce you to that you do not already know?"

"I understand you have a lady in your employ. A Miss Cosgrove?"

Marcus's expression went from wary to cold. Benedict's gaze bounced between the two men. The conversation had veered off the path and left him stranded on the roadside wondering what the hell had happened.

"Absolutely not."

"You do not employ her?"

"I will not provide you with a proper introduction to her."

"That's rather definitive," Hawksmoor said, taking a slow drink from his glass.

Marcus wasted no time in answering. "It is. Leave her be."

"Should that not be the young lady's decision?"

"Not while she is under my employ and my protection."

The two men stared at each other, neither budging an inch. Benedict stepped forward. "I do not see what Miss Cosgrove has to do with the matter at hand, nor do I feel comfortable using an innocent to barter for what I need. If that is the only stipulation that will convince you to yield the information I require, then this conversation is at an end."

As if to punctuate the point, a ruckus erupted beyond the doors to Hawksmoor's office. He let out a harsh breath. "Son of a—! Do I not pay these people enough to do their jobs?" He brushed past Benedict and Marcus and threw open the door. "What is it?"

Benedict took a step forward in surprise. "Pengrin?"

A quite inebriated and somewhat disheveled Lord Pengrin pulled against the constraints of the two burly men that held him and lunged toward Hawksmoor. Hawksmoor, for his part, did not so much as flinch.

"I demand an audience!"

"It must be my lucky day," Hawksmoor muttered.

Pengrin struggled to free himself, but Hawksmoor's men

refused to release him. This did little to curtail the haughtiness in the viscount's next statement, however. "I understand you have cut me off at the tables."

"Then I am certain you also are aware that you owe me a significant debt. Such debt you have made no provisions in which to pay. I do not run a charity, Lord Pengrin. You pay me what is due or there will be consequences, your inability to play at the tables is only the beginning."

The threat hung heavy in the air.

"I will have the money soon," Pengrin stated. "I have—" He stopped and looked past Hawksmoor to Benedict. Whatever he'd been about to say became lost in the space between them.

"Do not come back until you have settled your debt," Hawksmoor said.

"You will regret this!"

"Doubtful," Hawksmoor said and nodded toward one of his men. "Remove him from the premises and see he does not return unless his pockets are filled to bursting with the money he owes."

Hawksmoor's foot caught the corner of the door and slammed it shut in Pengrin's face before turning to face Benedict. "Is there anything further I can assist you gentlemen with?"

Marcus glanced at Benedict, disappointment and resignation written across his sharp features. "Shall we go?"

Defeated, Benedict nodded. "I can see no other alternative."

Whatever negotiation they had undertaken for information had come to an end. He had nothing to offer, and Hawksmoor, as he had said to Pengrin, was not running a charity.

When it came to uncovering his silent partner, Benedict was on his own.

Chapter Fourteen

"You seem more subdued than usual, my lord."

Lord Glenmor glanced up and smiled, and though the expression never truly reached his eyes, they remained warmly fixed on her and brought on the familiar tingling in her toes that quickly traveled up her legs to pool uncomfortably between them. Judith had been most happy to see him arrive at the musicale and though she had warned herself to avoid him, she could not. He pulled her like a moth dancing about his flame.

"Do I often seem subdued?"

She returned his smile. "You are often much more understated than some of the other gentlemen."

"I'm not sure if that is a good or bad thing."

She shrugged and came to stand beside him as they stood on the fringes of the crowd invited to the Staythams' musicale. The performances had left much to be desired, but such was often the case when one imbued one's family members with more skill than they actually possessed. Judith grew weary of the constant little celebrations and events that went on about town this time of year. One would think with the House of

Lords being out of session and the Season not yet begun, London would be quiet and dull, but those who had not settled in their country estates seemed determine to keep the party going year long.

"It is a good thing," she answered. "Some gentlemen feel the need to strut about brandishing their accomplishments and such like a peacock on full display, but I find such things rather tedious after a while, don't you?"

"You're not overly fond of peacocks?"

"Not anymore, no."

"Ah. Then I suppose I am just the man for you." He winced. "That is to say—what I meant is that—"

She laughed. "I know what you meant. No need to tumble over your words."

He joined her laughter and Judith relished the sensation of being insulated within it, just the two of them. But all too soon, the moment passed and they returned their attention to the crowd milling about in front of them.

"I see Lord Pengrin continues his pursuit of Lady Henrietta."

The joy of the previous moment extinguished as quickly as it had appeared. "Yes, I am afraid he does."

"You do not approve?"

"I find his motives questionable and his character even more so." She left it at that. Anything further drew perilously close to revealing her own truth. What hope did she have of enlisting Lord Glenmor's assistance in getting Hen to see Lord Pengrin's true nature if she revealed her own as less than respectable?

"You speak quite plainly, Miss Sutherland. Have you always done so?"

She glanced down at the floor where her toes pointed out from the deep lilac gown she wore. Another of Lady Henrietta's cast-offs altered to fit her, to make her more presentable to society and less like a *dowdy school marm* as Hen had maligned the effect of the rest of her dresses. Judith could not claim to be fully comfortable in such garb, but the thrill at the appreciative gaze Lord Glenmor had given her was worth any discomfort. Perhaps she had a little peacock in her as well.

She nodded and smiled. "I have never held the opinion that a woman's thoughts should be kept to herself. I have a mind and it seems a waste not to use it."

"I couldn't agree more. I find I have learned much from listening to women's opinions." He smiled again, and again the sensation of warmth swam through her.

How was it he could warm her from the inside out with nothing more than a curving of the lips? Lips she longed to feel upon her own. Lips that had touched hers every night in her dreams since that moment at the theatre. But no, those dreams had started well before that, hadn't they? They had begun in the carriage on the ride to London when the carriage axle cracked and tossed her into his arms. She had believed he disliked her back then, but somewhere along the way, had realized such was not the case. He had simply hidden his emotions.

Something she had vast experience in.

"You are staring, Miss Sutherland."

Heat seared her cheeks and she looked away, horrified at having lost herself, caught up in daydreams she had no business entertaining. "Forgive me!" The words squeezed out in a rush before humiliation strangled her.

Lord Glenmor held his hands behind his back and stared out at the other guests, his tone no more serious than if they were discussing the weather. She saw all this from the corner of her eye, for there was nothing that could make her meet his gaze now.

"No need to apologize. I find I am often fascinated by people's mouths."

She winced. Oh dear Lord above. Please make it stop. "Truly?"

What else could she say? Perhaps nothing, but it was such an odd statement and standing there silent, dying of humiliation at being caught out doing exactly what he claimed he enjoyed doing himself was more than she could bear.

"Truly. In fact I find myself staring at yours on a regular basis."

Her erratic heart pounded fiercely, bruising her ribs from the inside out. What did he mean? What did any of this mean? They had been having a lovely conversation and somehow it had veered off and placed her on unsteady ground.

"Lord Glenmor—"

"No, no. Don't respond. I just thought I would mention it, as it seems to be something we share. It is good to have common interests, don't you think? If we are being truthful," he continued, and in her fascination at his admission and the casual way in which he spoke, she forgot herself and lifted her gaze to meet his once again. "I find myself thinking of your lovely mouth quite often."

"You do?"

His gaze dropped to her mouth. "Yes. Too often to be proper, I'm afraid."

"How often is too often?" Perhaps such things were commonplace and she had simply been unaware. And perhaps if such feelings were commonplace, then she could convince herself they meant nothing and go about her life.

"Every minute of every day."

Oh dear.

"I cannot seem to help myself. You are in possession of a rather enticing pair of lips, Miss Sutherland. Ripe and pleasing with the most wonderful words always tripping off them. And when you smile, it is as if I have been lost in a fog and suddenly see a brilliant ray of light beckoning me out of the gloom."

The expression on his face turned painful and his brow furrowed. "And now I've gone and scandalized you, making it so you will never wish to speak to me again, haven't I?"

"Was that your hope?"

He gave an almost imperceptible shake of his head. "No, I'm afraid my dearest hope was to someday kiss those lips."

Now she truly was scandalized. It was positively wonderful.

"I see." Except that she didn't, not really. For how could a man like Lord Glenmor think of her in such a way? Ordinary, unremarkable *her*.

"Now who is guilty of speaking plainly? I owe you an apology. I do not know why I admitted all of this to you, except that the words sit on the tip of my tongue and whenever I am near you, I struggle to keep them from leaping off. Tonight, it appears, I have lost that battle. Can you forgive me? Or should I remove myself from your company with all due haste?"

"No, don't go," she whispered. Oh please, don't go. If she was a light in the fog to him, he was the sunlight that warmed her heart. Without his presence in London, surely she would have withered and died. Knowing he was near, that she had someone she could speak to, go to for assistance, had made her life here more tolerable. "I could not bear your leaving."

He glanced at her briefly then looked away and nodded. "Then I shall stay."

W hat had possessed him? Had he lost his mind? No. Not his mind. His mind was perfectly intact, if somewhat crowded with thoughts of Miss Sutherland that overlapped everything else. She would be thoroughly scandalized if she knew it was not just her beautiful mouth that occupied his mind, but every other inch of her body as well. No, it was something else he'd lost, more than his mind. His heart.

She had stolen it. Quietly and completely. And as much as he suspected it was in good hands, it was not in the hands of the woman it needed to be. He had meant to hold the fragile organ safe and give it to the woman he married, in the vain hope that he could turn a monetary exchange of vows into one that would grow into love, or at the very least, warm regard.

But his plans had faltered. Not intentionally. He had tried to prevent it. Tried to push her from his mind, but it appeared when he did so, his feelings for her had migrated downward and settled in his heart. Some went even farther along then that and settled in his groin, but that was neither here nor there. One torment at a time, thank you.

Perhaps he could have stayed on course if he hadn't caught her staring at his mouth with the same hunger he experienced whenever he stared at hers. Did she feel the same all-consuming need as he? Did she wish to throw caution and duty and every last speck of propriety to the wind and lose herself in his arms? To kiss him until every inch of her skin was aflame with desire and want?

Oh, bloody hell. He shifted in his seat.

This was not good. This was as far from good as he could get. In fact, it wasn't even on the same continent as good.

It was almost a relief when the guests began their departures from the Staythams' home. He had not taken the carriage. He spent too much time already in stagnant activity and any excuse to stretch his legs and move was more than welcomed. It would take all of five minutes to walk from the Staythams' to his own home if he kept up a brisk pace. If anything, he embraced the cold night air with enthusiasm, in the hopes it would cool his ardor over Miss Sutherland.

Though likely nothing short of an ice bath in the Thames would cure him of that.

He shook his head. What a fool he had been to speak with such open honesty to her. What if she believed there was a chance for something to develop? What a lark. As if something hadn't already bloomed between them.

But it could not go beyond words. Despite his claim, or his feelings, he must make it clear to Miss Sutherland that she could hold no hope in that regard. *If* she held such a hope. He could not be certain. His brow furrowed. Should he ask her? It would be nice to know he was not alone in this madness. To hear her say the words. To feel them wrap around his heart and—

He closed his eyes pushed the image away. No. No, absolutely not. It would not be fair. Would it?

The sound of a horse's hooves striking the road dragged him abruptly from his thoughts of Miss Sutherland. He looked up only to discover he was on the verge of being trampled. A large, black beast bore down on him. Its rider, dark as midnight, sat hunched over its neck and made no move to veer the steed from its course. The image imprinted in his mind as his brain screamed for him to move. He sprang backward but not quite far enough. The horse's muscled chest knocked against him with brute force, throwing him back. In the distance, someone screamed as he landed hard against the cobblestones and the air rushed from his lungs.

How much time passed as he lay there, flat on his back staring up at the star-filled sky? He could not say. Cold seeped through his coat and into his flesh and bones as his mind replayed the event over and over again.

He had come within seconds of being trampled to death.

A death, he was certain, that had been the rider's ultimate goal.

Chapter Fifteen

"Lord Glenmor!" Judith fell to her knees next to the earl's still figure. Their carriage had barely stopped when she'd opened the door and vaulted out of it, catching her balance on the slick cobblestones. She ran to him, heedless of how she may appear or who saw her, and grabbed his hand, afraid to touch him anywhere else. "Are you hurt?"

His eyes were open and staring up at the night sky. For a flicker of a moment she feared the worst, but then he blinked once, then twice and relief rushed through her.

"No, I do not believe so."

The words rasped out and he sucked in air like a man submerged too long underwater. Lady Dalridge and their driver arrived then, cutting off any further inquiry. "Lord Glenmor, are you quite all right? Can you stand?"

He didn't answer immediately. His gaze traveled down to his boots and Judith's followed with it. He tapped his toes together then apart. Lifted one leg slightly, then the other. "I appear to be in working order." He motioned to their driver. "Perhaps you could give me a hand up?"

By then, others who had left the party approached and

Judith could hear the whispers. Lady Dalridge turned and addressed them, putting an end to any erroneous supposition with her commanding tone. "A runaway horse. Frightful thing. His Lordship is fine, are you not, Lord Glenmor?"

Judith refused to release his hand as the driver assisted him up on one side and she the other. She leaned in. "Are you really?"

"Somewhat rattled, but otherwise in shipshape," he said before turning to address the onlookers who would likely be telling tales about the event for the next few days, until something else occurred to tickle their fancy. "Lady Dalridge has the right of it. Fine as a fiddle, I am."

"Did you see who was riding?" Someone called out.

"I'm afraid the only thing I had time to see was the broadside of a horse. But no matter. No harm done."

But there was something in his tone that caught Judith something that lingered just behind the confident words. He was rattled, though if not from the impact, then what? Had he seen what she had? From the window of their carriage, she had witnessed the horse barreling down upon him. The animal had swept past them in a blur and headed toward the walkway, straight for the earl. Her breath caught when Lord Glenmor stepped off to cross the road and the horse corrected its course as if the rider had intended all along to hit him.

She'd screamed then, called out in horror. Thankfully, the earl's quick reflexes had saved him from being trampled.

"You shall come to Harrow House with us, Lord Glenmor, and we shall call for the doctor to ensure you are as well as you say you are," Lady Dalridge stated, motioning for the driver to assist the earl to their carriage.

"I promise that is not necessary."

"I can assure you it is," the dowager said. "I will not have you returned home alone only to succumb to an unknown injury."

"Lady Dalridge is right," Judith said, still holding fast to his hand. She should let go. It wasn't proper, but she couldn't. Not yet. "You shouldn't be alone."

"I will not be alone," he said, squeezing her hand. "My mother is in residence and I guarantee once I tell her what occurred, she will hover over me like the staunchest of nursemaids."

He did not sound pleased by the notion of being coddled in such fashion. A shame, for she very much would have enjoyed doing just that. He always seemed to be carrying such a weight on his shoulders. How nice it would be to relieve him of it, if only for a short while.

"If you are sure, but we shall take you the rest of the way in our carriage," Lady Dalridge said.

But he protested even that. "I am only a few minutes' walk away."

Lady Dalridge reached the open door of the carriage and turned to them. Somehow, despite his superior height, she managed to look down her nose at him. "My dear Lord Glenmor, my offer was not a request."

"You might as well do it," Judith whispered. "She shall badger you relentlessly until you comply."

He managed a small laugh and inclined his head toward Lady Dalridge, acquiescing to her command. "Very well then. I suppose the best thing for any injury is a few moments in the company of three beautiful ladies, is it not?"

"Are you attempting to charm me, Lord Glenmor?" Despite the older lady's austere tone, humor lingered just beyond it.

He smiled and the corners of his eyes crinkled, and even if Lady Dalridge was not charmed, Judith could not help herself. "Perhaps a little."

The viscountess shook her head, but amusement danced in her light green eyes as she accepted his offer of assistance into the carriage. As Lady Dalridge settled herself, he turned to Judith.

"Miss Sutherland?"

"Lord Glenmor," she whispered, leaning into him. She had only a few seconds to reveal what she had seen. The sinister image had imprinted in her mind. She needed to make him aware. "I believe the rider meant to intentionally cause you harm. In fact, I'm sure of it."

He answered with a knowing glance and squeezed her hand as he lifted her into the carriage, the only acknowledgement he had heard her claim. Had he already come to the same conclusion? And if so, what did it mean?

Miss Sutherland's whispered words haunted him well into the night and continued to dog his heels come morning, dragging his attention away from more pressing matters. He pinched the bridge of his nose. He must concentrate. There must be some way to salvage the Glenmor fortune. But no. He had already robbed his other investments to fund the renovations of Maple Glen. Renovations that, now underway, could not be stopped.

Frustration filled him. He shoved the ledgers away and rose from his desk chair, his body stiff and sore from his run-in with the horse and rider the night before. He crossed the room to stare out the window into the street below. A light snow had begun earlier in the day and now dressed the world beyond in white.

I believe the rider meant to intentionally cause you harm.

Miss Sutherland's observations haunted him, her keen perceptions echoing what he too believed. The horse had not been a runaway. In retrospect, in the split second before he leaped out of the way, he recalled the rider, hunched over the animal's neck, had a firm grip on the reins. He should have been able to redirect the horse enough to avoid a collision. And yet, he had not. Nor had the rider stopped once the collision had occurred, or looked back to survey the damage he had caused. He'd simply kept going, disappearing into the dark like a specter.

Benedict dragged his fingers through his hair. It made no sense. What value was there in causing him harm? He had no greedy heir hoping to take his place and no fortune to inherit even if there was an heir to receive it. He was it. The last of the Laytham line. With the last hope of changing the family fortunes lost, if he could not sever his interest in the Western Trading Company and stop the bleeding of his investment. The only one who would suffer from his success in that matter was—

His thoughts arrested, stopped suddenly in their tracks.

His business partner.

He let out a small laugh. "Foolishness."

Based on the agreement Uncle Henry had signed, should the current earl die without heirs, his portion of the business would fully revert to his silent partner. Which, if the Western Trading Company had proven a profitable venture, would lean toward motive. But it wasn't profitable, not in the least and therefore, despite how things may appear, the incident had to be nothing more than the random act of a madman. He must remove the event from his mind and spend his energies where they were more suited—to finding a wealthy bride.

It did not bode well that the plan gave him no more peace than being run down in the street by a lunatic on a horse.

Behind him, the door opened and he saw his mother's image reflected in the window. He turned and crossed the room to greet her, her sunny presence a much-needed balm to his jumbled thoughts. He had told her of his mishap the night before, not wishing to have her hear about it from someone else, exaggerated to such a degree it caused her more distress than the truth.

"Good morning, Mother."

She met him halfway and took his offered hands, giving them a loving squeeze. "I should have known I'd find you here. You should be resting, Ben."

"I am perfectly fine, Mother. A little sore and with a few bruises. Nothing to worry yourself over." He loathed causing her any concern. She had already lost one son tragically. He did not want her to revisit those memories by worrying over his welfare.

"Nearly being trampled by a horse is hardly nothing. I fear even letting you out of my sight now." She waved off his protest. "It is a foolish notion, I know, but once you have children of your own, you will understand."

"I will need to find myself a bride first, Mother. And I am afraid that search is not going as well as I had hoped."

Mrs. Feeney arrived with tea and biscuits and Benedict led his mother over to the chairs near the hearth where a warm fire beat back the chill.

"Have you no interest at all in any of the young ladies?" she asked.

Yes, teetered on the tip of his tongue, but he bit it back. As much as his heart had turned in one woman's direction, his life must go in another. It had not been fair to say the things he had the night before, speaking to her of lips and kisses and such. It had been improper and out of character for him, but whenever he was in Judith's company, he forgot himself. Forgot what was proper and what was not and let down his guard to reveal his true self to her.

"Benedict?"

He gave himself a mental shake. "Yes. I mean—no." He could not tell Mother. For heavens' sakes, if he let her know he'd lost his heart to Miss Sutherland, she would begin a campaign to have them standing at the altar before Christmas, so firmly entrenched she was in her belief that love must come above all. A lofty ideal, and a lovely one, but not one he could indulge in given his current circumstances.

"What of Lady Henrietta? She seemed quite lovely, if a bit shy. And I wouldn't think her scars would be of a concern to you."

"She is and they weren't, however she appears quite over the moon for Lord Pengrin, to hear Miss Sutherland tell it."

"How unfortunate." His mother's voice changed and one eyebrow arched. "Please do not tell me you are still entertaining the idea of Lady Susan."

Benedict winced and leaned back in his chair, stretching his legs toward the fire. "I may have no other alternative. I know she is unpleasant, but perhaps once I get to know her, I will discover more pleasing qualities beneath the exterior."

His mother gave him a look. The one that clearly indicated he was mad, or severely misguided.

Benedict sighed. "Very well, likely that is not the case. But regardless, her dowry and lack of other suitors make her a viable prospect."

"The very thought of you tying yourself to her for life leaves such a bad taste in my mouth I cannot even describe it. Please reconsider, Benedict. Is there no hope at all that your investments will turn around?"

He had told her very little in that regard, revealing only enough that she understood the gravity of the situation and what he must do to reverse it.

"I have made every attempt to track down Mr. Crowley or this silent partner Uncle Henry tied us to, but so far all my inquiries have come to naught. I hold out very little hope in that regard. I fear I may have to involve the magistrate in order to sever the agreement, but that will take time I do not have. Marrying well is the quickest, most practical solution. I will need to do it either way, so I might as well make the choice worth my while. And I will begin in earnest this evening at the Lindwell fete."

"Then I shall accompany you. Perhaps I can uncover a better option than Lady Susan and her displeasing personality."

Benedict did not bother to dissuade her, though he could not shake the impression that marriage to Lady Susan was a penance he would have to pay for failing his family yet again. Time was running out.

A nother party, this one the grandest yet. The hosts, the Lindwells, were not of the aristocracy, but rather had come over from the Americas with their newly made fortunes and, as many of the ton whispered, badly acquired sense of what was appropriate. Only a loose familial connection to the Duke of Franklyn made them in any way acceptable, though even this did not prevent those with old fortunes and lofty titles from looking down their aristocratic noses at them.

Despite this condescension, however, these same titled lords and ladies arrived tonight to celebrate the two youngest Lindwell daughters as they turned twenty.

"It is a rather gauche display," Lady Dalridge said, looking around as their group entered the glittering ballroom that reminded Judith of a winter wonderland. "One would think Lady Franklyn would have counseled them on restraint."

"Perhaps Lady Franklyn thought to eliminate the competition by allowing the Lindwells to offend every titled gentlemen looking for a bride in the hopes it would leave at least one willing to take on her daughter," Lord Ridgemont suggested, an amused smile playing about his lips.

His great-aunt cast him a dubious look. "And if so, was she successful? Would *you* choose Lady Susan over one of the Lindwell girls?"

Judith suppressed a smile as Lord Ridgemont caught her eye and shuddered. "Heavens, no. But I am not currently in search of a bride."

Lady Dalridge harrumphed. "By the time you decide to find one, Lady Susan may be all that's left."

"Auntie," Lady Henrietta said, placing a hand upon the dowager viscountess's arm. "Don't chide him so. One would hope James will fall in love when he least expects it and all will end well."

"Love." Lady Dalridge shook her head. "Young people."

"Come then," Lord Ridgemont said, offering an arm to both his great-aunt and sister, leaving Judith to trail behind them. "Shall we assimilate ourselves into the masses?"

It was an apt description in Judith's estimation and in short order, the sea of bodies opened up for Lord Ridgemont and his family, then quickly closed over, separating her from them as if she were invisible. If not for Lord Ridgemont's dark head standing taller than most, she would have lost sight of them completely. Either way, she drifted farther and farther behind as they crossed the room, only coming close to catching up when they would stop to exchange pleasantries with friends, before moving on once again.

"Miss Sutherland!"

A hand caught her arm and Judith turned at the familiar voice. "Oh, Mrs. Laytham. How wonderful to see you." The words rushed out of her in relief. She despised these parties; bodies crushed into each other, leaving little space for thought or movement. The constant hum of voices reminded her of an angry hive of bees. To find a friendly face was a relief indeed.

Mrs. Laytham pulled Judith in close to her so she might be heard. "It is quite the thing, is it not?"

"Indeed it is. I've not seen so many candles lighting a room. I wonder that it won't set the room ablaze before the night is over. But it is rather pretty, I must admit." Not a popular sentiment to hear others speak, but Judith suspected the Lindwells could have arranged the room with all proper decorum and still have been the subject of ridicule for their efforts. The ton was not very welcoming to those beneath their ranks.

Mrs. Laytham opened her fan and waved it beneath her chin. "I understand the Lindwells are hoping to marry their youngest daughters off to titled gentlemen. It is said the dowry for each is nothing less than a small fortune."

"Oh?" It had been much the same information Lord Ridgemont had provided, but hearing it from Mrs. Laytham made the pronouncement sit a bit differently.

"Did Lord Glenmor accompany you this evening?"

Mrs. Laytham inclined her head toward the middle of the room. "Oh yes, he is making his way toward the Lindwells as we speak, in the hopes of receiving a proper introduction to their daughters."

Judith's heart sank. "I see. And you did not join him?"

Mrs. Laytham gave her a rueful smile. "I despise crowds, truth be told. Always have. I suspect if one of the daughters is to his liking I will meet her soon enough. I have already made up my mind to visit the Lindwells. I feel a certain kinship, knowing well what it is like to be on the outside looking in."

"Yes. I'm rather familiar with that sensation myself."

Mrs. Laytham patted her hand. "I suspect you are, my dear."

"Ah, Miss Sutherland, there you are!" Lord Ridgemont appeared through the swath of bodies and executed a brief bow. "My sister feared you were swallowed up by the masses, never to be seen again. But I see you have found safe harbor with Mrs. Laytham."

"I have. She most kindly rescued me and offered refuge."

"May I escort both you ladies to our party? Lady Dalridge is sitting down just on the other side of the room. I would be most pleased to have you join us, Mrs. Laytham, as I'm sure my aunt would as well."

Judith wasn't sure about that. Lady Dalridge was a bit of a stickler when it came to associating with anyone who lacked rank. She tolerated Judith, but only because Hen insisted she do so.

Mrs. Laytham smiled. "That is very kind of you, Lord Ridgemont. Please give Lady Dalridge my best regards, but I believe I will wait here for my son to return."

"Ah yes, I saw him speaking with one of the Miss Lindwells. Well then," He turned and offered Judith his arm. "Shall we make our way through, Miss Sutherland?"

"Of course," she said, slipping her arm through his, unsure which disappointed her more, that she did not get to see Lord Glenmor face to face, or that he was busy, actively courting an audience with one of the Lindwell girls in the hopes of procuring a potential marriage. "Thank you for rescuing me, Mrs. Laytham. I hope to see you again soon."

"I am certain we will," she answered. "It won't be long now before the wedding, will it?"

Judith smiled. "Not long at all."

As she and Lord Ridgemont skimmed the outer edges of the crowd, the marquess leaned down to better be heard. "I must confess, I was shocked when I heard the Dowager Countess of Blackbourne had agreed to marry your uncle."

Something in his tone piqued her. "And why is that, my lord?"

"Forgive me. I meant no disrespect to your uncle. I suppose I was simply surprised."

"You shouldn't be." She grew weary of the assumption those of Lord Ridgemont's ilk held, that anyone without title should only consort with those who shared the same standing. "My uncle is an exceptionally fine man and Lady Blackbourne a lovely woman. That two such people of enduring qualities have found love with each other should hardly be a shocking occurrence."

He winced. "I have offended you."

She pursed her lips. She should not have spoken so freely. He was her employer, after all, and she could not risk displeasing him and losing her position. Nor should she be surprised he held such a belief. As a member of the peerage he was no different from the rest of them in their views of who was worthy of their time and attention and who was not. Likely, it had been branded into him from the cradle and heartily enforced by Lady Dalridge since he reached the age of majority.

"Forgive me," she said. "I spoke out of turn."

"On the contrary, I have behaved the boor. It is I who should apologize. I hope Lady Blackbourne and your uncle find every happiness. We should all be so lucky, should we not?"

Judith nodded then stopped as her gaze fell upon a familiar golden head, burnished bronze by the candlelight raining down upon him. Lord Glenmor was engrossed in an animated conversation with a pretty young lady of similar coloring, who appeared equally engaged.

"That is one of the Miss Lindwells," Lord Ridgemont told her, leaning down again to be heard over the crowd. "Temperance, I believe her name is. Or Constance. I cannot remember which of them is which. She seems quite captivated by your Lord Glenmor."

"He is not—" She stopped suddenly and modulated her tone that had come out harsher than she intended, her emotions in an uproar over seeing the two together. A state not improved upon by the realization that they made a lovely couple. Where he was handsome, she was pretty. Where she was dainty, he was strong. "He is not *my* Lord Glenmor," she stressed. Nor would he ever be. When would she get that through her thick head?

"Forgive me, Miss Sutherland. I fear I cannot win with you tonight. Everything I say has brought you distress."

She pursed her lips. At this rate, he would be showing her the door by the end of the night, her trunk at her side and a one-way ticket back to Havelock Manor in her hand. "No, it is not you. I suppose I am feeling a bit tired from all the parties. I had not expected it when I took the position. I believe I envisioned a much quieter existence."

"As I feared it would be," Lord Ridgemont said. "But with your counsel and support I am pleased to see my sister has come out of her shell and taken her proper place in society. I worried such a day would never come to pass. To see that it has gives me a great deal of relief. I have you and my friend, Lord Pengrin, to thank for that."

Lord Pengrin. Hearing the name associated with Lady Henrietta only added to her misery. If Lord Ridgemont held the man in such high regard, how would she ever succeed in convincing him the viscount was not what he appeared to be, without exposing herself to ruin in the process?

Unease plagued her as she sat next to Lady Dalridge, ignored by the gentlemen present as a suitable dance partner and by the ladies who curried the dowager's favor. As midnight came and went, Judith wearied of sitting on her behind and made her excuses to escape to the ladies room. Afterward, heedless of the cold air, she slipped outside the first set of doors she could find.

Chapter Sixteen

J udith walked along the stone terrace, away from the doors and anyone who may come through them, until she found a little alcove cut into the side of the building that left her partially hidden. She breathed deeply as if the cool air could overtake all that felt wrong inside of her. It couldn't, of course. But for a few moments, she enjoyed the view of the starry sky and the illusion of freedom and tried to ignore the fact that as each day wore on, her discomfort in her position as companion grew. Lady Henrietta was a lovely young woman and Judith had grown quite fond of her, but being so acquiescent was not in her nature. It was like wearing a pair of shoes two sizes too small.

"I see we are of a similar mind."

Judith whirled about at the familiar voice behind her. "Lord Glenmor." She glanced around. He was alone. *They* were alone. A dangerous situation should they be discovered, yet she said nothing, greedy for any time she could have with him.

He bowed and kept a proper distance. Pity. "You look lovely this evening, Miss Sutherland."

She did not. She had exhausted her supply of dresses and was once again wearing one of Lady Henrietta's altered cast-offs. A gown she had worn two other times in the past fortnight. A fact pointed out by Lady Susan when she stopped by to pay her respects to Lady Dalridge.

"You are too kind, my lord. But I'm certain my appearance can in no way compete with the other young ladies."

"I beg to differ. While they're all quite lovely for the most part, I find they pale in comparison."

She raised one eyebrow, sad to discover that despite all his wonderful qualities, Lord Glenmor was, in truth, daft. Or blind. Or, more likely, gallant in the way gentlemen thought they needed to be.

"You do not believe me," Lord Glenmor said, taking a step forward. He appeared genuinely surprised, which in turn, surprised her even further.

"I am not beautiful, my lord. I never have been. My cousin, Patience, is the beauty in the family. I am the sensible one, nothing more."

An expression she could not quite pin down crossed his handsome features.

"Come with me." He held out a hand and for a moment, she hesitated. Going anywhere with him could spell her doom in more ways than one. He tempted her heart far too thoroughly. Yet, despite this knowledge, she slipped her hand into his, before her good sense could raise any further objection.

They did not go far. He led her to a nearby pair of French doors covered from the inside with heavy drapery and illuminated from the outside by moonlight. Their images reflected against it, she standing in front with Lord Glenmor behind her, his hands resting on her shoulders. Despite being taller than many of the young ladies, she reached just past his chin. What would happen if she leaned back against him? Would his arms slide around her? Hold her close until the warmth of his body turned her limbs languid?

"Tell me what you see," he said, his voice a soft command that cut through her imaginings.

Heat rushed to her cheeks and she glanced down to the stone at her feet. "There is nothing to see. Brown eyes, brown hair."

His hand left her shoulder and his fingers rested beneath her chin, gently lifting it up until they both stared at her reflection once again. The touch entranced her, sending fire racing through her veins and creating an ache deep within her.

"There is everything to see. For your eyes are not simply brown. They are deep and dark. Mysterious."

Her blush increased tenfold. "They are nothing of the—"

He cut her off. "And when you smile, a tiny dimple appears near the apple of your left cheek." His hand left her chin and touched lightly upon the spot where her dimple resided.

How had he noticed such a thing? A thrill danced up her spine.

"And your hair is anything but just brown. It is the darkest chocolate, long and glorious." He wound a loose curl around his finger. When he spoke again, his voice had changed, lowered to a whisper as if he were talking to himself, discovering as he went. "Soft to the touch. I suspect when you pull out your pins, it tumbles down your back in wild and uninhibited waves. Does it?"

She glanced at his reflection. His gaze had shifted to stare at the curl entwined around his finger. She swallowed. A deep ache throbbed between her legs. "Yes."

"Sometimes..." He hesitated for a brief second, as if considering his words; perhaps whether or not he should speak them, before continuing. "Sometimes I imagine pulling out every last pin and watching it fall. I imagine what it would feel like to run my fingers through your hair and discover if it truly feels as silky as it appears. Even now, the moonlight glistens off it."

Judith closed her eyes. It was too much. Her heart fluttered rapidly against her breast and her skin cried out, desperate for his touch. And then its cries were answered as his lips touched the curve of her neck with gentle precision.

She caught her breath and her eyes flew open. She should protest, but the words would not come. And even if they did, she would not mean them.

"Your beauty begins deep inside of you and it shines through everything you do. Every look you give, every smile you offer. You should not try so hard to hide it away. Let it out," he said, his hands returning to her shoulders, though she rested against his chest now and his warmth and strength radiated through her. "Let the rest of the world take note and wish with all their hearts that they could modify themselves to be even half as wonderful as you are."

Lord Glenmor, it turned out, was neither daft nor blind, but simply mad.

But, oh, what affection she held for his special brand of madness. How she longed to immerse herself in it until the rest of the world faded away.

He turned her around until she faced him and his fingers teased the sensitive skin of her neck, the line of her jaw. Her lips.

"You claim to be sensible, and you are. You are intelligent and reliable, as well. All of those things. But they are only half of the story. You skipped over all of the best parts and, despite my noblest attempts, I cannot help but be captivated by you, Miss Sutherland. Utterly and completely and to my everlasting dismay."

"Because nothing can come of it." She finished, speaking aloud the words that lingered between them in the hopes it would stop the insanity that had enveloped them. It didn't. If anything, the words only added urgency to the tension that had teased them from the moment he'd offered his hand and she accepted.

He nodded his acknowledgement. "No, it cannot. But I long to kiss you nonetheless. May I? Just this once, so I might have a lovely memory to carry with me. Something to hold tightly to when the days grow dark and empty."

She should say no. He offered her nothing in recompense for such liberties, made her no promises of a future. If anything, he made it clear one did not exist for them. She had been in this position once before, and been hurt as a result, deeply and egregiously. But somehow, this was different. There were no lies, no subterfuge. Only stark honesty.

"Yes," she whispered and lifted her head to accept his kiss, but it did not come. Not right away. Not where she expected. He kissed her brow. Her cheekbone. His fingertips explored the planes and angles of her face, finding new places for his lips to go. The feather-light torment made the ache at the juncture of her thighs almost painful, and had she been alone, she would have pressed her hand against it in the hopes of some relief. The image of him doing such for her appeared unbidden in her mind and her breath caught in her throat at the sinful imagining.

His hands stopped their exploration and cupped her face, leading her mouth to his and even then, even as she expected it, his kiss surprised her. Soft and tender, it teased and tempted before deepening and becoming all-consuming. Had the entire ballroom poured outside to witness the event, she would not have noticed. Nothing else existed. Only this kiss. Only this man.

Her hands twisted into the lapels of his coat. She needed to be closer, to crawl into him and stay there forever. But there was no forever for them. None offered. None accepted. They were nothing more than this moment.

It would have to be enough.

The kiss broke and he ended it with several smaller ones as if his lips were reluctant to leave hers. The truth hit her then. One kiss would not be enough. It would never be enough. The cruelty of their individual fates crushed down upon her and she bit down on her bottom lip to keep the tears at bay.

"I am the worst kind of reprobate." He whispered and in his voice she heard the shared anguish. "To ask for such a thing, when—"

"No more than I," she said, with a small shake of her head. The kiss had been a beautiful moment. A memory to cherish for the rest of her days. "You were not alone in wishing for a kiss. Let us not spoil it now with regret and recriminations."

He fell silent then nodded, his forehead pressed lightly against hers. "Very well. You must be freezing. I should not have kept you out here."

"I am glad you did."

"So am I." He gifted her with a small smile, but within it lived the sadness of their separate futures. His hands fell away and cold air rushed up and chilled her skin. "Off you go then," he said. "I have kept you too long."

She did as he bade her. It was for the best. They could not risk a scandal. But as she walked away, feeling his gaze follow her, she could not extinguish the deepest wish that he could keep her forever.

"Y ou've not heard a word I've said, have you, Ben?"

Benedict pulled his gaze away from where the morning sunlight spilled across the newspaper in front of him. Not only had he not heard his mother, he had not read a single word, but rather stared at the print until his vision blurred. His mind had been on something else.

Or rather, someone else.

"Forgive me, Mother."

She set her fork down upon the plate in front of her, concern etched into the fine lines around her eyes. "You have not been yourself lately, Benedict. I fear my leaving may not be the best thing."

"Leaving?" Heavens, how much of their conversation had he missed? "We have only just arrived."

"We arrived several weeks ago and I only meant to stay for a brief while. Honestly, I had hoped to talk you out of this foolish bride hunt of yours during my stay, though I fear I have failed in that endeavor." Mother sighed and sat back in her chair, giving him the look she often did when exasperation took hold.

"I need to marry regardless, Mother. As earl, I need an heir. What does it matter whether I marry a rich wife over a poor one?" But his words lacked conviction, for now he understood what was at stake, what he would be giving up.

Judith.

He should not have kissed her. It was the highest impropriety and she deserved so much better than to be used in such a way. But he had been unable to resist the temptation to touch her, to taste her. Such temptation he had willingly surrendered to, only to regret it later.

Not the kiss—that he would never regret. He would carry the memory of that moment with him until he took his last breath. But he mourned that he could not take it further. That he could not marry her and spend his days basking in her loveliness, inside and out. But the kiss had awakened in him the irrefutable knowledge that he would lament each morning he awoke to someone else, not her. And when he was blessed with children, a part of him would always wish that they had been borne of her, with dark hair and unfathomable eyes and her sweet, glorious smile and sensible nature.

Their kiss had unleashed a desire he could not quench, and yet could not drink from ever again. He had taken the first step on the road to madness, for certain.

Mother interrupted his thoughts. "One day you will wake up, Benedict, and you will realize that marrying for money mattered a great deal. That having saved the family fortunes proves a very poor substitute for love. Your father and I had little, but we were richer than most, because we loved each other. Do you not want that for yourself? Do you think your own happiness of no importance?"

Therein lay the crux of his dilemma. As much as he longed for happiness, for the kind of life his mother and father had, he could not pursue it. He had failed his family time and again. All he had left, the one thing he *could* do, was resurrect the family name—*Father's* family name—and bring the title and fortunes back to their former glory. So that when he passed them onto his son, they would no longer be tainted with scandal and struggle.

If that meant he must sacrifice his own happiness to achieve this, then so be it.

"I am the Earl of Glenmor now, Mother. I cannot think in such singular terms as if my actions have no effect on anyone else." She started to protest, but he held up a hand. He could not allow her to convince him otherwise. Ripe with the memory of last night's kiss, it would be too easy a feat. And how would he live with himself then? "Please, Mother. I do not want to argue with you and cause strife before you leave. I dislike animosity before a separation, you know that."

He and Father had argued the last time he'd seen him. Benedict had not wanted to leave for school. He'd wanted to stay home with his family. He loathed the constant separation and school had proven a lonely enterprise. No one had much interest in cultivating a friendship with the eldest son of a youngest son who had long been shunned by his family.

She sighed her displeasure, but relented. "As you wish. I have invited the Lindwells to pay us a call. Their daughters seem lovely and spirited and less likely to turn up their nose at a little scandal so long as they can marry a titled gentleman. They may be Americans, but still a far cry more amenable than Lady Susan."

"Very well then." Though while avoiding a marriage to Lady Susan pleased him, nothing would ever live up to the dream of a lifetime with Miss Sutherland.

———

"James has invited Lord Pengrin to accompany us to Lady Felliwig's dinner party this evening," Lady Henrietta said, clasping her hands beneath her chin as she entered the solar after finishing her breakfast. Hen's eyes, wide and expressive, radiated joy. But neither the sight, nor the news that Judith would have to suffer the viscount's company yet again, permeated her current mood.

"And has he accepted?"

Hen took a seat on the sofa next to Judith. "Yes, and he has also indicated he will stop by for a visit today. Is that not wonderful? Auntie believes an offer may come before the Season even begins at this rate. Oh, Judith, do you think she is right? Do you think it is possible he feels for me what I feel for him? I had settled myself to the idea of a life alone, but now— Oh, I had never imagined this could happen! And so quickly?"

Judith's stomach turned on itself making her glad she had begged off breakfast on the pretense of a headache. Heartache would have been a more accurate description of her true ailment, but claiming such would require a more thorough explanation and she certainly wasn't going to get into that.

Nor was she about to encourage the relationship between Hen and Lord Pengrin. A relationship that experience told her was doomed to failure. The idea that Lord Pengrin would cause Hen the same grievous humiliation he had caused Judith tormented her beyond measure. The worst of it was, she was now certain the viscount had every intention of going through with marrying Lady Henrietta, though not out of any sense of love for the young woman. He wanted her dowry. Needed it, if Lord Glenmor's insinuation about his gambling debts were founded in truth. And once he had it, the only thing he would need Hen for was to produce his heirs.

It was a dire prediction on Judith's part, but one established in experience. She had seen the calculating flash in Lord Pengrin's eyes when he looked at Hen. Unlike the passion and longing in Lord Glenmor's gaze the night before, Lord Pengrin's eyes possessed nothing but a mercenary gleam. Judith's blood ran cold. He did not love or care for Hen. To do so would require a heart, an organ the viscount did not possess.

"I cannot comment on what goes on in Lord Pengrin's mind, I'm afraid. I do not know the man well enough." The lie tripped off her tongue, leaving a bitter taste. If only she'd warned her off sooner, before Hen's feelings had a chance to develop. "But do you not think you should consider other gentlemen as well? To have a comparison as to which one is best suited to you? Or to hold Lord Pengrin off to at least allow you a Season?"

Judith reached for any reason she could think of, desperate to stop Hen from making the same mistakes she had, but it did little good. She wasn't even finished with her suggestion before Hen started shaking her head in the negative.

"My heart tells me he is the one. I feel beautiful with him, less afraid that others judge me. Is this not what you wanted for me?" Hurt colored her words and Judith's heart squeezed.

She reached out and took Hen's hands in hers. "Oh, yes. Of course it is. I want nothing but happiness for you. But marriage is forever and should never be entered into lightly or too quickly. I would simply suggest caution and time. If Lord Pengrin feels as strongly as you do, he will be only too happy to wait."

Though likely, if his debts were severe, he would latch onto a new, unsuspecting victim and leave poor Hen alone. It would break the young woman's heart, but she would recover. Far better than she would if he married her and discarded her once he had what he needed.

"But I do not wish to wait. I feel as if I have been living in a dark limbo for years and have finally come out into the light. I wish to embrace my future now, not hide from it. And I have you to thank for supporting me in this. If you had not been such a steady and encouraging friend, I could not have begun this journey. You gave me the strength to try, and now look at me!"

Judith forced a smile but the emotion behind it was anything but happy. Instead, it was mired in guilt and dread—and the certainty that if she was responsible for this then it must be she who put an end to it.

Chapter Seventeen

"**L**ord Pengrin." Judith called the man's name from the opposite end of the hallway, catching him as he left the receiving room. He turned on his heel at the sound of her voice and a triumphant smile spread across his handsome face.

At least it would have been handsome if she did not know the fiend that lurked beneath. But once the layers had been peeled back to reveal who he truly was, it was an image that could not be unseen.

"Ah, Miss Sutherland. Such a vision you present, lurking in the hallway of your employer in your dowdy little dress." His grin slowly grew and she could not shake the image of a snake about to strike as he slowly sauntered toward her.

The insult bounced off her. His opinion meant nothing now that she saw herself through different eyes. Benedict's words had wrapped themselves around her like a shield, washing away the stain of insecurity Lord Pengrin's actions had left in their wake and reminding her of the woman she had been before.

"I mean to have a word with you, Lord Pengrin."

"Is that so?" His voice slithered across the space between them. A space that shrunk with each step he took. She had stopped moving, preferring to be farther away from the receiving room in case Lady Henrietta and Lady Dalridge should overhear. "And what, pray tell, do you have to say to me that I would have any interest in hearing?"

He stopped a few feet from her. Uncomfortably close. Likely, just what he intended. An attempt to intimidate. Despite its effectiveness, she stood her ground.

"I must insist you stop courting Lady Henrietta." The words came out quick and clipped, before she lost her nerve.

"Stop—" He laughed and even that sound had a twinge of malevolence to it. Like the rattle of a snake before a deadly strike. Her feet itched to run, to take her to safety. She refused their plea. "Well, well. Miss Sutherland, do you still have such tender feelings for me that you cannot stand to see me with another?"

The very idea sickened her. "The only feelings I have for you are loathing, my lord. You are a contemptible individual, incapable of being decent. That is why I wish you away from Lady Henrietta. She is a kind, lovely young woman. I will not stand by and watch you destroy her in order to have want you want."

He took a step closer. "And what is it you think I want?"

"Money, I suspect. Rumor has it you have a bit of trouble staying away from the gaming tables." It was not something she should know about, certainly not something a proper lady would speak of, but she had already thrown caution to the wind. What was one more thing?

Pengrin's expression darkened and fear reared its ugly head. Still, she held her ground and continued. "Once you have what you need, I suspect she will see your true nature and wish she'd never set eyes upon you."

He sneered. "And just what do you think you can do

about it? Her family thinks us a suitable match, one they heartily approve of. I can't imagine the opinion of a lowly *servant* would change their minds in that regard."

She tossed aside his slight. What did she care of his opinions? "It might if I tell them what you did to me."

His face tightened. To anyone else, it might have been imperceptible, but she had been watching for it, looking for telltale signs that revealed whether her threat had merit. It did.

He glanced behind him at the receiving room door before turning back to her. His eyes blazed with hatred. She took a step back but he followed her. "You wouldn't dare. To do so would spell your ruin."

"It is a risk I am willing to take if it saves her from making the same mistake I did in trusting you to be a gentleman, when in truth you are nothing more than a beast. Lady Henrietta deserves far better than the likes of you and I will do whatever I must to ensure she gets it."

"You little bitch." The words bit out of him as he strode swiftly toward her. Judith attempted to evade him, but he grabbed her arms and propelled her backward down the hall. She opened her mouth to scream, but the sound arrested in her throat as he pushed her around a corner and threw her back against the wall. The impact knocked the breath out of her.

His hold on her arm tightened while his other hand grabbed her face, his fingers digging into her jawbone, preventing her from calling out. Terror paralyzed her. He was despicable, but now she understood it went far deeper than that. He was also dangerous. Deadly.

"Let me tell you something," he said, his face close to hers so that bits of spittle landed on her skin. She twisted her head to release his grip but he held fast. "If you breathe a word of your silly little story, I will destroy you. I will make it look as if you tried to seduce me to improve your situation. A sad little attempt to trap one of your betters."

"They won't believe you," she said, and though the words came out muffled, his smile indicated he'd understood them. A smile that had once charmed her. What a fool she had been!

"Oh, but they will believe me. But let me tell you a story of my own." He leaned in closer, his lips pressed against her ear. She tried to turn away from his touch, but could not escape it. "You see, I find myself in need of a considerable payment due to those gambling debts you so scandalously referred to. So I will marry that scarred little monster with her oh so generous dowry to get it and you will not interfere. Because if you do, I can assure you the consequences to you will be great and irreversible."

"There is nothing you can do to me." If he ruined her, so be it. She would retire to a quiet country life and find contentment in the fact she'd saved Lady Henrietta from a lifetime of misery.

"Oh, but I can." The words hissed in her ear. "I am not in the habit of leaving loose ends, I assure you. Should you make any attempt to stop me in my pursuit of this marriage, you will find yourself swimming in the Thames, do I make myself quite clear?"

The blood in her veins turned to ice. Something in his voice, in the pressure of his fingertips where they gripped her, told her it was not an idle threat.

He released her then and the sudden removal of his touch made her stumble, her quivering legs threatening to give out. By the time she regained her balance, the only view she had of him was a glimpse as he turned the corner and disappeared from view. But his threat lingered in the air.

No, not a threat. A promise.

He would see her dead and think nothing of it once the deed was done.

T he party played out around Judith, much like the others she had attended over the past several weeks. She tired of them already and the prospect of the upcoming Season did not cheer her as it did Patience, who had finally been given a reprieve from her mother and released from the purgatory she had been cast into after last year's debacle with Lady Susan.

Judith was happy for her cousin, but her happiness was tempered by yesterday's events. Lord Pengrin's threat still echoed in her mind and her jaw ached where he had held it tightly. She had worn long sleeves this evening as well, to cover the imprint of his fingertips where he had bruised her arm with his unyielding grip. She must decide on a course of action, but the fear of what he might do to her had become a greater stumbling block than the idea of revealing her past secrets.

Upon arriving at the party, she sought out a quiet corner to contemplate what she must do and how best to go about it to avoid further injury. Or worse. The other guests paid her no heed. The lords and ladies of the ton did not go out of their way to converse with her or draw her into their conversations. She was nothing to them. Nobody. An invisible companion that most did not deign to know or acknowledge.

Most, but not all.

"Are you quite well, Miss Sutherland?"

She glanced up into Lord Glenmor's handsome face and a brief respite chased away her anxieties. She never tired of seeing him. One would think such a feeling would wear off after repetition, but the more she saw him, the more she looked forward to future viewings. Even more so after the kiss they had shared stirred up a bevy of longing and desire she could no longer lock away or deny.

Despite having once considered all members of society to be worthy of her contempt, Lord Glenmor had shown her she could not paint everyone with the same brush. He was nothing like Lord Pengrin. He was not an ogre dressed in deceptive finery who believed himself entitled to take whatever he wanted. Instead, he had shown himself to be a kind man. A warm soul. And a bit of a kindred spirit. That he would remain forever out of her reach, relegated to nothing more but a friend, did not diminish these feelings. It was as if her heart refused to acknowledge the kiss had been but a one-time thing, never to be repeated. Her heart, obstinate organ that it was, continued to leap whenever he smiled at her. Continued to hope, even if it was in vain.

"I am entirely well," she lied, giving him a small smile. "And you?"

"Well enough." But something about his answer lacked conviction.

He motioned to the empty seat next to her and she nodded. Once he'd situated himself, he leaned back and stretched out one long, lean leg. She had learned he much preferred to be outside and spent many hours walking and riding when at Sheridan Park or the Glenmor estate, Maple Glen. Even while in London, he would often go for long walks at unfashionable hours to clear his mind. His physique showed his love for physical activity and her fingers itched to reach out and run her hand down the length of his thigh where the muscles strained against his breeches.

Heat flushed her cheeks and she glanced away. This would not do. She must regain control of her emotions where he was concerned. To allow them free rein would only lead to a broken heart. Lord Glenmor had admitted he longed to kiss her, but also that it could never progress beyond that one kiss. Unlike Lord Pengrin, who had promised her a future and then abused her trust and left her humiliated, Lord Glenmor had told her the truth.

"I only ask because as I watched you from across the room—"

He had watched her?

"—it appeared as if you were deep in thought. It occurred to me, if such were the case, you might want someone to talk to about whatever has caused you such dark ruminations."

She did not. Or rather she did, but she couldn't. Not about this. The truth would taint his opinion of her; of that, she was certain. If he discovered what she had allowed, what Lord Pengrin had done, likely he would believe that the kiss they had shared was something she did on a regular basis. That it hadn't been special. She couldn't bear it. Because it *had* been special. It had been the most special thing she had ever experienced.

"It is nothing of consequence, my lord."

"Benedict," he corrected. "I think we have earned the right to call each other by our given names, have we not? At least in private?"

She smiled. "Very well. Benedict." The name tasted like warm chocolate melting on her tongue.

"Very good. And I believe you to be a liar, Judith."

His blunt comment took her by surprise but when she looked up, the warm smile he wore and the way it lit his blue eyes softened his accusation, as did the sound of her name upon his lips. "You do not believe me?"

"I do not. You were fidgeting with your hands," he said, nodding toward the appendages in question where she held them in her lap. "I have noticed that you twist your fingers about each other when something distresses you."

"You have? I do?" She did not know what else to say. His words left her brain in a bit of a muddle.

"I have and yes, you do." His smile expanded and the

twinkle in his eye brightened. Or was that simply the candle-light reflecting in them? Regardless, the effect made her heart trip over itself as if she had imbibed a little too much sherry.

"And just how much time, exactly, do you spend noticing such things?"

He gave a sheepish shrug. "Far too much, I'm afraid."

She looked away, unable to hold his gaze, though she could still feel it upon her like a soft caress. Oh, how she longed to feel the real thing. Relive the sensation of his fingertips tracing the line of her jaw, the curve of her bottom lip. His mouth pressing against hers. She sighed then caught herself.

"I have shocked you. Forgive me. Perhaps I should have left that unsaid. I forget myself when I am with you." But he didn't sound sorry, not really. He sounded...well, he sounded wonderful. She had no doubt that if she looked at him now she would want nothing more than to kiss the words from his lips, breathe them in and let them live inside of her forever.

"You have not shocked me. I am glad you feel you can speak freely with me. It is good to be friends, is it not?"

"Friends." His smile turned rueful. "And will you tell this friend what it is that troubles you? Perhaps I can help. I'm quite good at solving other people's dilemmas. It's always so much easier than tackling your own."

Something in his expression pulled deep inside of her. Her heart insisted she could trust him, and though her heart had been wrong before, Benedict's good character had broken through her hesitancy. This time, her trust was not misplaced. His offer to help would stand regardless of what the problem was. It was tempting. She longed to speak of her dilemma, to have him share his insight as to what she should do with respect to protecting Lady Henrietta and keeping her away from Lord Pengrin.

But how did she do so without giving specifics as to the origins of her strong feelings in this regard? To speak of her experiences would no doubt ruin his good opinion of her. Perhaps she could keep it vague, yet give him enough information to allow him to provide his insight into the situation.

"Very well." She took a fortifying breath and chose her words carefully. "I feel I am at a crossroads of sorts and unsure of which path to take."

"Ah. And what are the options that have left you so tormented?"

"Whether to help someone at a personal cost to myself, or to leave it be, even though I know to do so would end up causing them great pain in the end." There. That was all that needed to be said.

"I see. And this person—do you have strong feelings for them?"

"Yes, I have grown quite fond of them."

"Hm. I see." Benedict reached into his coat pocket and pulled out his father's pipe. He rubbed its smooth exterior with his thumb the way another man might rub at their chin when giving a matter serious consideration. The realization made her smile. Perhaps she had been watching him in equal measure. "If you do choose to help this individual, will they welcome such assistance?"

Judith shoulders slumped. "No. At least not initially. But I am hopeful in the long term, they will look back and see the wisdom of it." She did not want to lose Lady Henrietta's friendship, nor make her feel as though she had misplaced her trust and been betrayed. Judith understood the pain of such a thing. But what else could she do?

"And what will the cost be to you if you go ahead with this?"

I will see you swimming in the Thames.

Fear rushed up and gripped her throat. She swallowed it back as best she could and glanced down at her hands. He had been correct in his observation. She did twist her fingers about themselves when stressed or worried. "The cost could possibly be great."

"And would paying such a high cost be worth the outcome?"

He had reached the crux of the dilemma, finding the one question she had been unable to answer since Lord Pengrin made his threat. Was she willing to prevent Lady Henrietta from making a grievous mistake at the potential cost of her own life? How badly she wanted to say yes—to act boldly and bravely and stand up to Lord Pengrin and his threats. But she had no wish to die and as much as it shamed her, she could not help but feel a strong sense of self-preservation.

"I do not know."

"Then perhaps that is the question you need to answer first, before you decide upon your course of action."

"Yes, you are right, of course."

His voice softened. "Is it as bad as all that?"

"I fear it might be." She had come to London to start a new life, now that life teetered on a knife's edge and no matter which decision she made, she would come away wounded by the sharp blade.

Benedict slipped the pipe back into his pocket and reached out to rest his hand lightly on hers. The scandalous touch rippled in waves up her arm and through her body, creating a deep longing. She cast a nervous look about the room. No one gave them any notice. And why would they? A paid companion and an impoverished lord with a title tainted by its predecessor's scandal. They were hardly the type to garner the attention of others.

"You know that if you need me, you have only to ask. Whatever trouble you encounter, you may count on my assistance." He squeezed her hand and her heart threatened to burst through her chest with each powerful beat. "I will be there for you."

His touch slipped away and it took every ounce of her will not to pull it back. She did not want him to let go. She did not want him to ever let go. But he must and, despite his kind words of comfort, it was for the best that he did.

"Thank you, Lord—" She stopped, smiled. "Benedict." Oh, but his name sounded glorious on her tongue. "Your kind words and counsel are greatly appreciated."

"Appreciated enough to dance with me?"

She laughed. "I do not believe there will be dancing tonight, my lord."

"No, but there will be dancing at some point in the near future, of that I am certain. And I would like to dance with you when there is. A waltz preferably. I must confess, I enjoyed myself very much the last time we danced."

His words surprised her. "I did not think you even remembered it."

"On the contrary. I remember every detail quite clearly. So much so, that I feel the need to repeat the experience to see if the second time might live up to the magic of the first."

His claim wrapped around her, warm as a secret whispered in one's ear. He had enjoyed their dance. He wanted to do it again. She had yearned for the very same thing since the moment the music had ended.

"You flatter me."

"I tell the truth. What say you? Will you save me a dance? I promise to be on my best behavior."

Was it wrong to hope he would break such a promise? A thrill shot through her. "I believe I would like that very much."

Chapter Eighteen

After much tossing and turning, Judith had made her decision. She must act. She must do something to stop the impending disaster should Lady Henrietta continue down this path with Lord Pengrin.

I will marry that scarred little monster with her oh so generous dowry.

His claim, his contempt for Lady Henrietta, stabbed at Judith's heart. She could not let it be. She could not stand by and watch him destroy Hen's tender heart. Unfortunately, Hen was too wrapped up in her infatuation to listen to Judith. Which left her but one other option.

She took a deep breath and pushed open the heavy door of Lady Dalridge's private salon, thankful to find the great lady inside. The dowager viscountess turned her regal head at the uninvited interruption.

"Miss Sutherland. May I help you?" Her cool greeting reinforced the distance between them. Despite Hen's insistence that they were friends and that Judith be treated as more of a guest than the employee she was, Lady Dalridge had not embraced the idea.

Judith stepped into the room and closed the door behind her. Lady Dalridge raised one eyebrow at this but said nothing.

"I wonder if I might have a word, my lady."

There was a brief hesitation, as if the dowager weighed the merits of such a conversation. Perhaps curiosity got the better of her as she motioned a hand laden with jewels toward the chair next to the settee where she rested, a heavy tome in her lap.

Judith hurried to the chair before the lady could change her mind or before the nervous knots in her stomach made her rethink her course of action. But she could not back down. She could not sacrifice Hen for the sake of her pride and allow Lord Pengrin to win. The cost was too high.

She sat, took a deep breath, and dove in before her courage failed her. "I feel it is my duty to inform you of a potential situation that may—" She stopped. No, not may. *Will.* "A situation that will cause Lady Henrietta a great deal of pain."

Lady Dalridge did not move and Judith wondered if she had heard her. She'd been about to continue, to repeat what she had said, when the older lady spoke. "And what is this potential situation that has caused you such concern you felt it necessary to interrupt my afternoon with it?"

The censure did not go unnoticed. Nor did the concern that edged Lady Dalridge's light green eyes. As much as she kept Judith in her place, she cared greatly for her great-niece and protected her the way a lioness did her cubs. Judith was right to have sought her out.

"It concerns Lord Pengrin and his intentions toward Lady Henrietta. I fear they are not honorable or honest."

Another long hesitation. "I see. And what do you believe his intentions toward my great-niece are?"

"To marry her."

Lady Dalridge offered up a patronizing smile. "And you do not feel marriage to be an honest or honorable state?"

"No, it isn't that." Oh, bother. She was making a mash of this already. "I believe marriage to be both honorable and honest. It is the intentions behind Lord Pengrin courting Lady Henrietta that worries me."

"I assume you refer to her dowry?"

Judith sat up straight. Did Lady Dalridge know? And if so, did she not care? "Well...yes. In a sense."

Lady Dalridge scoffed. "Heavens, Miss Sutherland. I realize you are but an inexperienced country miss, but even you must know our kind marry more for social and monetary gain than we do for love."

An inexperienced country miss. If only she knew. "Yes, of course. But—"

"Why, if we didn't, likely none of us would have married at all. It is hardly a desirable state for a woman, is it? To be deemed someone else's property? The best most of us can hope for is an early widowhood."

Lady Dalridge painted a rather dismal, yet depressingly accurate depiction of the matrimonial state. Though Judith had once expected to someday marry, she had hoped to choose someone who would be a partner, not a lord and master.

"Was there anything else, Miss Sutherland?"

This had gone completely wrong. She had thought to find a sympathetic ear, to collect an ally in convincing Hen that Lord Pengrin was not the one for her. "I am not making my concerns clear. Forgive me, my lady. But Lord Pengrin is—" She stopped. He is what? A pompous ass? A heartless cad? Hardly enough to convince the dowager of his unsuitability given the circumstances. A man who threatens to toss ladies into the Thames? No. That sounded too melodramatic to be believed, despite the truth of the statement.

"What is it, Miss Sutherland?" Lady Dalridge's impatience

192 · KELLY BOYCE

crackled in the air between them. "If you have something of import to say, I do wish you would hurry up about it so I might return to my book." She tapped her fingers against the leather bound volume sitting in her lap.

"It is just that Lord Pengrin is not the gentleman he presents himself to be." There. She let out a breath. Success.

Lady Dalridge chuckled deep in her throat, amused rather than concerned. "They rarely are, my dear."

Judith's spirits sank. Must she tell all to her in order to have her concerns validated? The idea of admitting what had happened, what she had allowed to happen, filled her with shame. "Yes, I realize, my lady, but Lord Pengrin is worst than most. He's...he's a reprobate of the vilest kind. A...philanderer and a profligate gambler."

The laughter Lady Dalridge had offered only a moment before, condescending as it was, disappeared in the blink of an eye, replaced with aggravation. "Good heavens! Do you fear he will cheat on Lady Henrietta? Take a mistress? Or that he might find himself from time to time at the gaming tables? Such is the way of men, Miss Sutherland. I understand you are too much of an innocent to know these things but I assure you—"

"I am not an innocent!"

Frustrated, the words blurted out before she could stop them, then echoed in the air around them until finally falling away to leave a cold silence in their wake. Heat burned through her.

Lady Dalridge's next words bit out like a bitter wind. "I beg your pardon?"

"I mean...that is..." Her vision blurred. She grasped her hands tightly together to try and stop their trembling. It was out. Her shameful secret. The private disgrace she had carried for the past three years. Where did she go from here? Where could she go? Nowhere. It was done. *She* was done. She could see it in Lady Dalridge's eyes. "Lord Pengrin compromised me."

Lady Dalridge straightened in her chair then rose to her feet, slowly with such poise and regality she might have been Queen of England. When she peered down her straight nose, Judith could not help but feel as if she were nothing more than a lowly subject who had displeased their matriarch. She lowered her head and tried to blink away the tears filling her eyes.

"I see. And now you are jealous that his attentions are directed at my great-niece so you think to destroy that."

Judith's gaze shot up. "What? No! No, that is not it at all!"

"How very unbecoming of you, Miss Sutherland. Lady Henrietta has formed a strong attachment to you. How distressed she would be to know you have behaved in such a despicable manner, using your own low character to rob her of someone who has brought her out of her shell."

Brought her out of her shell? For what? To send her back into it forever when she learned how Lord Pengrin truly felt? Why did Lady Dalridge not see this? Did her confession mean nothing?

"He thinks her a monster—he told me so!"

Hate, cold and pure, burned in Lady Dalridge's eyes and it took a moment for Judith to realize it was not over what Lord Pengrin had said, but was instead directed at her.

"Enough." The word sliced through the thick air between them and cut Judith's words off before she could offer a more proper explanation. "Your behavior is inexcusable. You have already admitted to your lowly comportment and lack of innocence, I am certain you are not the person you presented yourself to be when my nephew offered you employment."

"My lady—"

Lady Dalridge did not allow her to continue. "You will remove yourself from our home immediately. I will make your excuses so as not to ruin your character more than you have done yourself, though I cannot say you deserve it. Return to your room; pack your belongings and leave. I will have Cleveland ready the carriage to convey you to wherever it is you need to go. You will not speak to Lady Henrietta before your departure and you will not contact her afterward. Am I clear on this, Miss Sutherland?"

Judith tried again. "But you must—"

"I must do nothing more than what I am doing, which is to protect my great-niece from your petty jealousy. If you challenge me in this regard, rest assured the news of your lost innocence will quickly make its way outside of this room."

Fear stabbed at Judith's heart. It had been her greatest fear, and that fear now lumped in her throat and created a barrier that prevented any other words from breaking through. Not that Lady Dalridge would have listened. She'd made up her mind and Judith had little doubt that if she tried to thwart her, she would make good on her threat.

The dowager viscountess swept from the room without a glance back, obviously confident that her commands would be heeded. As they would be. What other choice did Judith have? She had been tossed out.

The question was—where would she go now?

———

When Titus entered the library to deliver a message, Benedict could honestly say the words that came out of his mouth were the last ones he had ever expected to hear from the man. So much so, that he inquired further, for surely he had heard incorrectly.

"Forgive me, Titus. But did you say Miss Sutherland was at the front door?"

"Yes, my lord." Titus inclined his head, though his eyes were opened wide enough to easily reveal what he considered a gross impropriety. A lady simply did not present herself on a gentleman's doorstep. "And she has brought her belongings with her."

"Her belongings?"

"So I would assume that is what is in the trunk Lord Ridgemont's driver left at her feet before he rode off, my lord."

Benedict took a step toward his butler, certain he must be dreaming. Titus's tale had a surreal quality about it and made as much sense as a jumbled dream, where anything was possible. Why, he'd had many such reveries where Miss Sutherland featured prominently, none of which were possible in real life, but which seemed perfectly acceptable in the world of his imaginings.

"I see." Except that he didn't. This was no dream. This was the bright light of day and as such, nothing Titus had relayed made one lick of sense. Benedict did not much care for things that did not make sense. He preferred his life to be orderly and sensible. It was much easier to manage that way. "And where is Miss Sutherland now?"

"I have shown her to the receiving room, my lord. It would not do to leave a lady standing at your front door with her belongings, given the circumstances."

"Yes. Indeed. The circumstances." He gave Titus a strange look. "What circumstances would that be again?" Beyond the obvious, of course.

Titus lifted one eyebrow. "Mrs. Laytham's departure to Sheridan Park, my lord."

Bloody hell. How could he have forgotten that? "Did you happen to mention Mrs. Laytham's departure to Miss Sutherland?"

"No, my lord. I thought I might leave that to your discretion."

"Wonderful. Of course. Proper thing." He did not look forward to that particular conversation. "I suppose I should greet her and determine what it is that has brought her here." But still he made no move to leave the safety of the library. His legs remained leaden posts driven into the floor. The moment he left this room, the second he informed Miss Sutherland that they were alone in Glenmor House without proper chaperone, it was all over. He would have no alternative but to marry her to save her from ruination.

A lovely prospect, if not for the fact saving her from ruination would mean to mete out his own, creating one last and final failure without any hope of putting things back to right. Worse still, it would mean dragging Judith down with him in the process.

His mind worked furiously to find a way around the inevitable. "Did anyone see her arrive?"

"I cannot say, my lord. The street was quiet, however. Though whether Lord Ridgemont's driver is the chatty sort, I cannot claim any knowledge of."

"No. Right. Naturally."

Why in heavens was she here? With her belongings? Had she been sacked? Questions he had no answers to tripped over one another until he gave his head a shake to send them on their way. Only Judith could provide answers.

"Shall I inform Miss Sutherland you will be along directly, my lord?"

"No, that will be unnecessary, Titus. But...perhaps you could have Mrs. Feeney stay with her until I arrive." It wasn't ideal, but having his housekeeper in the room with them would lend a modicum of propriety to the situation that may prove the only saving grace they had, thin as it was.

"I have already requested such, my lord."

Of course he had. Titus was the bastion of all things proper. Likely, he was dying quietly inside at the unseemliness of the current situation. "Very well, then."

He could put it off no longer. He must go to her.

Benedict made his way to the other end of the hallway, glancing down the long staircase that led to the foyer. For a fleeting moment, the idea of running down the stairs and out the front door crossed his mind. But then what? Unlike many of his counterparts, he did not possess bachelor apartments. He had deemed separate lodgings an unnecessary expense. Perhaps he could hunt down Charlie. He was Miss Sutherland's cousin, after all. Which begged the question—why had she not gone there, instead of here, if she was seeking sanctuary?

But he could not run. Had he not told her if she needed him, he would be there for her? What stronger cry for help was there than to arrive at his door, belongings in hand, without warning or invitation?

What had happened?

"You could perhaps open the door and ask her," he muttered.

His hand rested on the door handle, the brass cold beneath his touch. Whatever her answer, the action itself had tossed them into a beastly morass they may not get out of. Odd that his biggest worry in that regard was what this would do to her. On one hand, if he did not marry her, she would be ruined. And if he did, she would share in his ruination.

Either way, her fate was sealed unless he could come up with some solution that saved them both.

He pushed open the door and his gaze found her pacing in front of the fireplace. His housekeeper sat poker straight in a chair near the window, standing when Benedict entered and gifting him with the same disapproving look as had Titus. Honestly, you would think both of them would be better accustomed with scandal given his family's close acquaintance with it.

Miss Sutherland turned at the sound of his arrival, myriad emotions rushing across her lovely face. She stepped forward, then hesitated, casting a nervous look at Mrs. Feeney.

"Forgive my intrusion, Lord Glenmor." She appeared drawn, distraught. His gaze dropped to her hands where they were clasped against her belly, her fingers squeezing and twisting about each other. The situation must be dire indeed.

"It is no intrusion, Miss Sutherland. Is something wrong?"

"Y—yes. I suppose you could say so." She cast another look toward their chaperone and said nothing more.

He understood the silent request for privacy. To grant it, however, put him in a rather delicate position. "Mrs. Feeney, perhaps you might sit just outside the door?"

His housekeeper's look of disapproval deepened. "With the door open, my lord?"

It was kind how she framed it as a question, when it was anything but. "Yes, Mrs. Feeney. Of course."

He waited for her to remove herself from the room before turning back to Judith. Before he could ask her to continue, however, she spoke. "Is Mrs. Laytham not at home this evening?"

He swallowed and cleared his throat, clasping his hands behind his back though he would have much preferred to reach for her, pull her to him, and kiss the pinch of worry from those ruby lips. He closed his eyes for a brief moment and prayed for strength.

"No, I am afraid Mother has left for Sheridan Park just this morning."

Judith grew paler, if such a thing was possible. "Oh." She looked about her, though for what, he wasn't certain. Salvation? It was too late for that. "Oh. That is..." Her voice dropped to a whisper. "Oh dear, I did not know. This is very improper."

He did not bother contradicting her. There was no way around it. He had an innocent young woman who was not family under his roof without proper chaperone. But there was nothing to be done about that now. He could hardly send her back out into the encroaching night unprotected. "What has brought you here?"

"An ill wind, I suppose." He started to inquire her meaning but she held up a hand and continued. "I have been relieved of my duties as lady's companion to Lady Henrietta. Lady Dalridge insisted I pack my belongings and leave immediately. She provided me with a week's wages as recompense and the Ridgemont carriage to convey me to my desired location. I sought out Aunt Beatris, but when I arrived, I discovered she and my cousins had already left London for Havelock Manor. The housekeeper indicated Patience had experienced another run-in with Lady Susan and my aunt decided it best to put a distance between the two. She had sent me a message to that effect, but I did not receive it before my departure from Harrow House."

"Ah," Benedict nodded. The explanation did little to ease his anxiety over what to do now.

"I did not think it proper to stay alone without chaperone, so I came here, thinking perhaps Mrs. Laytham could provide such."

"Except that she, too, has left to assist with the wedding preparations at Sheridan Hall."

"Yes. So you have said. If anyone took note of my arrival..." Her gaze dropped to her clasped hands. The reality of their situation lingered between them in the silence.

If anyone took note. Benedict's mind churned over the possibility until an idea formed in his head. It would be risky, fraught with peril should the truth be discovered. But *if* she hadn't been seen, then no one would be the wiser and there existed the possibility they could come out of this unscathed.

"I'm afraid I cannot allow you to leave here."

"You cannot—forgive me?" Judith looked up sharply and one curl slipped from its pin and bounced against her cheek. He curled his fingers into his palm in an attempt to prevent reaching out and tucking the recalcitrant lock behind her ear, where he would linger, perhaps lean in close and whisper—

Hell and damn! He clasped his hands more tightly behind him.

Perhaps his insistence that she stay was a bad idea. Then again, likely even the best idea was a bad one at this point. But since it was the only plan he could come up with that had a chance of success, slim as said chance might be, he saw little sense in changing course now.

"If you are amenable to the idea, I can keep you here under my protection, provided you remain within these four walls."

"You expect me to stay? But I cannot. Not with your mother no longer in residence. It wouldn't be proper."

"Judith, you are here now without chaperone. The damage is done. If you step beyond that door, you risk being seen departing. But if no one has noticed your arrival given the early hour, perhaps we can still save your reputation."

"How?" She did not sound convinced.

"If you stay here, we can secret you inside of this house until the time comes for me to depart for Sheridan Park later in the week. At that time, we can leave in the wee hours of the morning when no one is about and make our way out of London, no one the wiser. But you must commit to staying within these four walls."

"You mean I cannot go outside? At all? Not even to the gardens?" She waved a hand in the direction of the gardens that resided at the back of the house. He wasn't sure what she wanted to see in the gardens. The flowers had long since succumbed to the colder temperatures, leaving behind tangled stems and roots in their wake. Perhaps, like him, she simply preferred the fresh air to being trapped inside all day.

"It is too risky. The garden walls are not so high the neighbors might not look down from their upper windows and see you there."

"And what about your staff?"

"They can be trusted." They had kept Uncle Henry's secrets, hadn't they? And Abigail's, when she had ventured off into Madame St. Augustine's den of inequity to seek her revenge for their uncle's death. Saints preserve him, but could his family do nothing without courting disgrace? It made him question whether he should not just surrender to the inevitability of it all.

But he could not set Judith on such a path. No matter how desperately he wished she was the one he could surrender to scandal with.

Her shoulders lifted and fell upon a sigh. "I suppose I do not have a choice in the matter, do I?"

He didn't answer as she glanced around the room. Did she see the shabbiness edging in? The wear upon the furniture? The faded rugs? The repair required to the hearth? If she did, she gave no indication. He wished he could offer her finer lodgings, but his circumstances were what they were, and if he ever hoped to improve them, he must keep her under wraps or risk losing any opportunity for claiming a well-dowered bride. He had enough strikes against him as it was without adding a new scandal to the mix.

"Now, before we get settled, perhaps you would like to tell me exactly what occurred that gave Lady Dalridge cause to sack you so unceremoniously?"

Chapter Nineteen

W hat did she say? What *could* she say? Judith certainly wasn't about to reveal to Benedict what she had blurted out to Lady Dalridge. What would he think of her if she revealed the innocence he so carefully attempted to protect had already been compromised? Would he toss her out on her backside and wash his hands of her?

She looked at him for a long moment. No. Of course he wouldn't. He was a kind man, after all. A good man. But even a good man could not help but react when he learned his perception of someone was wrong. Would he understand? Or would he hold it against her, forever looking at her just a little bit differently than before?

"Would you be upset with me if I told you I did not wish to speak of it?"

He tilted his head to one side and his mouth twisted. Heavens, but he had the most kissable mouth. She did not blame herself for being unable to resist it. She challenged any woman to feel differently.

Though the real challenge would be resisting him while

holed up in Glenmor House with him like clandestine lovers. Which was exactly what everyone would believe they were should her presence be discovered. Then poor Benedict would be cast in the role of debaucher of innocents, and she would be forever ruined. Not exactly the reputation either of them wanted, and one that would likely prevent him from attaining a wealthy bride and her any future employment.

"I suppose it is your right," he said, pulling Judith from her reverie. "But if you change your mind, I am all ears."

Which he wasn't, of course. Why even his ears were perfect. But he was all heart. A truth she never expected to believe about a titled gentleman of the ton, yet Benedict had changed her mind in that regard. Perhaps she had been wrong to view all men with the taint of what Lord Pengrin had done. The difficulty was determining which gentlemen upheld their honor and integrity and which did not. She had once considered Lord Pengrin to be a good man, only to find her trust to be egregiously misplaced.

"You are very generous to do this for me. I'm not certain how I can ever repay your kindness."

He smiled and his warm blue eyes crinkled at the corner, thin lines fanning toward the tips of his cheekbones. "You can ensure no one knows you are here and that will be repayment enough."

Because he must marry another. How many times would she need to remind herself of that unpleasant truth? Daily? Hourly? More?

"I promise you, I will do nothing to endanger your future plans."

Behind her, the fire crackled, casting its warmth against her legs. When he did marry, would he sit on the sofa to her left, curled up like cats with his chosen bride? Would they talk like old friends well into the evening, perfectly at ease with each other's company? And when they retired for the night, would they hide beneath the covers and enjoy the secrets to be found in the marriage bed, sharing their bodies as easily as they had their conversations?

The mental image of him indulging in such intimacies with another woman cut so deeply into her heart, it could mean only one thing.

She had, despite all her best intentions, fallen desperately in love with the Earl of Glenmor.

The situation could not have been more calamitous. It was sheer lunacy to allow her to stay, but what other choice did he have? He could hardly send her on her way, leave her alone and unprotected in London. Even with the funds Lady Dalridge had paid her for services rendered, what she had would barely keep her for a week, even if she managed to find a respectable place that would take in a single lady.

No, he had done the right thing. It was just that...

Benedict stared blankly at the ledger in front of him and sighed for about the sixth time in ten minutes. It had been three days since Judith's arrival. Seventy-two long, torturous hours. He had no clue how to exist in this house with her. He could not turn a corner without fear she would be coming from the other direction. And when she wasn't, he could not stop the wave of disappointment that greeted him in her absence.

He dropped his head to rest against the pages of the ledger that detailed, in perfectly ordered columns, the dire circumstances of the family's finances and groaned. She was a prisoner in his home and yet he was the one locked away in his study for fear seeing her would cause him to lose the tenuous grip he had on his self-control. Because what he really wanted

—what he imagined whenever he walked the hallways of Glenmor House—was not only finding her around the next corner, but also pinning her to the wall then kissing her madly until he'd ruined them both.

Ah. He smiled. Now that was a lovely, *lovely* idea.

His head shot up. No! No. Not lovely. Awful. Horrible. Disastrous!

He pushed away from his desk and stalked to the door. He needed air. Fresh air, but London in the early evening would have to do. He must clear his mind of Judith Sutherland and erase all thoughts of touching her or kissing her or—

A vision of her splayed across the soft linen sheets on his bed, her dark hair curled seductively around her generous breasts, teasing the nipples while she looked up at him with a knowing smile, filled with mystery and promise filled his head.

Dear sweet Lord!

He yanked open the door and rushed down the hallway, taking the steps two at a time and practically leaping upon the floor of the foyer, his boots skidding against the polished marble.

"Good heavens, my lord!" Titus jumped back, the silver salver he always seemed to be carrying in his hand nearly upended in surprise, forcing him to slap a gloved hand over the envelopes laid out on its surface.

"My coat, Titus. I must leave. I need to—" No. Best he not actually state what he needed aloud. "I must take some air."

Titus recovered himself. "Now, my lord?"

"Yes, now. Immediately. This very second." Bloody hell. He sounded like a raving lunatic. Calm yourself, man!

But the teasing vision of Judith, naked beneath him, had sent his blood boiling and his heart racing and only the cold December air had any hope of setting things back to rights. And he must set things back to rights, even if he had to walk all night to do so. He was being abominably rude, after all, avoiding her as he did. What kind of host treated a guest in such a disparaging way? His mother would be shocked at his behavior.

Although, likely the bigger shock would be the fact Judith was here at all under such circumstances. And should his mother become privy to the scandalous notions he'd entertained since first issuing his invitation for Judith to stay, she would be thoroughly horrified and likely call for his head on a platter.

Titus returned with his coat and held it out for him to slip his arms into. "Shall I put these in your study, my lord?" He nodded toward the salver he'd set on a small table near the stairs.

"Is there anything of interest?"

"The Lindwells are hosting a dinner party and wish your attendance, my lord. As well, there are several other invitations of note and a letter that bears the Blackbourne seal and appears to have been addressed by your sister, Lady Blackbourne, if my eye does not deceive."

Likely another missive insisting he cease his ridiculous bride hunt. How desperately he wished he could take her up on it. "Put them on my desk, Titus. I will see to them upon my return."

The Lindwells. Both daughters were lovely to look upon. Both had dowries significant enough to make his life much easier. He should decide upon one of them and court her, make an offer. Get it over with. It made sense. They wished a titled gentleman; he wished a fortune in exchange. It was a fair swap. Yet he could not think of it without his insides turning cold. Hardly a brilliant start to a life together.

If only—

But no. He did not allow the extravagance of *if onlys*.

"I will return later, Titus. Do not hold dinner for me."

Yet another meal Judith would take alone. He really must

gain control of his desires or risk having her hate him for his inhospitable nature by week's end.

"But my lord, it is—"

"Whatever it is, I will deal with it later." He needed to get away, to let the fresh air clear his head. To—holy sweet Jesus!

The harsh wind whipped across his face like a hard slap, cold and bitter, pulling the air from his lungs, and leaving him reeling. He blinked but it did nothing to rid him of the wet snowflakes sticking to his lashes, all but blinding him. When had this happened? Granted, he had spent the better part of the day enshrouded in his study and took little notice of the weather. But when had it gone from a dreary, gray day to the ungodly white hell unleashed from above? Why, he could barely see to the other side of the street.

He stumbled back into the foyer, shaking the snow from his hair and coat. Titus awaited him on the other side in silence, although his single, raised eyebrow spoke volumes.

"It appears to be snowing."

"Yes, my lord."

Benedict cleared his throat. "Likely that is what you were about to tell me."

"Indeed, my lord."

"Right. Very well then." He forced a tight smile. "It appears I will be staying for dinner after all."

"I shall alert the kitchens, my lord."

B enedict's presence at dinner surprised her, given his studious attempts to dodge her over the past few days. Not a coincidence, she was certain. Glenmor House was not so large that he could avoid her unless attempting to do so. Not that she blamed him, really. She had shown up on his doorstep unannounced with every intent on staying here, putting them both in a precarious predicament. Granted, she had believed Mrs. Laytham in residence at the time, but her erroneous assumption did not alter their present dilemma.

She was a prisoner of her own making, filling the endless hours reading and doing needlepoint. After three days, she was bored to tears and would have greatly appreciated some conversation. A little interaction with her host. She would have even settled for a hint of his smile as they passed in the hall.

Except they never passed in the hall. Although she could have sworn that yesterday afternoon, she heard his approach only to then hear a hasty retreat. When she turned the corner, no one was there, but the door to Mrs. Laytham's bedchamber was slightly ajar. Perhaps it had only been one of the maids, but the footfalls had sounded too heavy.

Now, with dinner at an end, she'd barely been able to coerce more than a few words out of Benedict. Had he come to the conclusion her presence in his home was a horribly flawed idea? If so, she had but one recourse available.

"I think it best if I leave," she announced, glancing sideways to where Benedict sat at the head of the table.

His fork, filled with succulent roast beef, stopped halfway to his mouth, which hung open, waiting to accept it. The fork hovered for a moment before he lowered it back down to his plate. "Leave? But you've barely touched your meal?"

"No, not the meal. The house."

Surprise registered on his features doing nothing to mar his handsomeness. "You can't. We discussed this. It is too risky. If you are recognized, you will be ruined. Whatever you need, I will have someone fetch it for you."

"You misunderstand. It isn't that I need something. It is more that you have made it clear you do not want me here and I do not blame you. I arrived without warning and cast us both into an untenable situation. It was wrong of me to stay here. I should have left immediately and not involved you in my problems."

"I told you to come to me."

And she had taken him up on it without considering the price they would pay for it. She'd had no right to jeopardize his future in such a way. It was not fair. He had his own problems and her presence here only compounded them.

"I appreciate what you have done, but I cannot in good conscience continue to put you in harm's way. It was selfish of me not to consider this beforehand." But in the moment, all she'd been able to think of was finding a safe place to go and she could think of no place safer than with Benedict. "I will use my earnings to hire a carriage and convey me home."

His hand cut through the air. "Absolutely not. I cannot send you on such a journey unprotected."

"It is not your decision, my lord."

"It is very much my decision. You came to me for protection and are now under my care. As such—"

"Leaving is my prerogative and there is nothing you can do to stop me, short of barring the doors and windows to prevent my departure. I have taken up enough of your time and put your ability to find a suitable bride in peril. I cannot allow this to continue. I will leave at an early hour of the morning while your neighbors are still tucked in their beds and spirit myself out of town before anyone is the wiser."

"Which does nothing to address you traveling without chaperone or protection."

"I can hire that as well."

"You do not have the funds to cover such an expenditure."

"If you were to arrange such, I am certain Uncle Arran will—"

Benedict's hand cut through the air, nearly brushing his wineglass that the footman had already refilled twice. "No. I will allow no such thing. Sir Arran would have my hide if I did not personally ensure your safety. I cannot—*will not*—hand such a task over to someone else."

"Uncle Arran may well have your hide if he sees us arrive together, knowing we do so without a proper chaperone."

"I will bring Mrs. Feeney."

"And what of the time I spent here in the interim?"

He shrugged, though looked uncertain, as if he had not quite considered this part of their dilemma. "We will conveniently leave that part out. We can tell him I brought you directly from Lord Ridgemont's. He will be none the wiser in that regard."

She scoffed. Did he really believe that? The ton treated gossip like the air they breathed. Necessary to sustain life. "Word will get out that I was relieved of my position by Lady Dalridge, I can assure you. Once Lord Pengrin notices my absence he will ensure it reaches all the right ears."

A muscle in Benedict's jaw jumped, drawing Judith's attention. She had been trying not to look too closely at him, afraid if she did her insistence that she leave would falter. Her silly heart would whisper how much it truly wanted to stay, to haunt the rooms and hallways in the hopes he would appear and gift her with a smile. A kiss. More.

Heat rushed to her face and she looked away.

"Do you truly wish to leave me?"

"No," her rebellious heart whispered and the truth slipped off her tongue before she could stop it. She would have been fine if he had simply asked if she wanted to leave, but he'd asked if she wanted to leave *him* and somehow that made all the difference. Because she did not want to leave him. She didn't ever want to leave him.

Silence lingered in the air crackling with a tension she could not put a name to. Need? Desire? Something else? Something more.

"Then stay, and let us not speak of this again. I will

endeavor to conclude my business quickly and we will leave directly thereafter. A couple of days at most. We shall put our heads together and concoct a reasonable story to appease your uncle's concerns and keep your reputation intact."

She wanted to argue, to refuse, but her heart was not in it and too easily her mind was swayed with the seductive promise of a few more days in his presence.

"Very well then."

———

A wise man would have let her go. Then again, a wise man would never have allowed her to set foot in his home under such circumstances to begin with. But Benedict could not blame Titus in that regard. Had it been he who had opened the door, he would have ushered her in for no other reason than because he wished her to be there. And now here she was. And here he was. And she'd presented him with the perfect opportunity to let her go and he'd refused.

No, not just refused. Demanded that she not go. He gave every reason he could throw at her, none of which were the true reason he fought so hard to keep her here.

And that, quite simply, was that he did not want her to go. Ever.

He played with fire, fulfilling a need with one hand and courting destruction with the other. There was no good that could come of this. None. He needed to stop this madness before it went too far. Yet, when she joined him in the library shortly after the meal ended—on his own invitation, no less— madness was not the first thing he felt. Nor the second. Not even the third.

Unless one considered the fact he was mad for her. About her.

He closed his eyes and took a breath, then opened them

again to watch her peruse the stack of books, her fingertips lightly caressing the spines as she passed over them. He imagined those fingertips touching him in such a manner, skimming over his chest, stomach, lower.

He caught a groan as it attempted to escape and swallowed it back. Dangerous thinking, but he was powerless to stop it. He could not look at her without thinking how much he wanted her. Longed for her. He could think of nothing but her.

He stood and walked toward her, his steps muffled by the worn Aubusson rug beneath his feet.

"Miss Sutherland?"

She gave a small jolt of surprise and turned, her fingers falling away from the books. She smiled and it passed through him like a breath of warm air on a summer's eve. "I thought we agreed to call each other by our given names in private?"

"We did at that."

A brief silence passed between them. "Did you have a question to ask? You have that look about you."

He lifted one eyebrow. He had a look? "And what look might that be?"

Her smile grew and with it the beating of his heart. "The one filled with expectation."

Benedict glanced down at his feet and pursed his lips together. She had no idea the expectations he longed to have fulfilled. But that was not his purpose. He had a far more chaste plan in mind, one that would fulfill the desire to have her close, to hold her in his arms one last time before he must let her go forever.

He looked up and took a deep breath, holding his hand out to her. "I wondered if you might allow me the honor of that dance you promised."

"A dance?" She gave a small laugh. It reminded him of the

sound twinkling stars might make if they had the ability to do so. "But we have no music?"

Did they not? Because he was quite certain he could feel sweet melodies coursing through his veins while haunting harmonies seeped into his heart with such intent he suspected they would linger there long after the moment passed.

He hummed a few notes and watched her eyes light up with surprise. What a glorious creature she was. Anyone who had ever considered her plain or unremarkable had never spent more than a moment in her company. They had never taken notice of the expressions that traveled through her eyes or the hundred different smiles that played upon her lips. They'd never spoken to her or heard her laugh or experienced the stirring pleasure when their name tripped off the tip of her tongue.

They'd never kissed her as he had. Never tasted and savored and devoured her.

They'd never loved her, and for that he was eternally grateful, because had they, she would not be here now. And he could not imagine a more magical place existed in the world than in this library, in this moment, with him standing there, his hand held out as he hummed a tune just a little off key.

And they would never know the distinct pleasure of the instant her ungloved hand slid into his and accepted his invitation of a dance long overdue.

Chapter Twenty

B enedict gave himself strict orders to keep a proper distance between them. Such restrictions lasted only long enough for him to finish the first third of the song, however, and by then he had inched closer. Or perhaps she had stepped closer. He could not be sure. Nor did he care, as the result was that mere inches were left between them as they slowly waltzed about the section of the library where no furniture collaborated to impede their efforts.

"What is the song?" she asked him. "I do not recognize it."

"It is one my father used to hum to my mother whenever he wanted to entice her into a dance. It has stuck with me all these years, but I'm afraid I cannot claim to know its name or origin."

"What a lovely memory." Her soft voice was like a caress.

He smiled. It was a lovely memory, though not one he'd allowed himself in recent years. The sudden elevation in his status to earl and the burdens that had come with it often left him scrabbling for purchase and allowed little time to remember the way things had once been. In truth, he tried not to think of those days, for as warm and familiar as the memories were, they shared with them the pain of loss. A loss he had not been able to prevent or been there to provide comfort against as it ravaged the other members of his family.

"Did your parents often dance about?" Judith's calm voice chased his demons back to the shadows, but their footprints lingered on his heart. Had she sensed his sorrow? He squeezed her hand gently, a silent thank-you, just in case.

"They did," he said. "My father was a firm believer you should dance with a lovely lady every single day of your life, for if you did not, you risked making waste to a day."

"Your father sounded like a very wise man."

He nodded. "Far wiser than I."

Odd that he should consider Father wise. After all, he had failed to perform the one duty his family expected of him—marrying to enhance the family's standing and connections. Much like Benedict, he had fallen madly in love with the wrong woman and been so captivated by her he had ignored his family's dictates, pleas, threats, and ultimate renouncement to be with the woman he loved. He had left the life of comfort and privilege and struck out on his own with little more than the small pittance of savings he had managed to stow away.

It had been nothing short of insanity.

Yet Benedict had never known a man more insanely happy than his father.

"I think you do not give yourself the credit you deserve," Judith told him.

Sometimes it was as if she could read his mind, an ability he wouldn't put past her. She had to possess some unusual power to have so positively ensnared him despite all his best efforts.

Fine. Perhaps his efforts had not been his best. In fact, giving said efforts a cursory review, he could not even claim to have tried all that hard to avoid such. Truthfully, he had run to her at every chance, making up one excuse after another to be in her presence. Was it any wonder he found himself in this predicament now?

"Benedict?" He looked at her and realized they had stopped dancing. "Are you quite all right?"

He did not know how to respond. He should tell her yes. She did not deserve to be burdened with his troubles. But when he opened his mouth to give the prudent answer common sense dictated he respond with, the words from his heart muscled past and leaped out instead.

"I'm about to kiss you."

Her eyebrows lifted. "You are?"

He nodded, unable to remove his gaze from her lips. "Yes. I thought I should give you fair warning, in case you'd prefer that I didn't and wished to express as much."

She smiled and heat shot directly to his groin. "I see. And will you abide by my wishes?"

"I will."

"Then I wish you to kiss me as you did before, so that I might feel it all the way down to my toes."

He swallowed. She *had* felt it too then. He feared he might have been mistaken, that he had simply projected his own wants and needs onto her to justify his ungentlemanly like behavior.

He touched her face, the soft, smooth skin beneath his fingertips sending shards of fire spiraling up his arm before spreading across his chest and then diving downward to pool much lower. He could not. Should not. Would not.

And yet, he did.

What sweet ecstasy she was! How desperately her touch reminded him of all the things he would miss if he continued to follow the path he'd set for himself. And to what end? To recapture everything Henry and his father had lost in their own pursuit for love? Such a strange circle he'd found himself in, the proverbial snake devouring its own tail.

The touch of her lips upon his was like a sigh, the kind that only someone who has come home after a long journey could possibly understand. He enfolded her in his arms, held her tight, let the warmth of her body and her heart fill him. She tasted of the sweetest honey and he explored her with his tongue, gently until she joined him and they teased and tangled and tormented together.

"I must have you," he whispered, the words harsh. Painful. He did not want to want it so much. He wished to be a stronger man, but to his utter dismay, he discovered such was not the case. She was his weakness. She took him out at the knees and left him beggared at her feet.

"I am yours." The words kissed upon his lips, a promise. A destruction. He could stop now. Step away and beg her forgiveness. She would never hold him accountable. She had too much pride to marry a man who did so only out of duty or sense of obligation.

He quickly dismissed the concern as it stole through his mind. He would not stop. Not without her express wish that he do so.

J udith caught her breath as Benedict swept her up into his arms and carried her from the room. He stopped at the door to the library and peered left and right, but the hallway and staircase ahead of them remained blessedly empty. Not that it would matter. She had said the words, surrendered herself to whatever scandal followed.

I am yours.

She would be ruined after this, a truth she could not escape. Nor cared to.

Why should she? She wanted no other but he, yet fully understood such could never be, not for the long term. But for this moment, he was hers, and she his. And when this moment ended, she would take the memories and pack them around her heart to protect her for when he took another as his bride. She would live out her days at Havelock Manor and do her best to live a life of service to others. Perhaps, if she filled her life with purpose she would not feel the loss of him quite so acutely.

But such ideas and plans were for later. For now, she gave herself over to the exhilaration of being carried up the stairwell, Benedict taking the stairs two at a time as if she weighed but a stone. He stopped abruptly and set her on her feet before pulling her into an alcove lost to the darkness. A maid passed by farther down the hallway but their presence remained undetected. Once she was gone, Benedict took her hand.

"Come," he said with a smile, giving her a glimpse of the mischievous boy who had been lost to the ages, squelched by duty and circumstance. Oh, how she would have loved to have seen him then. How she loved all the more to catch a glimpse of that boy now.

He led her past her own room and around another corner until they reached a door. He opened it swiftly and stepped into the dark interior, turning to face her as he pulled her to him. A small fire smoldered in the hearth in anticipation of its master's return. The bed too, had been turned down as if expecting them. A faint light spilled out from the low-burning fire and trickled across the floor and two candles flickered beneath glass sconces on a nearby table. It was enough to both light the room yet cast it in shadows. Even so, the masculine feel of its décor enticed her. Beckoned her to explore.

She pulled away from him and walked farther into the room. For the most part, the décor told her little about the man. Touches one would expect to see, that gave a room a distinct flavor of the person it belonged to, were notably absent, save for a book set on the nightstand next to the bed. It was turned over, marking where he'd left it last. She picked it up, careful not to lose his spot, and read the cover. *The Wanderer* by Frances Burney. Not exactly the type of novel one would expect to find a gentleman of the ton reading.

She smiled at him over its edge. "I am impressed."

He crossed the room to join her and slowly pulled the book from her hands, closing it with a smile, a glint of humor in his eyes. "It belonged to my sister, Abigail. She suggested it to me and it seemed a far more entertaining read in the evenings than a thick tome on crop rotation."

How solitary his world must be, now that both Abigail and Caelie were married and his mother spent her time between here and Sheridan Park with her new grandson. What had once been a home busy with people and activity had been reduced to a household of one. Perhaps the idea of marriage held other benefits to him beyond financial. Did he long to fill the house with life and laughter once again? To have someone to spend his days and nights with and fill the emptiness that echoed off the walls? What a shame it would be if he were to find a bride who did not offer the companionship he craved or accept the love he offered.

She pushed such concerns from her mind. She did not want to think of him married to another. It would come soon enough and her heart would break in two, of that she had no doubt. But for now, they were here, just the two of them. She rested her hands upon the lapels of his jacket, his chest solid beneath the superfine wool. He had taken care with his appearance for dinner this evening, yet now that dinner had ended and the evening had come to a close, she wanted nothing more than to see him out of his finely tailored clothes. She longed to peel his jacket off his shoulders, pull his shirt over his head, and press her mouth to his warm skin.

Her heart raced and she reached for a distraction. "And are you enjoying the book?"

"I am enjoying you more." He tossed the book onto the table and wrapped his strong arms around her. His lips dropped to her neck and teased against her pulse until her head fell back to give him full access. His mouth glided downward, trailing a line of kisses across her collarbone then across the rise of her breasts where the scooped bodice of her gown left them exposed.

When he lifted his head and pressed his mouth against hers a fever heated within her veins and rushed throughout her body, igniting a fire that raged beyond her control.

"I cannot think rationally when I am near you," Benedict confessed, pressing his lips to hers. She understood the sentiment. Returned it. His kiss left her breathless. Hungry, yet gentle, it reached somewhere deep inside of her, touching upon the part she kept hidden from others for fear of being hurt. But she did not fear him.

He broke the kiss, his chest rising and falling. He leaned his forehead against hers, a gesture so simple and yet so intimate. "There is so much wrong with this," he said.

But she disagreed. "Nothing has ever felt more right than this."

Perhaps society would call what went on between them sinful or scandalous, but Judith had learned the hard way that those opinions were built on hypocrisy. The ton set their puritanical rules, but few actually lived by them, yet most did not hesitate to cast stones at others who did the same.

"Should I stop?" Benedict's voice whispered in her ear, an edge of desperation dancing around his words.

"No. Do not." The answer came easily, definitively. She had been unsure about so much lately, but not this. This was true and real. Her feelings could not be denied even if circumstances allowed their relationship to go no farther than tonight. She held him to nothing beyond this.

He did not argue with her, a fact that both surprised and delighted her. "Turn around."

She did as he bade and felt the pull against the fabric of her dress as he undid the long row of buttons down her back. Within a few minutes, he pushed the gown over her shoulders and let it fall down her arms, until it tumbled into a heap at her feet.

She did not move, unsure of what to do. Benedict's arms wrapped around her waist and pulled her against him. The length of him warmed her. His hardness pushed against her bottom and a thrill shot through her, robbing her of breath.

Benedict's lips kissed a trail of heat across her shoulders and upper back where it was left exposed by her chemise and stays. The ties of which he soon loosened until that garment, too, fell away. She shivered. No man had ever touched her with such gentleness and reverence. Had touched her at all really, save for—

But no. She refused to think of that now. Refused to sully this wondrous moment with a past she could not change.

Benedict's hand slid over her hip before reaching down and pulling the hem of her chemise upward. Cool air rushed to meet her exposed skin and a familiar ache between her legs begged for relief.

"Lift your arms, my love."

The words skimmed across her skin and she obliged, being undressed before him both exhilarating and frightening. The linen disappeared over her head and dropped onto the floor next to her stays until she was left with nothing covering her save for her stockings and drawers. Benedict's touch disappeared. She glanced over her shoulder to find he had stepped away.

"Turn around. Let me see you," he said softly. She did, modesty forcing her arms across her chest. "Don't cover yourself. Let me see."

She kept her arms in place and tilted her head to one side. "But what of you?"

"Me?"

"Yes." She smiled through her shyness. "I am standing here in my drawers and stockings and you are still fully clothed. It seems rather imbalanced, wouldn't you say?"

A slow grin spread across his face, brightening his eyes as the candlelight flickered over him. "I suppose you have me there." He reached for the buttons on his jacket but stopped before undoing them. "Should I call in my valet to assist me?"

Judith laughed. Oh, how she loved hearing the ease in his voice, as if he'd sent his worries on holiday and allowed the lighter disposition his sister had attested he once possessed to take center stage. What she wouldn't give to make all his days like this.

"I think enlisting your valet at this point would be ill advised."

"Very well then, but I may require your assistance."

"I'm hardly dressed for it."

"You're hardly dressed at all," he teased as he undid the buttons of his jacket. "And I find I quite like you this way. But if you are shy, I promise I shall allow you your privacy."

"And how will you do that?"

He closed his eyes. "Like so. Now pull my coat down my arms."

She moved to stand in front of him and pushed the superfine wool over his shoulders, her hands brushing the breadth of them, running over the hard muscle beneath. He had spoken to her often about his preference for pursuits that took him out-of-doors and such active living had left him in fine form. A thrill raced through her at seeing him in his full glory and she hurried to push and pull at the jacket until it met the same fate as her own clothing and lay crumpled on the floor at their feet.

Benedict undid the buttons of his waistcoat and disposed of it, as well as his shirt, with far greater speed than she had his jacket. She took in a swift breath. Saints preserve her, but he was a fine, fine specimen of the male form. Hard planes and sculpted ridges reminded her of the statutes that populated Sheridan Park's gardens. Her fingers itched to reach out and touch him, to see if he was composed of flesh and blood, or cool marble.

He continued undressing, undoing the buttons on his trousers and pulling them down, stopping abruptly when he hit the top of his boots. He straightened, his eyes remaining closed and his hands upon his hips. The image both comical and enticing all at once. How was such a thing possible?

"It appears I have reached a bit of an impasse."

The absurdity of her previous shyness struck her as Benedict stood before her, his trousers bunched at his knees and the evidence of his need for her evident in his drawers. Laughter bubbled up inside until it escaped. "I suddenly feel a little silly being shy, given what we are about to do."

He opened one eye and his gaze roamed over her. She made no move to cover herself this time. "And what is it that we are about to do?"

Heat from his gaze burned into her bare skin until the need for his touch upon it became too much to bear. She wanted him. Wanted him with a desire that went beyond anything she had ever experienced.

She smiled at him, reaching up to pull the pins from her hair. Her heart filled with love and want and a hundred other things she would examine later, when she had less pressing issues to deal with. For now, there was only one thing she wished to do.

"Perhaps we should wrestle you out of those boots and discover the answer to that question."

Chapter Twenty-One

B enedict thrilled at how quickly Judith overcame her initial shyness, though the true thrill came when she bent before him to pull his boots off. The gentle sway of her lovely, full breasts was almost more than he could handle. The temptation to say the hell with his boots and pull her onto his lap and let her ride him until they both found their release became overwhelming, but he held himself in check. He did not want to rush this. He wanted to savor every tormenting moment of it. More than that, he wanted her to savor every moment of it as well.

It took several minutes, and far more laughter than he ever recalled being involved in dispersing of a pair of boots and trousers, before he too was left in nothing but his drawers. He kept them on for now afraid of moving too fast, though the evidence of his need for her had become more than apparent.

"Shall I remove your stockings, my lady?" How he longed to touch those long, shapely limbs. As beautiful as she was, he had not expected such magnificent curves to be hidden beneath the plain gowns she insisted upon wearing. Such a glorious surprise, she was.

"I suppose we shall need to, won't we?" She stepped her feet out of her slippers.

"Not necessarily." There was something about the idea of taking her while she wore nothing more than her stockings that was rather appealing. Though not nearly as much as having every inch of her delectable body bared to him. "But for now, let us rid ourselves of any barriers, shall we?"

She nodded and he knelt before her as if worshipping at an altar. Perhaps, in a sense, that was what he did. She had saved him in a way, taking him away from his worries and creating an oasis where he could escape. She became his safe haven and no matter how hard he'd tried to resist her siren's call, he had failed.

Failure had never been so glorious.

He undid the ties holding up her first stocking and slowly rolled it down, kissing the soft skin of her inner thigh, relishing the catch of her breath as he drew nearer the juncture of her thighs. How tempting to stay there, to lavish such delights upon her. He swallowed. All in good time. She lifted her foot for him to remove the garment and he tossed it aside, then returned to the remaining stocking. Her skin was pure silk and a part of him wished he had more time to cover every inch of her with his mouth. But another part of him pleaded for release.

He reached for the ribbon holding her drawers in place and slowly pulled it until it gave way. The soft cotton slid over her hips like a tantalizing whisper, revealing her most private parts. Judith lowered her hand to cover herself, but he caught her wrist.

"No, don't," he said and she relented. He kissed the palm of her hand before releasing it to place his hands on the curve of her hips. He leaned in and gently pressed his mouth against the nest of curls between her thighs. She gasped and her fingers threaded through his hair. He waited several heartbeats but she did not pull away and so he kissed her again, sliding his tongue against her moist center.

Her head dropped back and she groaned, deep and guttural. "Benedict." She breathed his name. It had never sounded so splendid.

"Should I stop now?"

"No." She shook her head. "I do not think you should."

And so he didn't. Nudging her legs apart to allow him better access, he kissed her again. His hands slid to her rounded bottom as he lavished her with slow strokes of his tongue until she writhed in his hold, whimpering as her fingers pulled at his hair for purchase. He brought her to the brink, the taste of her a sweet nectar.

"Are you ready for me, my love?"

"Oh, yes. Yes."

He stood, tossing aside the last stitch of clothing he'd had on and lifted her against him, her long legs wrapping around his waist as he caught her in a passionate kiss. Her bottom brushed against his cock until he feared he'd lose his mind if he did not have her. Any hope he'd had of taking this slow tossed out the window the moment he'd touched her. He could not wait and from the way she clung to him, kissed him with such passionate desperation, he sensed she shared his need.

He carried her to his bed and laid her upon it. She shimmied up the mattress, her hungry gaze never leaving his as he followed, covering her with his body once he reached her. She rained tiny kisses upon his cheeks, eyelids, and edge of his jaw until finally she found his mouth.

Her kiss stripped him of rational thought. She nibbled at his lips, explored him with her tongue then nipped playfully at him until madness hovered, threatening his sanity. The warmth of her body seeped into him, penetrating all of the dark places where he kept his secrets hidden. She laid him bare and he had no defense against her.

She enthralled him and the truth of the moment settled deep within him. There was no going back, no other future for them but the one where they were together, come what may. The reality of it hit him all at once. It could destroy him as well as her, liberating her from one ruin only to deliver her into another. Yet he could not let her go. He had tried. God knows, he had tried. But fate kept bringing him back to her as if it was trying to tell him something he was too foolish or blind to see.

But he saw it now.

This was what was meant to be. Whatever else befell them, they would get through it. Like his parents had done before them.

Love will win in the end. It always does. His father's words spoken firmly and often. Benedict had never paid them much heed when he was younger, but their meaning hit him full force now. He should have known. He should have seen it. He *had* seen it. He'd just been too stubborn to acknowledge the truth. Yet now the truth lay beneath him, smiling up at him, her dark hair tumbled around the white sheets much as he had imagined night after night in his dreams.

Love had won.

But would it be enough? Because when all was said and done, it may be the only thing Benedict had left to offer Judith.

He kissed her again, erasing the worry from his mind and losing himself in her. She wrapped herself around him and pressed her hips against him, urging him on. He could not hold back. He needed her, needed to know what it was like to become part of someone else's body, mind and soul. He pushed inside of her, slowly and with care. She stiffened at the intrusion and he stopped despite his body's yearning to throw caution to the wind and lose himself inside of her.

"Did I hurt you?"

She gave a rueful smile. "Perhaps a little, but it's easing now. It was more surprising than anything else." She moved against him and he groaned. She would be the death of him. "Sorry."

"Don't be. It felt wonderful," he said. If wonderful was categorized as a wrestling match between torment and desire. He touched the line of her jaw with his fingertips. How lovely she was. How fortunate he was that he would now be able to gaze upon her loveliness for the rest of his days. "We can stop if you wish."

"I wish no such thing." She lifted enough to capture his mouth with hers and the torment he suffered increased tenfold. Without thinking, he began to move inside of her with slow thrusts until she broke the kiss and let her head fall back against the pillows, her long hair surrounding her like a dark halo. Her breath came in rapid gasps and her hands clenched his shoulders, her fingers digging into his flesh. He moved quicker, his body taking over and creating its own rhythm, meeting hers until their passion melded together, twisting and tangling them in its clutches until there was no ending or beginning.

Everything within Benedict became lost in her until his body and mind exploded and she shuddered beneath him, a cry of surprise erupting from somewhere deep within before they collapsed together, entwined, nothing left but breath and wonderment and a fulfillment he had never known or experienced before.

This was his life now. *She* was his life now. And a luckier man did not exist.

. . .

J udith's heartbeat slowly returned to normal as Benedict shifted to rest next to her. He had said nothing since the cataclysmic event that had sent her body reeling, tumbling...soaring. She had never experienced anything more wondrous. It defied all description, becoming a hundred different things all at once. Sensory and sensual, physical and emotional. A complete blending of everything she knew and all the things she didn't until, at its end, she was a different person. How was such a thing possible?

And what did she do about that now?

She glanced over at Benedict. His gaze rested firmly upon her, but something about it seemed far away, as if she had lost him to his thoughts.

"What are you thinking?" She turned to face him, drawing her hand down his cheek, her thumb resting against his lips until their touch brought a smile to them. Such an amazing thing to be able to touch him freely like this.

"I was thinking of you. Of how many nights I have lain awake imagining you here, just like this."

A blush heated her cheeks. "You did not!"

He chuckled and the sound rumbled deep in his throat. "I did. Repeatedly. It made for some rather uncomfortable nights."

"And how did those imaginings liken to this?"

"They paled in comparison."

She smiled, her heart close to bursting. If only she could spend the rest of her life right here, wrapped up in bed with him, the rest of the world held at bay. But such a dream could never come true. Her smile faltered and she searched for a distraction. She would not allow the world to intrude on them, not yet. It would come soon enough.

"Tell me about the pipe I always see you carry."

"My pipe?"

She nodded. "Your mother told me it belonged to your father. I noticed you carry it with you and often take it out when you are worrying over something. Does it help, having it?"

Benedict's brow furrowed and Judith worried perhaps she had chosen the wrong topic of conversation, but she couldn't help herself. She longed to learn as much about him, about the lingering pain that lived in his blue eyes, about the influences that informed his decisions, the history that made him who he was now. Soon the time to discover all of these things would draw to a close and if she did not learn them now, she would forever wonder.

"Yes, I suppose it does," he answered, capturing a lock of her hair in his hand and twirling it loosely about his finger. "It's a reminder, more than anything."

"Of your father?"

His gaze remained fixed on the lock of hair, his thumb caressing it where it curled about his fingers. She resisted the urge to reach out and smooth the twin lines that had formed between his eyebrows.

"Of his strength. His dedication to our family above all else. The faith he put in me to continue to do so in his stead."

The pain in his eyes intensified as his voice drifted off. The words resounded within Judith, echoing inside of her with the answers she had searched for. Benedict did not believe he had lived up to the faith put in him by his father, the man he idolized above all others. The man he wanted to be.

"I think your father would be exceptionally proud of who you've become and the things you've accomplished."

Benedict scoffed and let her curl go, rolling over onto his back. "I doubt that. I have let my family down time and again."

"In what way have you possibly failed your family?" He had worked diligently to resurrect the family's finances and reputation after his uncle had all but destroyed both with his scandalous obsession over Madame St. Augustine. The story was legend, and even she had been privy to it, all the way out in the country. Despite his family being ostracized from society shortly thereafter, no one had a bad thing to say about Benedict, from what she'd witnessed. Save perhaps for Lord Pengrin, but she hardly considered him a credible source when it came to judging character, given that he had none of his own.

Benedict let out a slow breath. "After Father and Roddy died, I refused to return to school after their funerals. Mother was still quite weak and the loss had hit her hardest of all, as one can imagine. I could not leave her and Abigail to fend for themselves. So I stayed and tried to keep a roof over our heads. But eventually what little money we had ran out and I could not find a decent enough job to support us all."

Judith turned onto her side and nestled next to Benedict, placing her hand on his chest near his heart, a bandage for the wound she had inadvertently opened. "What did you do?"

Color stained his cheekbones. "I had no choice but to ask Uncle Henry to take us in."

"Was he not happy to do so? You said he ensured your schooling. He must have had an interest in your family's well-being."

Benedict nodded. "Yes, I think so. Uncle Henry had always had a soft spot for my father. Though I had the impression he preferred this affection to be dealt with from afar, for the sake of family harmony. His wife despised us. She considered us interlopers and treated us as such. It did not make for a warm welcome. Uncle Henry did not care to incur her wrath and so we spent years navigating around Aunt Edythe's anger and resentment. I hated that my inability to provide for them put Mother and Abigail in such a situation. Father would never have allowed such a thing had he survived. Nor would he have allowed Uncle Henry to destroy himself and the family finances over his insane obsession for his mistress."

"You don't know that," she said. His expectations of himself, given his age and experience at the time, were beyond what he—or anyone else in that position—could accomplish. He had been all of seventeen when his father died. Eighteen when they'd arrived in London to a world he had never experienced. She knew what that was like.

His hand came up to cover hers, his fingers absently caressing the back of her hand. "I do know. My father had an uncanny way of always landing on his feet, no matter what you threw his way. And he did it all with a smile. I swear, he was the happiest man I have ever known."

The stories Benedict's sister and mother had told her of Roderick Laytham bore these facts out. But the reason behind his happiness had always been rooted in his love for his wife and children. Perhaps if Benedict found this as well, he would stand a chance at recovering the happiness he had once known.

But how could he do such if he must continue to struggle to get his feet under him? At least a rich bride—such a loathsome thought—would provide him a leg up in that regard. Something she could never give him. All she could give him was now, this moment, this night.

"Perhaps I shall endeavor to make you happy while I can. Would you like that?"

His smile returned and the pain in his gaze receded, though did not disappear entirely. Judith leaned up on her elbow and pressed her lips to his. His hand sank into her hair and pulled her closer until her body covered his and his growing erection pressed against her. It took little effort to stoke the embers of their earlier passion into a raging fire and soon enough Benedict rolled her onto her back and filled her until they lost themselves in each other once again. Judith gave herself over to him, to the oblivion their lovemaking created, to the hours they had left together to create memories to carry for a lifetime.

Chapter Twenty-Two

"We will marry, of course."

The words were said in a matter-of-fact way and, at first, took Judith by surprise. But as the shock wore off, they only served to make her angry. Forcing Benedict into proposing marriage was not her intention when she made the decision to give herself to him. She had not wanted their night together to be about duty or sacrifice. It had been about love. About a moment in time she could tuck away and keep in her heart to comfort her in the years ahead. She did not want those memories stained by him thinking what they had done was something that required fixing. Of course, most of society would consider what they did sinful, but given that none of them were privy to such things, what reason was there for him to trot out such nonsense now? He could not marry her. She understood. She had asked for naught but what he gave last night and expected nothing more beyond that.

"We will not marry," she answered, her words as plainly spoken as his. She would not rob him of his need to come through for his family, no matter how wrong or misguided it was.

He turned his head to look at her, the sheets rustling beneath the movement. "There is no other option. I understood this going in."

His claim surprised her, but did not change her mind. He made what they had shared sound like an end. A sacrifice. Whatever warm and wonderful feelings she had woken up with in the morning sunlight dispersed as if dark clouds had slipped into the room unnoticed and snuffed out the light.

"There is another option and I plan to take it. No one knows anything has happened between us and therefore there is no reason for you to throw yourself upon the sacrificial altar on my account."

"I have ruined you."

Funny, she did not feel ruined. Nor did she think of what they had shared as ruination. Ruination evoked the sense that something had been destroyed. As if *she* had been destroyed. She had not. If anything, what they had shared bolstered her strength. At least now, she had a lovely memory to carry with her; one shared with the man she loved.

Or so she believed. Now, however, his words tainted that belief. He had turned what they shared into a duty that now must be dealt with.

"I went into this willingly and do not hold you responsible. Please do not concern yourself with trying to remedy the situation. There is nothing that requires fixing. I will go my way and you will go yours and that will be the end of it." It was a sad but true fact.

"What if you are with child?"

She really wished he would stop talking.

Benedict turned onto his side to face her, propping his head up with his hand. Sleep and their lovemaking had left his hair mussed and she longed to reach up and put it back to rights, but she refrained. Perhaps five minutes ago, before he had begun this line of conversation she might have, but now a strange tension destroyed the closeness they'd shared.

"Judith?"

She held her tongue and refused to move her gaze from the canopy above. What did he expect her to say? Of course, if she carried his child she would have little choice in the matter. She was willing to risk her own ruination, but not that of her child. Their child. Her fingers twitched where they rested against her flat belly. Could it be?

"If I am with child. But only then."

"You're speaking madness. If you do not marry me what hope do you have of marrying at all?"

His question cut into her like a barbed spear, slicing through her tender flesh and embedding itself in her heart. "I thank you for your pointed observation."

He sighed. "That is not what I meant."

"But it is true nonetheless." Because of course, he was right. What hope did she have? What he didn't understand was that she had never had any hope. She was not the type to attract the kind of gentleman her family wished her to marry. Her first and only Season had been a complete disaster. How she had captured Benedict's attention remained a mystery. An anomaly not to be repeated.

"Why do you not wish to marry me?"

Judith turned on her side to face him finally. "Why do you wish to marry me?"

"Because we—" He motioned to the bed with his free hand. "What other choice can there be?"

Hardly the romantic declaration she had hoped for. If he had claimed he loved her or that he would give up his fortune for her, perhaps she would be swayed. But he had not. Instead, he spoke of duty, lack of choices, necessity. All the things she wished to save him from.

She turned away and slipped her legs off the edge of the bed. She needed to escape. If she did not, his words would destroy whatever tender memories the night had created and she could not bear that. It was all she had left.

"Judith." He called her name as a plea. "Come back to bed. We need to discuss this."

"There is nothing to discuss," she said, pulling the sheet with her as she went and leaving him laying a top the soft down mattress in all his glory. She refused to let her gaze linger. Instead, she rummaged about the floor for something to cover herself with so she could quickly slip from his room to hers. She found her drawers and pulled them on, then grabbed his shirt and slipped it over her head. The sleeves hung past her hands, its length nearly reaching her knees. It would have to be enough.

"Come back here." She heard him move and did not hesitate, hurrying to the bedchamber door. Surely, he would not chase her down the hallway undressed. She opened the door and took a quick glance in both directions before bolting down the hallway.

"Judith!" His harsh whisper reached her, but she did not turn around. She couldn't. There was no going back.

How could she not agree to marry him? Benedict stared out the window, but saw nothing save the memory of Judith's shapely rear end as she'd scrounged about the floor for clothing to cover herself with before making her escape down the hallway. A bold move, he would give her that. Why, at this time of the morning, the chance of running into one of the maids readying the house for the day was fairly high. It was that fact alone that kept him from chasing down the hallway after her. If her state of undress had the servants' tongues wagging, finding the lord of the manor sprinting after her naked as a babe would do nothing to improve matters.

Had any of the servants noticed she'd not slept in her bed last night? Or had she reached her bedchamber before her absence was discovered? If she hadn't, the servants weren't talking. At least not yet and he hoped such would continue. He could not afford to have idle gossip leak out to the other houses and destroy her reputation.

At least not until she came to her senses and let go of this foolish notion not to marry him.

But what if she didn't?

The possibility lingered like a bad dream in the back of his mind. When he had asked her to dance, his motives had been pure. Well, perhaps not pure, but he had not intended for things to go as far as they had. Regardless, once they had, he could not dispute the rightness of them being together, despite all the evidence to the contrary.

Mother had been right, as had Abigail. As had his own instincts that had protested from the moment he'd decided to marry for financial gain and not love and companionship. And despite his repeated denial, his instinct on this matter had steadfastly refused to be silenced. The first moment he'd held Judith in his arms, something had stirred inside of him. The more he got to know her, the stronger those feelings became until the truth could no longer be disputed. She was meant for him.

Unless, of course, you asked Judith's opinion on it, for apparently the idea of marrying him appalled her to such a degree she was willing to sacrifice her reputation to avoid it and would only consider marrying him if she had his baby growing inside of her!

He growled and pushed himself up from his chair by the

window to stalk the floor of his study. The woman was obviously mad. What had possessed her to let him take her innocence if she had no intention of accepting his proposal? And why did she act so surprised when he announced they would marry?

Granted, it was not the most romantic of proposals, but were they not past that, given what had transpired last night? He stopped in the middle of the room and let his head fall back as he stared up at the intricate patterns carved into the ceiling. He was a fool. Of course, she deserved a more romantic proposal. He should have professed his feelings. Told her how much he cared about her. Loved her. Needed her.

But bloody hell, was that not implied by the fact he was throwing away any hope of recovering the family fortunes in order to make her his and keep her in his life forever? Was it not enough he was doing the unthinkable and failing his family yet again in order to save her from public scorn and ridicule?

Even if he did not say the perfect words or express himself as he should have, was that reason enough to subject oneself to ruination and public disparagement? Was he to wait until she discovered whether she carried his child and, if not, suffer a second rejection? What kind of man did not make right the situation they found themselves cast into?

Cast into. As if it had happened by accident. It hadn't. Last night had been the culmination of a passion that had started building the night of Lady Blackbourne's birthday party, when he had held her in his arms and within moments become captivated by her intelligent observations and kind heart. He had tried to ignore it, avoid it. Avoid her. It had all been for naught.

His mother had once warned him this would happen. He'd asked her if she had ever considered remarrying. Father had been gone a decade by then and Mother was still a lovely and vital woman. But she had given him a sad smile and her answer remained fixed in his memory even now.

The heart wants what it wants, my dear. And my heart wants your father. Someday you will know what I mean."

He hadn't believed her at the time, but now her words rang true. His heart wanted Judith. It would consider no other. Yet she would not consider him. Where did that leave them?

"My lord?"

Benedict turned to find Titus standing in the doorway of his study. "Yes, Titus, what is it?"

"Lord Ridgemont, my lord. I have put him in the receiving room and requested tea and biscuits be brought."

Ridgemont? What did he want? To beg forgiveness for the way his family had cast Judith out when she'd tried to do them a good turn? "Very well, Titus. I will be along in a moment. Can you see that Miss Sutherland—"

"Mrs. Feeney has already ensured she is returned to her room for the duration of the marquess's visit."

"Thank you, Titus." No doubt she would dislike being quarantined, but he was not about to have her discovered. He strode down the hallway to the receiving room, taking a calming breath before he entered. There was no point going in angry until the marquess revealed the purpose of his visit.

"Ridgemont."

His guest turned at the sound of his name. "Glenmor. Good to see you again, old man. I hope it was not an inconvenience, my stopping by unannounced."

Benedict didn't answer right away. Ridgemont was nervous. There was an unexpected edge to his voice and a tightness about his eyes. "What can I do for you?"

Ridgemont's hands flexed at his side, reminding Benedict of the way Judith would tangle her fingers about each other when stressed over something. But what did Ridgemont have to be upset over?

"I expect you have heard of the unfortunate incident with respect to Miss Sutherland's employment?"

Benedict nodded. "Your great-aunt sacked her. What of it?" He did not bother to keep the curtness from his tone. He had considered Ridgemont to be a good man and that Judith would be kept safe under his roof. Instead, she was cast out without warning or protection. They had not even offered to see her safely home. It was unconscionable.

Ridgemont's fists tightened. "You have every right to be angry. I was too when I arrived home to find her gone. I have tried to locate her to no avail. I simply wish to ensure her safety and offer to provide her with a proper reference should she require such. I have sent a letter to Havelock Manor, assuming that is where she has gone, but I wish to confirm such and that she arrived safely."

"That does not explain why you are here."

Ridgemont raised one eyebrow. "I came here because my driver instructed me this is where he brought her. Was he incorrect?"

Hell and damn. "He was not." He said nothing more.

"Is she still here? If so, I would like to speak with her."

Benedict dodged the question with one of his own. "To what end?"

Ridgemont proved equally as evasive. "I do not see what business that is of yours. It is a private matter—"

"I can see no reason for you and Miss Sutherland to share a private matter."

Anger peaked along the edge of Ridgemont's prominent cheekbones. "Are you suggesting something inappropriate? I can assure you it is nothing of the sort and I resent the implication. I wish to thank her, nothing more. She revealed something about Lord Pengrin's character I had not been privy to.

Had she not done so, I would have happily agreed to his marriage proposal to my sister and unknowingly consigned her to a life of misery. I had hoped to express my gratitude that she did so at great peril to her own reputation, and to make amends for Lady Dalridge's behavior."

Benedict let the words sink in and tried to make sense of them. What information had Judith revealed to cause Ridgemont to withdraw his long-time friendship from Pengrin? Surely, Ridgemont was already aware of the man's love of the gaming tables, it was hardly a secret, although perhaps the weight of his debt was not fully known to most. It hadn't been to him until Pengrin had barged into The Devil's Lair and been humiliated by Hawksmoor. But how did any of this put Judith's reputation at risk?

"What is it Miss Sutherland revealed?"

Ridgemont pulled his shoulders back and clasped his hands behind his back, every inch the proper gentleman. Gone was his usual affable manner and in its place a sternness Benedict had not seen in him before. "I do not feel comfortable speaking of it."

"Yet you felt perfectly comfortable tossing her out of your home."

"I did not—" The words barked out of the marquess before he caught himself. He took a deep breath then continued. "I did no such thing. I was away on business. Upon my return, Lady Dalridge insisted she did the right thing. Regardless, from what I had witnessed of Miss Sutherland's character, I found it difficult to believe she would make such assertions without cause. I investigated her claims and discovered she spoke the truth. Pengrin is a cad and a liar and I no longer consider him a friend. You would do well to do the same."

"I never considered him a friend in the first place," Benedict said.

Ridgemont rubbed a hand across his forehead and weariness invaded his voice. "Do you know where Miss Sutherland is?"

"I do."

"And she is safe?"

He did not answer. Would not until he had some answers of his own. "What did Miss Sutherland tell you?"

Something had happened between Pengrin and Judith. Charlie had told him they had courted, though Charlie believed she had taken the affair more serious than Pengrin had and ultimately the lord withdrew his interest before a proposal would have been deemed imminent. It was an ungallant thing to do, no doubt, but not completely uncommon or unheard of and, as Pengrin had not proposed, there were no promises broken.

So what was it then?

Ridgemont stared at him a long moment. "I thought as her friend and self-imposed protector, you already knew. Pengrin compromised her."

Ridgemont's words set Benedict back on his heels. It was a lie. She had not been compromised. He had lain with her only the night before and could verify her innocence had been, without a doubt, intact. Had been. For he had not simply compromised her, he had ruined her. Which made him a far worse cad than Pengrin, did it not?

"Miss Sutherland said this?"

"She did," Ridgemont verified. "I know not of the details of her claim, nor would I tell you if I did, but this is what she spoke of to my aunt when attempting to convince her to keep my sister away from him. I trust you will not repeat this."

Benedict wanted to hit him in that moment, to plant his fist hard and fast into the marquess's perfectly sculpted face until it was bruised and bloodied. What did he think? That Benedict was about to run through the streets of London yelling such claims from the top of his lungs?

Ridgemont held up a hand as if to ward off any oncoming blows. "Forgive me. That was uncalled for. Of course, you won't. Your loyalty to Miss Sutherland was obvious from the start and I should not have doubted its veracity. Just please tell me she is safe and put my mind at ease."

"She is safe."

Ridgemont glared at him. "See that she stays that way."

The words came as a warning, as if he already suspected she remained under his roof, but that was impossible. Benedict had kept her well hidden. "Good day to you, Ridgemont. I am certain you can see yourself out."

The marquess nodded and Benedict stood stock still until he heard the man's footfalls on the stairs leading down to the foyer. He waited a few moments more before turning on his heel and heading in the direction of Judith's room.

Whatever had happened between her and Pengrin, he was going to get to the bottom of it, and he was not leaving her bedchamber until he did.

Chapter Twenty-Three

A short rap on Judith's door gave her a start, but she had no further time to react as the door flew open and Benedict stormed inside like a winter squall, the bitter wind of anger swirling about him. She had never seen him in such a state. There was something elemental about it and in that moment she glimpsed the man who lived beneath the normally calm, controlled exterior.

"You cannot come barging into my room in such a manner!"

He didn't bother responding.

"What did Pengrin do to you?" The words shot out, pelting her one by one. Benedict's hands clenched and unclenched at his sides. Despite his anger, she did not feel threatened. Not as she had with Pengrin when his anger had piqued. Benedict would not hurt her. At least not physically. The certainty of this lived deep in her bones. But if she spoke the truth and he turned away from her in disgust or disappointment, the pain from that would cut far deeper than any physical blow.

"That is none of your concern." She had spent the better

part of three years trying to forget that episode. Coming to London had opened the old wound and brought it back to the surface, but she was leaving now, with the hope of never returning, and as such, she planned to bury the memory in a deep, dark corner never to be touched upon again.

"Ridgemont paid me a visit." His blue eyes blazed with accusation. Her heart shuddered to a stop. Had Lady Dalridge revealed her confession to him?

"Why was he here?"

"To apologize. His driver informed him he had brought you here." Benedict hesitated. "Ridgemont investigated the claims you made to Lady Dalridge."

Fear raged through her. Ridgemont knew. Humiliation scalded her skin. Had the marquess confronted Lord Pengrin with her claims?

I will see you swimming in the Thames.

Judith covered her mouth and held in the gasp of fear that threatened. She turned away and walked toward the window. The weather remained bleak, a perfect facsimile of the strange turn her life had taken of late.

She watched Benedict's approach from the reflection in the glass. His demeanor softened as his hands rested upon her shoulders. She closed her eyes, briefly, and absorbed the warmth of his touch, pulling as much strength as she could from it. From him.

"He has broken off all ties with the man and will not allow him further access to Lady Henrietta." He hesitated before continuing. "That was the dilemma you were struggling with when we spoke that time, was it not? How to keep Pengrin from hurting her?"

She nodded.

"And you knew he would because he had already hurt you and shown his true colors?"

What did she say? What could she say? She simply nodded again, struggling to hold back her fear and humiliation.

"What did he do to you? What is it you are hiding? You need to tell me. I cannot protect you if I don't know what I am protecting you from."

She wanted to tell him she did not require his protection but the words would not come. She was a long way from home in a city she neither liked nor trusted. Benedict was her only ally, yet if she told him the truth of what had happened, her part in it, would she lose him too?

He turned her around to face him. "Judith, you must tell me."

"He compromised me," she whispered then shook her head. "No, that is not the whole truth." And that was the crux of it, the guilt she carried. The shame.

"What is the truth?"

"The truth is, I let him. He had charmed me, made me believe he shared my feelings. He spoke to me of marriage—"

"He proposed?"

Judith dropped her gaze to the narrow strip of space between them. "No. Not formally. But he spoke of it and I believed it to be a foregone conclusion. Why else would he say such things?" And he had said many things. Risqué things about what he wished to do to her. Things that startled, yet titillated her. Things that made her body pulse uncomfortably.

"Then what happened?"

"Please," she pleaded. "Must we speak of this?" She did not want him to know, to think she was the type of woman who gave herself freely to any man who paid her the slightest bit of attention. She did not want to cheapen what they had shared last night. Her brief dalliance with Lord Pengrin could not compare to her feelings for Benedict. It was the difference between fading candlelight and a raging fire.

"We must. You fear him. I can see it in your eyes. What has he done to you?"

She lifted her head, embarrassed by the sheen of tears that blurred her vision. "That is not fear you see, it is shame."

"You have nothing to be ashamed of."

But she did. "You don't understand. I let him...compromise me. I could have stopped him, but I didn't." She swallowed the bile that rose in her throat as the memory rushed back. "It was at Lord and Lady Dunhaven's ball. He said he wished to speak with me in private. I believed he meant to propose, so I made an excuse of going to the ladies' room and let him lead me away to the library. When we arrived, he kissed me."

She dropped her gaze and noted the way Benedict's fist had clenched once again, the bones of his knuckles pulled white against the skin. Her heart withered at what he must think, how low his opinion of her would become once the full truth was revealed. She took a breath and continued. She would finish what she started.

"I had never been kissed before and it quite swept me away, so I let it continue. He took this as an invitation, I assume. Why would he not? And so he pressed it further and put his hand on my breast." She crossed her arms over her chest. "I protested, but he said such things were normal between a husband and wife. His words made me believe his intentions honorable, that whatever happened it mattered not, because we were to be married. He had all but said so. Or so I thought."

"A reasonable assumption," Benedict said, but she did not believe him.

"He pulled my bodice down," she whispered, tightening her arms. "And put his mouth on my bared flesh. It felt strange...nice..." How she hated to admit such. She closed her eyes, squeezing them tightly shut, unable to watch Benedict's reaction to her shameful admission. "So I did not stop him. And when he lifted my skirts and put his hand on my thigh, I did not stop him then either." The words came out, strangled and painful and a tear burned a path down her cheek.

"Judith—" His thumb brushed away the tear. She jerked at the unexpected gentleness of his hand on her face. "You are not the first person to lose yourself to an expert seducer and sadly, you will not be the last."

"No." She refused to accept his understanding. She did not deserve it. "I knew better. Part of me wanted to stop. I was unsure. But he cajoled and insisted it was the natural course of things, so I relented. It was as if...my mind had disconnected from my body."

"When did you realize he had no intention of marrying you?"

She winced. How stupid she must appear to him, to not have seen through Lord Pengrin sooner. Even now, looking back, she wondered such herself. She had always been smart, sensible. But in this...in this, she had played the part of fool with embarrassing expertise.

"When he tried to untie my drawers, it was too much. It frightened me how far things had gone so quickly. I tried to push him away. I told him I wished to stop."

"What was his response?"

"He tried to coerce me, saying pretty words, but suddenly everything felt wrong and I wanted him to release me. When he didn't immediately respect that, I grew afraid. Angry. I pushed at him again with all my might and he stumbled back. His expression changed then. He became angry. Frustrated. I don't know." She shrugged.

"Did he leave you be?"

"In a sense. I tried to placate his feelings, to explain I wished to wait until we were married. Instead of offering his understanding, he laughed at me." The sound had been caustic and cutting. And the words that followed had seared into her soul. "He told me he had no intention of marrying a cheap little piece of baggage like me. That this had all been in fun. He'd made a wager with another that he could trick me into believing he cared for me and convince me to—"

She stopped, the vileness of Pengrin's words like knives digging beneath her skin.

"What did he say?" Hate filled Benedict's voice, though whether directed toward her or Lord Pengrin she could not say and was too afraid to ask. "Tell me."

She did not want to, but she had kept the words locked away for so long now, they had burned a black hole deep inside of her. If she did not get them out, they would consume her.

She swallowed and mustered her courage, but even then, the confession only whispered out of her. "He said he'd wagered he could convince me to spread my legs for him like a common doxy. That someone so beneath his notice would be only too happy to receive his attention and do anything to keep it."

Pure, unadulterated fury blazed like an inferno in Benedict's eyes. Even the skin of his face appeared to have been pulled tight against the bones as if trying to contain the violence that roiled beneath the surface. What would happen should his tight control snap? Would he hunt down Lord Pengrin and make him pay for his sins? And what of her? Would she be held accountable as well, for had she not provided an easy target for such folly?

"With whom did Pengrin make this disgusting wager?"

"After he made his...declaration, I slapped him and in the silence that followed I heard someone laugh. There was someone else in the room watching us. That is when I realized the entire episode of bringing me to the library had been orchestrated. I quickly covered myself and looked about the room. I found Lady Susan lurking in the shadows."

"Lady Susan?" Benedict cursed under his breath. "She is a despicable individual to be certain, but I had never considered she would stoop to this level of depravity."

"The woman has a black soul, if she possesses one at all. But regardless, I allowed myself to be taken in and made the fool. Am I really any better?"

He shook his head. "You gave your heart freely and trusted Pengrin to be genuine. How could you have known what a heartless bastard he is?"

His understanding stunned her. She had expected disappointment, rejection. Yet he placed no blame at her feet. "I did not want you to think what we shared...that it didn't mean anything. It did. It meant everything."

"I cannot claim to be pleased at the notion of another man laying hands on you. In truth, the thought sickens me, but I do not hold you responsible. You were caught in a trap set by a despicable blackguard who fostered your tender feelings, then twisted them to his advantage. But what Pengrin did, and what we shared have nothing to do with one another."

"Then you don't think me—?" She couldn't say the words. Not a second time.

"I think you the most beautiful woman that I have ever had the pleasure to encounter, inside and out. And I stand firm on my desire to take you as my bride if you will come to your senses and accept my proposal."

The sob she had held back choked out of her. Benedict reached out and pulled her into his arms, surprising her with the warmth of his embrace. How wonderful was this man, who heard the worst about her and did not judge her less worthy. He did not scoff at her stupidity, or mock her for how easily she'd allowed herself to be duped and led astray. He did not call her names or turn away from her in disgust.

Instead, he offered her his hand, and with it, a lifetime of happiness. All she had to do was say yes. Yet she could not. As

252 • KELLY BOYCE

she rested against the length of him and allowed the rise and fall of his chest to calm her sobs, the knowledge of what their marriage would cost him could not be refuted. He needed a wealthy bride.

If she married him, if she robbed him of his one chance to save his family's fortune and resurrect their reputation from the ashes of scandal, he would eventually grow to resent her. How could he not? Saving his family, finding redemption for what he deemed as his past failures, was the driving force behind everything he did.

She could not consign them to such a future. She would not destroy what they shared now by heaping disappointment and resentment onto it until it curdled and soured.

As he cradled her head against the crook of his neck, the warmth of his cravat and the skin beneath seeped into her and gave her courage.

"I love you with all my heart, Benedict Laytham, but I will not marry you."

B enedict could not believe what he was hearing. Again, she had rejected his proposal. What exactly did he have to do to convince this woman to marry him?

"Judith—"

She pulled out of his arms, just enough to look up at him, to torment him with her touch as her hand rested upon his cheek. Her eyes were rimmed red from her tears, her skin still damp from the path they had created. None of which detracted from her beauty, from the strength and goodness he saw beneath it.

He did not know how he would manage without the dowry he needed from a wealthy bride, but it seemed an easier path than managing a life without her in it. With Judith by his side, surely they could tackle the hardships in their path and make their way through, just as his mother and father had done. He believed in her. Even more than that, he believed in them.

"No, Benedict. We both know what it will mean for you—for your family's future—if we marry."

"And I know what it will mean for you if we don't." He could not allow her to sacrifice herself in such away. Not for him. But she refused to be swayed.

"It will mean nothing. Not really. I do not plan to marry and therefore the state of my innocence will not be called into question. No one beyond us will ever know."

"But what will you do?"

She smiled at him, confidence radiating from her despite all she had been through. It dazzled him. *She* dazzled him. "I think I would like to give my life toward doing charitable works rather than become the property of someone else. Rather than do what my husband pleases, I will do as I please."

It was obvious she had considered the matter even before they had shared their bodies and their hearts. Her reasoning was sound; he could neither fault it nor find error in it. Given the limited options available to women in this day and age, he would have made a similar choice.

The only hitch he found in her plan was that he had no wish to control her. She had a mind of her own and the intelligence to put it to the best use. He rejoiced in the opportunity to be a part of that, to see where it led her. Unfortunately, where it led her, was away from him.

"But what of children?"

She shrugged. "Children would have been lovely. I do adore them. But perhaps I could convince Uncle Arran to allow me to use my dowry to fund a home for orphaned children, to give them a better start in life than the one they had been set with. I think I would like that."

Benedict could think of no better role model for a

houseful of children than Judith, but he had hoped the house would be their own, the children running about bearing a striking resemblance to the woman pulling away from him now.

His arms slipped away from her as she crossed the room to the window overlooking the gardens. With each step she grew farther and farther away from him until finally he had to admit she had moved beyond his reach. She remained firm in her convictions, her strong mind unwilling to bend or change. She believed she did him a service, freeing him to marry a bride of far more significant dowry. His head counseled to jump at the chance, but his heart and his body refused. He could no longer deny the truth.

If it meant a life with Judith, he would walk away from it all.

"And if you are with child?" It was the only hope he had left and it was a thin one at best. So far, the odds stacked against him showed no signs of relenting.

She glanced over her shoulder at him. "Then we will revisit the issue."

Revisit the issue.

Hardly the response he had hoped for. His heart ached. How had everything gone so horribly wrong? He was willing to give up everything for her. The only problem being, she was giving up everything for him, and those two sacrifices did not work in concert to create a happy ending.

"I am tired." She turned around and crossed the room. He'd yet to move, his feet rooted to the spot where his life had staggered to a standstill. She touched his arm lightly and leaned up to plant an all too brief kiss on his cheek. "I think I shall rest for a bit."

He said nothing, only nodded. He had no words left.

Chapter Twenty-Four

*Ⱦ*t occurred to Benedict that the only kind of luck he'd had in the past several years had been bad, and given Marcus Bowen's sudden appearance on his doorstep and the news he presented, that status did not appear to be changing any time soon.

"I beg your pardon?" Perhaps if he asked Marcus to repeat himself, the news would change. Unfortunately, it did not.

"Crowley's body was fished out of the Thames this morning. It appears he was stabbed several times, though with the state of the body, it may be difficult to tell—"

Benedict waved Marcus off. He did not need the gruesome details of how the man met his end. The fact that he had was troublesome enough—for both Crowley and himself. "Do they know who did it?"

"No. They are looking into his associates, but my guess is a man like Crowley did not keep copious notes on the people he dealt with. Or if he did, he kept them well hidden and likely we will never find them."

Benedict squeezed the bridge of nose as his hand slipped into his jacket pocket and squeezed the smooth wood of his father's pipe. "I need a drink." He didn't often imbibe, but after the past two days he'd had, he had earned one. "Care for one?"

"No. And you should keep it to one. You'll need to keep your head about you until we figure this out."

Benedict let out a bitter laugh as he poured the brandy. "What is there to figure out? Crowley is dead. Any hope we had of discovering the identity of my silent partner died with him. By the time we go through the courts in an effort to have my partner's identity revealed, it will be too late. My finances will be beyond repair." He downed the brandy and poured another.

"I'm not so sure."

"That my finances teeter on the precipice of utter ruin? Oh, I assure you, they do." It was gauche to speak of such things, but given Marcus had taken on the role of financial advisor to him—a little too late for it to do him much good— he didn't bother himself with the breach in etiquette.

"No," Marcus joined him at the bar and covered the top of Benedict's glass before he could lift it to his lips. "That we have lost all hope at revealing the identity of your silent partner. Or that it was he who had your money in the first place."

Benedict's blinked. Whatever he'd thought Marcus was about to say, that had not been on the list. "I beg your pardon?"

"When did you receive notice from Crowley that the investment had gone bad?"

"Shortly after I returned to London. A little over a fort-night ago."

"And previous to this, the money for the investment was given to him directly in his capacity as intermediary?"

"Yes. The last payment was given to him in the form of a bank draft. He required it be made out to him so that he might disperse it properly. He indicated my partner was giving him an equal amount. I voiced my hesitation, but he insisted it needed to be this way for the sake of expediency, claiming they were on the verge of a sharp rise in profits but required an influx of money to make this happen." Benedict gritted his teeth until his jaw ached. His desperation had made him blind and foolish.

Marcus rubbed at his chin. "And then we discover Crowley planned to move to new lodgings and had bought himself several expensive new suits. Shall we hazard a guess as to where he got the money to do so?"

"Bloody hell."

"Do not beat yourself up too harshly. Crowley was a master manipulator and you were forced into making the best of a bad investment entered into by your uncle. You did the best you could under the circumstances with the information you had. But now is not the time to wallow in the past. We must stay focused on what we know."

Benedict took a deep breath. "Yes, of course. You're right. So what do we know? Crowley is known to have made expensive purchases and was moving to new lodgings. Clearly the money given to him to invest into the Western Trading Company did not go where it should have."

Marcus nodded. "The date on the receipt for the suits showed they were purchased *before* his letter where he indicated the investment had not gone as expected and refused to meet with you."

"Yes. His letter stated there would be no payout this quarter." Benedict did not like where this supposition was going, but the clearer the picture became, the less he could deny the facts. "And according to his landlord, this was around the same time where he announced his plan to move onto better, more expensive lodgings."

"And then he disappeared only to be found floating in the

Thames, his body in a state of decomposition. There is no telling how long he'd been in there."

Benedict pushed the drink he poured away. "Are you suggesting perhaps it was not Crowley who sent the letter refusing to meet with me? That he may have already been dead?"

"It is a possibility we need to consider."

Benedict pinched the bridge of his nose. A throbbing pushed against his skull just behind eyes. How could this be happening? Had his letter to Crowley, stating his wish to sell his shares in the Western Trading Company—a fact he'd insisted Crowley relay to his silent partner—been the instrument of his death?

Hell and damn.

"This silent partner of mine," Benedict said, letting out a long breath. "Safe to say he would be a prime suspect in Crowley's untimely demise? That he discovered Crowley was keeping some or all of my investment?"

Marcus nodded. "That would be my guess."

"And that this discovery led him to retaliate with violence then dispose of Crowley's body in the Thames?"

"Benedict?"

He looked up sharply to find Judith standing in the doorway of his study. Despite the disastrous news brought by Marcus and the dark tide rising against him, seeing her put a little wind in his sails, until he realized Marcus now knew of her presence under his roof.

"Judith, you shouldn't—"

Marcus stepped forward. "Miss Sutherland. I did not realize you were here."

She didn't address Marcus's statement directly. "Good afternoon, Mr. Bowen. Forgive my intrusion. I was in the hallway and could not help but overhear." She walked farther into the study, her hands clasped in front of her. Her fingers fidgeted against each other in agitation.

"It is nothing to worry yourself over," Benedict told her, his pride bruised at her witnessing the depth of his downfall. What a fool she must think him to have allowed himself to be duped so.

"But indeed, I may be able to help."

Unless she had squirreled away a small fortune, Benedict did not see how such a thing were possible. He crossed the room to usher her out of his study. This was not something he wanted her involved in. But Marcus's voice reached her before he did.

"Miss Sutherland, what help do you believe you can offer?"

She pulled in her lips and glanced at Marcus before bringing her gaze to rest on Benedict. Her distress troubled him. She had been equally upset when she'd revealed the truth of what Pengrin had done to her. An event he preferred not to think about.

"It is something I heard," she confessed. "Or rather, something that was said to me."

Benedict started, ushering her from the room quickly forgotten. "What was said to you? And by whom?"

"By Lord Pengrin."

He clenched his fist and silently wished it had been Pengrin's body fished out of the Thames instead of Crowley. The world would be well rid of a bastard such as him.

"What did he say?"

"When I told him I planned to expose him to Lord Ridgemont for the cad he was and ruin his chances at making a match with Lady Henrietta, he threatened me."

Benedict took her hands in his, heedless of Marcus standing behind him and any assumptions he may make with respect to such an intimacy. "Why did you not tell me this earlier?"

She gave a small shrug. "It is of no matter. But what he said...in light of Mr. Crowley's untimely death—"

"You heard that?" Guilt tormented him. He had meant to bring her here to protect her, to keep her safe. Yet time and again he exposed her to things no lady should be exposed to.

She nodded. "The thing is, when I told Lord Pengrin what I planned to do, he indicated I would regret my actions. He said he was not in the habit of leaving loose ends and that he would see me swimming in the Thames before he allowed me to ruin his chances at marrying Lady Henrietta."

Bile roiled in Benedict's gut. Marcus's description of what was left of Crowley imposed over Judith's beautiful countenance sickened him. "Swimming in the Thames? He said those exact words?"

"Yes. He had this wild look in his eyes. I quite believe he meant every word of what he said." She squeezed Benedict's hand and he longed to pull her into his arms, to take away her fear. And his own at what might have happened to her had she not sought his protection. He silently cursed Marcus's presence and every stricture of society that prevented him from doing so.

Marcus joined them, but Benedict refused to loosen his hold on Judith's hands. In truth, he drew as much strength from her as he gave. "Miss Sutherland, do you mean to say you think Lord Pengrin responsible for Mr. Crowley's death?"

She looked at Marcus, her usual calm reinstating itself. "While I cannot imagine what situation may have instigated such an outcome, I am not a big believer in coincidence, Mr. Bowen. That Lord Pengrin should speak of loose ends and threaten to toss me in the Thames, only to have Crowley's body show up in the same place soon after seems a little suspect, don't you think?"

"And you believe him capable of such?"

"I have seen the man's black heart. He is a monster with little regard for anyone or anything outside his own selfish needs. Though why he would consider Mr. Crowley a loose end I cannot say. I do know he was desperate to marry and I can assure you it had everything to do with financial gain. The complete disregard with which he spoke of Lady Henrietta made this perfectly clear."

Marcus reinforced Judith's sentiments. "We saw for ourselves the desperate straights Pengrin is in with Hawksmoor. He mentioned a large payment coming his way. Do you think it possible he meant Lady Henrietta's dowry? Or—"

Benedict finished his friend's thought. "Or it is Pengrin who is my silent partner and the money he expected as my investment. Crowley would have been only too aware of this and when he sought to keep the money for himself, he became one of those loose ends Pengrin did not like to leave dangling."

The idea sounded fantastical, yet rang with possibility. Worse, probability. The missing pieces of the puzzle started to fall into place.

Marcus nodded. "If we assume Crowley's greed got the best of him and he decided to cut Pengrin out of whatever shady deal they were involved in, it is a strong likelihood."

Benedict let go of Judith and ran his hand through his hair. His brain worked furiously to find a solution, more answers to their questions. "Unfortunately, Crowley has been silenced for good, but Hawksmoor is alive and well. If Pengrin disposed of Crowley then used the money to pay off his gambling debts, it may bring us one step closer to the truth of where my investment went. Although, I am beginning to wonder if The Western Trading Company was even a true investment to begin with."

"Or just a front to fund Pengrin's profligate lifestyle."

Marcus scowled. "Who knows how many other gentlemen have been swindled into such a scheme only to find the investments they were promised such high returns on took a sudden and inexplicable downturn."

"Do you mean," Judith said, "That Lord Pengrin and Mr. Crowley would have basically stolen from one to pay another just enough to keep them hoping, like a vicious circle?"

"It would not be the first time I have seen such greed perpetrated," Marcus said.

Benedict's guilt at being fooled turned to anger. "If Pengrin orchestrated the entire thing with Crowley's help, and Crowley turned on him, taking him to task would not be sufficient. Crowley would know too much, making him—"

"A loose end," Judith finished.

An uncomfortable realization hit Benedict then and the air rushed from his lungs. "And when Hawksmoor called in his debt, it is possible Pengrin went to collect from Crowley only to discover his deception."

"Not a situation that would have sat well with Pengrin, I'm sure. Especially with Hawksmoor breathing down his neck." Marcus said.

"I think we need to pay another visit to The Devil's Lair. If Pengrin has a brain in his head, he'll know better than to cross him and not pay his debt. Hawksmoor is not a man to be trifled with."

"Have you considered, Lord Pengrin may view Lord Hawksmoor as another loose end," Judith said. "As he did you."

Benedict spun on his heel to face her. She had grown pale and he hated that she had been drawn into this. "Me?"

She nodded slowly, as if the realization of what she'd just said surprised even her. "The broken axel on the carriage transporting us to London? Your driver said it was a clean break, as if it had been cut. And the horse and rider who attempted to run you down in the street?"

Benedict pulled his mouth into a grim line. "But to what end?"

"You have no heirs," Judith said. "If something were to happen to you, the Glenmor title and entailed properties would return to the crown. Perhaps Lord Pengrin believed that with no one to inherit, no one would think to look into the particulars of the failed investment and he would be free of any suspicion."

"She has a point," Marcus said. "You had indicated to Crowley before leaving for London that you had concerns about the partnership and were reconsidering your investment in the company. If he relayed this to Pengrin, the man may have decided to take matters into his own hands, fearful you were onto him or on the verge of discovering his identity."

The suggestion sickened him. Both Mother and Judith had been in the carriage with him. If anything had happened to either of them...

No. He couldn't think like that. Not now. He needed to stay focused.

He turned to Marcus. "The more desperate Pengrin grows, the more treacherous he becomes. We need to get to Hawksmoor, to find out what he knows and warn him of any danger." He looked to Judith, Pengrin's threat to her ringing in his ears. "I cannot leave you here unprotected."

Marcus nodded his agreement. "He's right. We will need to take you with us. Do you have a cloak? Something to mask yourself with?"

"Yes, of course."

"Fetch it," Benedict instructed. "We must leave immediately."

The trip to The Devil's Lair took longer than Judith had anticipated. Snow that had been falling relentlessly all afternoon had given way to sleet, making the roads difficult to travel. Beneath her, the carriage wheels slipped on the slush covered cobblestones and the driver was forced to slow down to prevent an accident. The roads were mostly deserted. Shops had closed for the day and patrons had emptied from the streets and headed home. Likely, many of the entertainments scheduled for this evening would find themselves cancelled or postponed as guests opted to stay within the safety and warmth of their own homes this night.

Judith didn't blame them. She very much wished she could do the same. This day had taken an unexpected, and unwelcomed turn. With each moment that passed, fear concocted ugly scenarios in her head. Would Lord Pengrin be desperate enough to continue his pursuit of Lady Henrietta or had Lord Ridgemont put an effective end to the matter? And what of Lord Hawksmoor? The mysterious gentleman held a lofty title but shunned polite society. It was intimated he was a dangerous man, a sinful one. Whether such claims were true, the notion did little to settle her nerves as they approached the gaming hell where he spent the majority of his time.

Next to her, Benedict reached over and took her hand, heedless of Mr. Bowen's presence. She did not pull away. She had learned enough of Mr. Bowen to know he did not cater to all of society's rules and Benedict trusted him above all, a recommendation she did not take lightly.

"When we arrive," Benedict said, "I want you to stay in the carriage and wait. I do not wish to expose you to such a place nor risk you being seen."

"But I may be able to help." She didn't know how, exactly. What could she do, after all? Resurrect Mr. Crowley? Drag a confession from Lord Pengrin? Demand Lord Hawksmoor reveal all he knew?

Helplessness gripped her. She despised the feeling as much as she loathed the idea of letting go of Benedict's hand only to watch him disappear inside The Devil's Lair. Even the name did not inspire confidence or do anything to quell her growing sense of unease.

"We will be better served if I know you are safe," he said, squeezing her hand. "I could not bear it if anything happened to you."

She shared the feeling with respect to him. What if things went awry? What if this was the last time she ever saw him? She swallowed her dread, forcing it down. Now was not the time to allow fear to overtake her mind. She must stay calm.

"Promise me you will be safe. Do not do anything to put yourselves at risk. It is not worth it in the end." It was just money after all. And while Lord Pengrin had no right to it, she did not want any harm to come to Benedict or Mr. Bowen because of it. "Would it not be better if we waited for the proper authorities and allowed them to deal with this?"

She had suggested the idea earlier and Benedict had sent a hasty dispatch to that effect but with the weather being as it was, how soon they would receive the missive and be able to respond remained to be seen.

"Time is of the essence, I'm afraid," Mr. Bowen said. "Pengrin will know Mr. Crowley's body has been found. If he is as desperate as we believe, then Hawksmoor is the only loose end he has left with respect to who can point the finger in his direction. I fear if we do not act now, we may lose our chance to put an end to this matter and regain the money Crowley and Pengrin have stolen from Glenmor."

"Is it worth it?" She gripped Benedict's hand with both of hers. How she wished she could touch his face, kiss his mouth, do whatever necessary to convince him not to go through with this. But resolve was written into the expression on his face. His mind was set upon its course. To him, it wasn't about money. It was about family. About doing the right thing.

He leaned in and kissed her forehead. "I will be safe. I promise."

But it was an empty promise as there was no telling what awaited them on the other side of the hidden door. Maybe nothing more than disappointment. Maybe something far more treacherous.

Chapter Twenty-Five

W hat awaited them as Benedict pushed through the open door was utter mayhem. Hawksmoor's two bodyguards lay crumpled on the ground just outside the door to his quarters, the floor slick with their blood. Marcus bent and pulled his glove off, touching his fingertips to each neck. He glanced up at Benedict and shook his head.

Beyond the doors, no sound could be heard.

Benedict swallowed, the metallic stench of blood seared into his senses. This was the deed of a truly desperate man and it did not bode well for Hawksmoor.

"Pengrin could not have done this on his own," he said, nodding toward the fallen men. "He must have hired men."

"Likely promised them a nice sum for their expertise. Curious what they'll do when he tries to run out on paying. He's playing a dangerous game." Marcus nodded toward the door, motioning for Benedict to open it. "Be careful."

The scene on the other side of the door offered no improvement.

"Pengrin!" Benedict barked out the name, horrified by

what he saw. Pengrin held a battered Hawksmoor pressed against the edge of his desk, a pistol leveled at his head. Two more men, likely those Pengrin had hired, lay unmoving on the floor. One stared sightlessly up at the ceiling, a hunting knife embedded deeply into his chest. The other man rested face down a few feet away from Marcus. Hawksmoor's work, Benedict surmised. Given his current state, he'd put up one hell of a fight before being overcome.

"Don't come any closer," Pengrin said, his frantic voice cutting through the death soaked air.

"Gentlemen," Hawksmoor attempted a smile, but his split lip did not allow it. "It appears you have found me in a rather precarious predicament. I don't suppose you brought any weapons that might be of use, did you?"

They had not. In their haste, they had rushed over, hoping to get there before Pengrin arrived. Hawksmoor read the answer in their expressions.

"Pity."

"Put the gun down, Pengrin. It is over. We know what you have done," Benedict said, struggling to keep his voice calm and controlled.

"What he has done—" Hawksmoor stated flatly. "—is killed my men and tried to rob me."

The pistol quivered in Pengrin's hand. "It is my money!"

"It is nothing of the sort. You and that toad, Crowley, stole it from Glenmor. That you hired a man to be your intermediary who was as untrustworthy as you is hardly my fault."

"He should have never come to you!" He pressed the gun against Hawksmoor's jaw but it did not silence him.

"Where else was he to go when he discovered you were hunting him down, desperate to get your hands on the money? The man knew you to be unhinged." Hawksmoor's gaze slid to Benedict and fixed there, revealing a tale he may not get a chance to finish. "Crowley feared for his life and figured if he left the money with me as payment for your rather immense gambling debt, all would be square. Given Crowley's body was found floating in the Thames, I take it you did not agree with his assessment in this regard. Now you have the audacity to show up and demand I return the money to you as if you have a right to it? Have you gone mad?" Hawksmoor laughed then winced. "But yes, obviously you have. Mad as a hatter from where I stand. You'll hang for this, you bastard. Your father has already cut you off and will not save you this time. I promise you, I will see you every bit as dead as Crowley."

As Hawksmoor's diatribe drew Pengrin's attention, Marcus and Benedict took slow steps to circle around him. Pengrin noticed their movements and shifted his position to keep his back to the wall. But Marcus and Benedict had moved far enough apart that he could not look at them both at the same time, his gaze volleying between the two as he kept his pistol leveled at Hawksmoor's chest.

"He's right," Benedict said. "You will not get away with this. There are too many loose ends. Too many people who know what you did. You may have disposed of Crowley, but you can't kill us all."

Pengrin's eyes narrowed. "Crowley was a common criminal in a fancy suit. No one will care about his absence or ask questions about his death."

"They will when we show them the letter he sent Glenmor," Marcus bluffed.

Pengrin's gaze swung to Marcus and Benedict used the opportunity to get closer. Escalating tension rolled off the viscount. How much time did they have before he acted, before he realized the only way for him to escape this situation was to give up, or attempt a grand escape?

"Lies!"

"He knew we were onto your scheme, stealing money

from desperate lords using a sham of an investment to dangle in front of them," Marcus continued. Benedict took another step closer. "Turns out Crowley did not trust you. He decided you were desperate enough to try and swindle him out of his share, so he came to Glenmor and offered him a choice—lose his entire investment, or allow Crowley to turn the tables and swindle you, then split the difference. He thought Glenmor would be happy with some, rather than none."

Uncertainty clouded Pengrin's expression. Had the situation not become so fraught with peril, Benedict would have applauded the tall tale spinning out of Marcus and the calm, reasonable manner in which he delivered it. Under different circumstances, he would definitely have been swayed to believe him.

Marcus kept talking. "We know there was no investment. The Western Trading Company is nothing more than a false front. Tell me, were you surprised when Crowley refused to hand over the bank notes? Did you truly think he wouldn't turn on you? Honestly, Pengrin, you are a fool to have trusted in the loyalty of a man who sells himself to the highest bidder."

"Well, he got his in the end didn't he? The rotten little turncoat won't be swindling anyone any longer. But before I disposed of him, he tried to buy back his life by telling me he left the bank notes with Hawksmoor." Pengrin glared at Benedict. "And once the viscount divulges where he has hidden your tidy little fortune, I will bid you all *adieu* and begin a new life in France."

"Except that Hawksmoor is not about to tell you anything," Benedict's mind raced. Why had Crowley given Hawksmoor his fortune? Was he involved in this mess? He pushed the questions aside. He'd dwell on the particulars later. Time was running out. He could feel it in his bones. "There are three of us and your hired thugs are dead. Your pistol has one shot and no more. Even if you take one of us down, there remain two—"

It happened in an instant and in retrospect, Benedict would never quite understand the sequence, as in his mind's eye it all transpired at once. Pengrin jumped back and aimed his pistol as Benedict lunged forward. A shot rang out and pain seared across his upper arm. From the corner of his eye, Hawksmoor crumpled to the floor like a dropped stone. Propelled by momentum, Benedict drove his shoulder into Pengrin's midsection, taking them both to the floor.

"Hawk!" Marcus's voice echoed behind him.

"Benedict!" The unexpected sound of Judith's voice rippled through him, stealing his attention and allowing Pengrin to land a solid hit to his jaw that sent him reeling backward. His shoulder screamed as he landed hard against where the pistol's bullet had found its mark. Benedict pushed himself to his feet but not fast enough to breach the shorter distance between Pengrin and Judith.

Pengrin grabbed the knife from the dead man on the floor, yanking hard to dislodge it from his chest. Benedict tried to reach Judith, but his brain buzzed with pain and his movements had turned slow and sluggish. Blood trickled down his arm inside the confines of his coat sleeve. How badly had he been hit? He couldn't think of that now.

"Let her go." Fear cut through him as Pengrin caught and held Judith tight against him as a shield, the bloody knife's tip pressed against the tender skin at her throat. For her part, she remained outwardly calm, but he could see the terror in her eyes. She, above anyone else, understood what Pengrin was capable of.

"Oh, I will let her go," Pengrin said with a smile that reeked of malevolence. "But not until I reach the docks and only if you remain here. If I see hide or hair of you, I will slit this little doxy's throat from end to end and toss her into the Thames like I did Crowley."

The image forced bile to rush up Benedict's throat, but he held himself in check. His head swam and darkness bled at the edges of his sight. Not now. He needed to hang on. "I will let you go if you leave her here."

Pengrin snorted in derision. "Will you now? I don't believe any of you are in a position to bargain."

Benedict wished he had a ripe argument against such a claim but a quick glance behind him showed Marcus had removed his cravat and had it pressed against Hawksmoor's head, the material already soaked red. Benedict's arm had turned into a useless lead weight hanging from his torso.

"It is fine, Benedict. I will go with him. When I reach the docks, I will have the driver return me here. It will be fine." The pitch of her voice was higher than usual and despite her composed demeanor and reasonable words he could see she didn't believe a single word of it. Pengrin didn't leave loose ends.

Dammit, why hadn't she stayed in the carriage as he'd instructed! His head spun and try as he might, it would not stop. The pain in his arm radiated throughout his body and his grip on consciousness grew tenuous. He struggled to hang on. He had to keep her safe. He had promised Sir Arran. Promised himself. Promised her. He could not fail.

"I will be fine," she repeated. Her words echoed as if from far away. "It serves Lord Pengrin no purpose to harm me."

Not that such a sound reason would stop him. The man had already killed three men and tried to murder both him and Hawksmoor.

"No," he said, but the word whispered out of him and his legs faltered. His knees hit the floor. He attempted to push himself back up, but his limbs refused to respond to his commands. From the corner of his eye, he saw Marcus stand but Pengrin's voice halted his movements.

"Ah-ah. I wouldn't do anything rash, Mr. Bowen." The tip of the knife dug into Judith's flesh and she straightened against Pengrin to evade it, but his hand followed her movements. Impotent rage coursed through him as he tried to push the encroaching darkness away.

"Please," Judith pleaded. "Let us go."

"No." If she went, it could spell her doom. Benedict tried again to stand, but the motion proved his undoing. Blackness mocked him, then claimed him.

Pengrin propelled Judith out of the room as Benedict lost consciousness. She tripped over the bodies by the door when she tried to look over her shoulder, but Pengrin refused to stop, his grip on her arm unrelenting. Panic swept through her. How badly hurt was Benedict? Had she done the right thing, getting Pengrin away from them? It had been a rash decision, but with two men injured, she couldn't risk him doing anything further. She only hoped to convince him to let her go unharmed, but the hope was thin.

Pengrin hauled her up the short staircase to the door. They came out to the alleyway where the Glenmor carriage awaited, the sleet soaked wind hitting her full force. The driver stood when he saw them, but Pengrin flashed his knife at her throat and barked his orders.

"If you veer even minimally from the path, you will see Miss Sutherland's lifeless body thrown from the coach. Now move and do so with all due haste!"

Pengrin yanked open the door and shoved her inside. Her knees smacked against the floor and she had no time to react or lift herself into a seat before he jumped inside behind her and the carriage began to move at a rapid pace. She stayed on the floor and gripped the edge of the seats to hold herself steady. They went too fast and the wheels skidded and slid beneath the slick, wet snow on the ground beneath them.

"You should have left well enough alone," Pengrin said, his voice filled with hate. "This is your fault. Had you not thwarted my plans to wed your little monster, I could have disposed of Crowley and left London quietly after the wedding. No one would have been the wiser. But you had to interfere, didn't you? You never did know when to just go along."

He had the reasoning of a mad man. "Did you honestly believe I would not speak up? That I would stand by and let you abuse Lady Henrietta in such a fashion? What do you think Lord Ridgemont would have done if you disappeared and abandoned his sister?"

He did not answer, but instead glared down at her with a sick smile. "Perhaps I won't kill you directly. Maybe I will take you with me, hmm? Get a little taste of you first, before I make good on my promise."

Her stomach heaved but she refused to give into it. "I would rather take a swim in the Thames."

His smile grew with a twisted sense of glee. "Oh, that can be arranged my dear. That can be arranged."

Time eluded her and Judith lost count of the amount of times the carriage skidded and tipped as it rushed along. Benedict's driver had taken Pengrin's threat seriously and he had not slowed down once, despite the danger it posed to all of them. Even Pengrin had cursed more times than not, but he had not shouted for the driver to slow.

"If you do not stop the carriage, we will all end up dead!"

"If Glenmor catches up with me, I am dead anyway. I'd rather die by my own hand than his. If you suffer in the process, I care little. You have brought this on yourself."

He'd become unhinged. "In what possible way? Because I had the audacity to reveal your true self to Lady Henrietta's family?"

"Her dowry was the only thing standing between me and ruin!"

"What of the money you stole from Lord Glenmor? It was a small fortune. All he had. If you planned on marrying Lady Henrietta for her dowry, why steal from him?"

Pengrin glared down at her, his face twisted in madness. How had she ever thought him attractive? When held up to Benedict, there was no comparison, not just on the outside but on the inside as well. Where Benedict was filled with goodness and heart, Pengrin had only darkness and hate.

"My father has cut me off and refused to pay my debts. The dowry would pay my creditors and Glenmor's sorry excuse for a fortune would allow me to set myself up nicely without relying on my father's largess. The man is as pious as a vicar and far too healthy to die any time soon for my liking. I needed immediate relief. And your friend, Glenmor, was only too happy to assist in that regard."

"Until your lies began to fall apart," she reminded him. Benedict had revealed his trepidation over the investment from the beginning and was on the verge of pulling out of it. How dismayed he must have been when he learned the money was gone and his hopes of a financial recovery dashed. "You are a thief and a murderer and will not know a moment's peace from this day forward, you black-hearted swine!"

Without warning, his hand cracked against her cheek, its full force lessened as the carriage skidded once more. But this time, the driver was unable to correct it. The horses screeched and the side of the carriage hit something hard and solid, scraping along it. Pengrin fell against her, but as they slid in the other direction, he was thrown back against the door. The force of the impact knocked the door open and it swung loosely from its hinges before being torn off completely, leaving a gaping hole at Pengrin's back. Behind him, Judith had a frightening view of the Thames. The only thing between them and the water was a low stone barrier.

Instinct took over and she lashed out with her feet, kicking at Pengrin in the hopes of knocking him out of the carriage, but he gripped her leg with one hand and the side of the carriage with the other. She struggled against his hold, but his size gave him the advantage and he forced his way back in, shouting at the driver to stop. There was no response.

"You little bitch!" He yelled and his hand came down again but this time Judith was ready and threw her arms up to ward off the blow. She kicked out and her foot caught Pengrin somewhere soft. He cursed and keeled over, his hands clenched over his private parts. She lashed out once again. As her foot smashed into his knee, the carriage skidded away from the stone wall, throwing him backward and out the open door. For a fleeting second, Pengrin appeared suspended in mid-air, hovering there as terror and surprise stamped themselves over his features.

And then he was gone.

Chapter Twenty-Six

Marcus claimed he was out for no longer than a few minutes, but it was a lifetime to Benedict. Judith's lifetime. What monstrous things would Pengrin do to her? Where had he taken her?

"Head to the docks. That's where he'll go," Marcus instructed after removing Benedict's cravat to bind his arm. "They'll have the horse ready for you outside."

The sounds of shots had brought one of ladies who offered solace to those whose luck at the tables took a downturn. Marcus promptly sent her to the mews to have one of Hawksmoor's horses saddled and brought around.

Benedict nodded. "What will you do with Hawksmoor?"

"I'll stay with him. He'll be better served if I can continue to apply pressure to the wound to keep him from bleeding out. The authorities should be here shortly. Can you manage without me until then?"

"Yes." His ears rang and his head felt fuzzy, but he would find a way. He would not fail. Everything he loved rode on his shoulders as he vaulted onto the horse and urged it toward the Thames.

He would find Judith, get her to safety, and ensure Pengrin paid for what he had done.

His crimes would not go unpunished.

It took a lifetime before the carriage came into view, though the grooves it left in the newly fallen snow made the job of finding it easier. The cold air revived him and cleared his head, though it did little for the pain shooting through the left side of his body. The trajectory of the bullet as it burst from Pengrin's pistol had seared the side of Benedict's arm and cut deeply across Hawksmoor's skull.

He cared little of the pistol now. It was the knife in Pengrin's hand he feared most. In the distance, the carriage swung wildly from side to side, bashing itself against the low stone wall that kept it from skidding into the Thames. One hard blow sent his driver flying in one direction and the door of the carriage in another. The man landed on the snow-covered cobblestone, rolled once then stopped. He did not move again.

Benedict shot him a look but did not stop. His horse charged onward as if it sensed the urgency of his mission. The snow-covered cobblestone offered little traction, slowing his progress. He urged the animal on, fear clawing at his insides.

His heart hammered against his chest as the carriage swung wildly away from the wall and a body flew out, hitting the wall then tumbling over it. It had happened too fast and the snow blew too thickly to allow him to discern whether it had been Judith or Pengrin.

He pulled up on the reins and the horse skidded to a stop. Benedict jumped from the saddle and ran to the wall, leaning over it. Several feet beneath him, Pengrin dangled, his hands gripping the jagged stone at the base of the wall. Beneath him, the Thames churned and beckoned, crashing against the barrier.

"Don't just stand there! Help me, dammit!" Panic edged

Pengrin's demand, but the emotion did not serve to move Benedict. If Pengrin was here, Judith was still in the carriage. "Bloody hell, man, pull me up! The stupid chit tried to kill me!"

If any part of Benedict had been swayed by the man's plight, his words cut such feeling off. "Go to hell, Pengrin. It is nothing more than you deserve."

He pushed away from the wall and mounted once again. The carriage hobbled now, one of the wheels broken, leaving it dragging along the wall, the gaping hole left by the door perilously close to its edge. If Judith fell out, she would risk tumbling over the wall into the water below much like Pengrin had done. Or equally as horrible, be thrown beneath the jagged spokes of the wheel.

Benedict dug his heels into the horse. The speed of the carriage reduced as he drew closer, the broken wheel slowing the runaway horses. He passed the carriage and leaned in the saddle to grasp the bridle of the nearest horse. His arm screamed in protest where he held the saddle's pommel, every muscle in his body stretched to maintain his hold on the other horse's bridle.

A lifetime passed before they finally stopped and when they did, Benedict feared letting go. Feared they would spook again and run away. He dismounted and ran to the side of the carriage that had expelled Pengrin. Inside, he found Judith on the floor, white as snow and eyes wide. Both of her feet were wedged against either side of the seats, and her hands pressed into the seat cushions for purchase.

She was alive and unharmed. He had never seen a more beautiful sight.

"You're safe," he said, reaching for her.

She nodded, her chest rising and falling in rapid succession, but she made no move to release her hold. "I—I—" It was all she managed before the fear caught up with her and a sob bubbled up her throat and broke free. He wished to join her, though his would have been tears of joy. Relief. She was alive. And God help him, he was never letting her out of his sight again!

With gentle movements, he pulled her feet free. "Let go. Come to me."

She nodded through her tears. "I'm sorry. I don't mean to cry. I am not a crier," she said, as if it mattered. As if he would think less of her.

She slid into his arms and despite the pain the pressure of her weight sent shooting through him, he held onto her with everything he had, burying his face into the thick waves of hair that had come loose during the treacherous ride. He breathed in her scent and for a moment simply stayed there while the horror of what had happened settled around him and clarified all the things they had tried to deny each other.

Things that would no longer be denied.

"I love you, Judith Sutherland, and you are going to be my wife and I'll not hear another word about it."

She remained silent a moment as she clung to him and he feared she might be forming a rebuttal to his proposal. "Not a single word?"

"No." If he said it firmly enough, perhaps he could convince her. "Not one."

Again silence. Then, "But what if that one word is *yes*?"

Despite the rightness of it all, her easy acceptance took him by surprise. He had expected a fight, to argue against her insistence that he needed to do what was best for his family. Hogwash, that was. The truth of the matter was the best thing for his family would be making her a part of it. With her intelligence and strong will, her clear head and beautiful heart, he could accomplish anything. *They* could accomplish anything. He was certain of it.

"Do you mean it?"

"I do," she whispered. "With all my heart."

His heart soared in response and for a brief respite joy overrode the pain barraging his body.

He pulled away just enough to stare down into the face he loved more than life itself. A smile filled his heart. "Then I wholeheartedly accept your answer, Miss Sutherland."

She returned his smile and the warmth that radiated from it warmed him despite the storm raging around them. "I promise to make you very happy."

"You already have. More than you can ever know."

He leaned down and captured her mouth in his, putting everything in that one kiss that had filled his heart these past weeks, removing all the fear and worry and pain and replacing it with hope and certainty and love. Was there a more wonderful thing to surrender to?

He did not think so.

Epilogue

The wedding was the loveliest of affairs. Judith had never seen Uncle Arran happier and the Dowager Countess of Blackbourne, who now insisted upon being called Mrs. Sutherland, had never been more beautiful. Love was truly a wondrous thing.

It made Judith all the more excited for her own wedding to follow after the holidays, once her uncle and new bride returned from their honeymoon. Which, considering the time of year, would take place no farther than Havelock Manor, as travel during the winter could be arduous. And, as the new Mrs. Sutherland put it, she much preferred the idea of spending her time curled up in front of the fireplace with the man she loved than braving the elements to do the exact same thing somewhere else.

"Ah, my lovely bride-to-be, there you are." Benedict joined her at the refreshment table, lifting her hand to kiss the back of her knuckles through her gloves. "I was just speaking with your uncle," he murmured, laughter in his tone.

Judith smiled. "And how did that go?"

Uncle Arran had threatened to divvy the parts of Benedict

up and bury them throughout the village for what Judith had been put through during her time in London. It had taken a full week of everyone banding together to convince her uncle that Benedict was not at fault. That when needed, he had not hesitated to come to her aid, at his own peril.

"He has stopped threatening to kill me, which I take as great progress."

"Wonderful." She held his hands, unwilling to let him go and caring little if it made them a spectacle amongst the guests that consisted of villagers and local gentry, family and a few close friends. "I'm sure, in time, he will come to love you as much as I."

"Let us simply be content if he does not carve the Christmas ham while staring me threateningly in the eye."

She laughed and lightness filled her, something she had not experienced since she was a young girl and everything was still right with the world. As it was now, once again.

"Good day, Miss Sutherland. It is lovely to see you again," Mr. Bowen said, joining them. "Still determined to marry this old boy, are you?"

"Indeed I am. I've quite lost my mind in that regard," she said, happy to see Mr. Bowen again. He had stayed behind in London following their statements to the authorities, indicating a need to tie up a few business matters before joining them. "Have you any good news for us?"

Benedict shot her an odd look. "Good news? Were we expecting news?"

Mr. Bowen smiled. "Indeed we were, and I do."

Judith clasped her hands at her breast. "Tell us."

"Pengrin's insistence that Hawksmoor had the bank notes you had given Crowley seemed worth exploring. I searched Hawksmoor's offices and discovered he kept very detailed journals on any number of topics, including Crowley and his mystery employer. It appears our reclusive viscount had heard rumblings about their scam of collecting so-called investments from desperate gentlemen with the promise of strong returns. Most of the gentlemen in question were, according to Hawksmoor's notes, not overly deserving of his interference in this regard, but it appears he took a special exception when the scam involved Glenmor."

Benedict shook his head. "But why? I barely know the man."

Mr. Bowen shrugged. "Hawksmoor has always had a strange sense of justice. According to his journals—"

"You read the man's journals?"

Judith nudged him. "Do you want to hear Mr. Bowen's news, or not?"

"Yes, please continue."

Mr. Bowen gifted them with a rare smile. "Hawksmoor made a short-list of who he believed your silent partner might be. He suspected it had to be a gentleman privy to those whose finances were in dire straights and would be willing to risk much to improve their lot."

"And he figured it out from that?"

"He'd narrowed it down to three, but according to his notes, he leaned heavily toward Pengrin being the culprit, though he had no actual evidence to bring against him as yet. He confronted Crowley, but the man refused to give Pengrin up. It wasn't until Pengrin discovered Crowley had double-crossed him thereby putting Crowley's life in danger, that he went to Hawksmoor promising information in exchange for protection."

"But Pengrin got to him anyway," Benedict said.

Mr. Bowen nodded. "But not before Hawksmoor took your bank notes as collateral."

Benedict let out a deep breath. "Then that explains why Hawksmoor had my money."

"Yes," Mr. Bowen said and his grin widened to such a spectacular degree, Judith wondered why he did not allow the expression more often. It quite suited him. "According to Hawksmoor's notes, he had intended on returning it to you. But it appears Pengrin reached him first."

Benedict rubbed at his forehead. "And it was all there?"

"Save for what Crowley spent at the tailor and a few sundry items, it appears your investment was barely touched. The other gentlemen were less fortunate, but they had invested prior to your uncle becoming involved and I suspect it wasn't until the late earl passed away that Crowley got the idea to keep it all for himself and cut Pengrin out completely. Unfortunately Pengrin's debts made him a very dangerous man, hence Crowley's untimely demise."

The twisted turns created by two men's greed and the lives they'd nearly torn apart in the process sickened Judith. Both Crowley and Pengrin had been determined to keep the fortune Benedict and his uncle had invested, to the point both had died for it in similar fashions.

After Benedict had rescued Judith from the carriage, they went back to where Pengrin had fallen over the edge, but he was no longer there. Two days later, his body was fished out of the Thames, much as Crowley's had been. Judith held no sympathy for either of them, not after all the pain their greed and duplicity had caused.

"I see smiles," Lady Rebecca said as she joined their group, looping her arm through Mr. Bowen's. "Has my husband told you the wonderful news then?"

"He has, indeed," Benedict answered, though his voice continued to echo the wonder of it all. Judith was less surprised. Mr. Bowen had informed her of his plans to stay behind and see what else he could discover from Lord Hawksmoor's files, but both agreed not to raise Benedict's hopes in that regard until the outcome was certain.

Relief swept through her.

"And the letter?" Lady Rebecca asked. "Did you deliver it?"

"Hush. You'll ruin the surprise," Mr. Bowen admonished, yet did so with such warmth in his voice and love in his eyes that Lady Rebecca laughed and kissed his cheek. How Judith counted the days until she and Benedict could share such affection in public without worry of raising eyebrows.

Benedict's brow furrowed. "What letter?"

Mr. Bowen reached into the pocket of his jacket and pulled out a vellum letter, handing it over to Benedict. He glanced down at the seal then over to Judith. "It is the Earl of Dungrave's seal." Pengrin's father.

"Open it," she urged.

Benedict slipped his finger beneath the seal and unfolded the letter, holding it up so Judith could read along with him. In the letter, the earl issued a heartfelt apology for his son's actions as well as informing him he had purchased, in Benedict's name, a substantial amount of shares in the Liverpool and Manchester Railway as compensation for crimes perpetrated by his late son.

Judith lifted a hand to her mouth as she stared down at the amount the earl had gifted to Benedict.

"I cannot accept this," Benedict said, his gaze fixed on the letter.

"You can and you will," Mr. Bowen said. "The shares have been purchased in your name. That cannot be undone. And it is small compensation for everything Pengrin put you and your family through."

"Marcus is right," Lady Rebecca said. "The man tried to kill you both. It is a miracle you survived. And Lord Dungrave can more than afford it. Allow him to assuage his guilt and ease your hardship in the process. This will go a long way to starting your new life together on the right foot and allow you to put this sordid mess behind you. Heavens, how either one of you avoided scandal in this regard is beyond me!"

Judith looked at Benedict and heat bloomed in her cheeks.

Benedict caught her eye and cleared his throat, a smile pulling at the corners of his mouth. "And Lord Hawksmoor, how does he fare?"

Mr. Bowen's smile disappeared. "There is no change, I'm afraid. I have moved him to Northill to convalesce, but it is hard to say how much improvement we can expect. The doctor has indicated head wounds can be tricky devils."

Lord Hawksmoor's lack of progress was the only black spot remaining in this whole affair and it hurt Judith's heart to think the man still suffered. Had it not been for his machinations, likely Benedict's fortunes would have been lost completely.

"His family did not take him in?" Benedict asked.

Mr. Bowen's expression darkened further. "They did not. He remains *persona non gratis* in their eyes."

His answer took Judith aback. "But he is the heir to Ravenwood. What could possibly have occurred to turn them so harshly against him?"

"Hawksmoor has never said," Mr. Bowen said. "I suppose that is a tale to discover another day, is it not? Today we are here to celebrate a joyous occasion, and one soon to come, yes?"

"Indeed," Judith smiled and turned toward Benedict.

He took her hand. "With a lifetime of happiness to follow."

Heat seared her insides as he squeezed her hand and brought it to his mouth to kiss her once again. His passionate gaze promised untold delights and she, for one, could not wait to discover every aspect of what that entailed.

A Sneak Peek

~∞~

BOOK 6: A SINNER NO MORE

There were a few things he knew for sure. To start, he had an unwavering awareness of the pain in his head that refused to relent and give him even a modicum of peace. Following that, was the fact that when he attempted to rise up out of the bed he'd been laying in for days on end, his head swam as if caught in a whirlwind, forcing him back down into a prone position. He also knew his name was Lord Hawksmoor, as that was how the servants referred to him when they came to fluff his pillows, change his sheets, feed him, and assist him to the privy, ensuring he did not fall into the pot when his legs gave out. He did not care to think about that rather humiliating event as it ruffled his pride, which he apparently possessed in abundance.

But beyond these few, rather limited truths, the wealth of his knowledge dropped into a rather embarrassing deficit when compared to what he did not know.

Such as, where he was. Or why. Or how and when the wound to his head had occurred, or who had inflicted it. The rather serious-minded gentleman who checked in on him periodically was of little assistance in any of these matters. The man said little and gave away even less. Mostly he asked questions to which Hawksmoor had no answers. Not that he admitted to such. Acknowledging his mind had become a sieve through which all the things he had once known had leaked out served no purpose that he could ascertain.

What did one do with someone who had lost his mind? Send him off to Bedlam to be forgotten? And how was it he could remember that a place like Bedlam even existed and yet not recall his given name? Or who had given it to him?

Not a stellar commentary on his sanity.

He reached up and touched the bandage wrapped around his head, careful to avoid the area along his temple and beyond as that gave him the most pain. He must look a fine picture.

Ah, there was that pride again.

He had requested a looking glass from one of the servants, but they had shuffled off without promising anything. He should have asked the pretty young woman with the blonde hair. She seemed a nicer sort than the others. At least she looked at him instead of averting her gaze, though he doubted she was aware of his scrutiny. She only came late in the evenings and he always pretended to be asleep, watching her through his lashes.

Awaiting her arrival became a game of sorts, albeit a rather one-sided amusement. He'd pretend to be fast asleep, and then attempt to guess what she was doing based on the sounds she made. Some were easy. The pouring of fresh water into the ewer on the bureau. Straightening the blankets around him. That was a particular favorite. She smelled of wild roses freshly bloomed on the vine, which led him to discover that wild roses were his most favorite flower. At least they were now. Other movements were more difficult to ascertain. One time, the chair in the far corner out of his line of sight creaked only to be followed by a long silence. Had she sat there? If so, why?

He'd longed to open his eyes and inquire, but feared if he

did, she might slip away like a wraith and not return. A horrible thought, as her arrival provided the highlight of his day. There was something about her. More than her obvious beauty, which was indeed remarkable. But her appeal went beyond that. Something in him wanted to reach out to her. To keep her safe. Which was rather ridiculous given he did not know her any more than he knew himself.

He had, however, given her a name. Rose, naturally. It seemed fitting. He hadn't done that with any of the other servants, but she was special. He wasn't sure why, but there it was.

The door to his bedroom opened slowly and he immediately shut his eyes. The delicate scent of wild roses drifted in to greet him as she quietly moved about the room like a whisper. She conducted her duties, pouring fresh water into the ewer, straightening the blankets at the end of the bed. As she drew closer, he shut his eyes completely so as not to give himself away.

She hovered over him like a little hummingbird. He held his breath. Waited.

He stilled as the tips of her fingers pressed lightly against his chest, just above his heart that beat a little faster at her touch. Such an intimacy had not occurred before and he did not know what to make of it. No one had touched him in such a way in—well, he did not know how long.

"Thomas? Are you awake?"

Also by Kelly Boyce

THE SINS & SCANDALS SERIES

THE BRIDES OF FATAL BLUFF

SALVATION FALLS

Dear Reader

Thank you so much for reading **SURRENDER TO SCANDAL**, Book 5 in *The Sins & Scandals Series*. I hope you have enjoyed reading Benedict and Judith's adventures on the road to happily ever after as much as I loved writing it.

If **SURRENDER TO SCANDAL** is the first book in The Sins & Scandals Series that you have read, I hope you will check out the earlier books in the series. And if you are curious as to the fate of the enigmatic Hawksmoor, might I suggest you pick up the 6th book in the *Sins & Scandals Series*, **A SINNER NO MORE.**

For the most updated booklist, check out my **website book page** or sign up for my **Newsletter** at **www.kelly boyce.com.** I send out notifications to all subscribers to let them know when a new release is on its way, as well as provide the opportunity to win a prize with each new edition. Be sure not to miss it!

I love to hear and connect with my readers through social media and email and you can find all of my social media links on my **website**!

Again, thank you for reading **SURRENDER TO SCANDAL** and I hope you will consider leaving a review at your favorite online retailer to help others discover **The Sins & Scandals Series!**

Wishing you all the best ~ *Kelly*

Acknowledgments

The biggest acknowledgement for this book needs to go to my dear friends and family who recognized I was burning out under the schedule I had set for myself and suggested I might want to take a step back and re-think things. I didn't particularly *want* to do this, but I trusted these people to have my best interest at heart so I took their advice. In doing so, I realized I had become too consumed with page counts and timelines that I had lost the joy of the process in the rush to *get 'er done.* As it turned out, it was sound advice and I'm glad I took it.

SURRENDER TO SCANDAL was the first book I tackled on my less rigid writing schedule and I'm happy to report the joy of writing has returned, along with my sanity.

So, a big thanks to those of you who gave me a gentle (and sometimes not-so-gentle) talking to.

I'd also like to thank the crews at Starbucks Scotia Square who understand I want a sugar-free vanilla latte with soy when I show up in an ungodly hour of the morning having left my ability to speak at home, likely still in bed. Verbosity at that early hour is not a skill I possess. Also, to the Second Cup crew on Portland Street—thanks for not kicking me out when I spend hours hiding in the corner, sipping lattes and making liberal use of your free Wi-Fi. Coffee shops are my second home and you guys and gals make it a comfy and welcoming one.

As always, thanks to the people that helped me pull this book together: My editor, Nancy Cassidy, who helps me write the best book possible. Kim Killion (cover designer) and Amy Atwell (formatter) – thanks for your remarkable skills. You ladies are awesome!

And, as always, to John – for going on this crazy journey with me. You're the best!

About the Author

Kelly Boyce started writing stories in Grade 2 when her favorite teacher, Mrs. Matheson, showed up with a box filled with plot ideas and she was immediately hooked. But it wasn't until she read Lisa Gregory's *Bitterleaf* that she fell in love with historical romance. Once she discovered Romance Writers of Atlantic Canada and learned how to turn those stories into books, it was full steam ahead.

A life-long Nova Scotian, Kelly lives near the Atlantic Ocean with her amazing husband and a clownish golden retriever with a stubborn streak a mile wide. She loves writing stories about relationships and creating a sense of community around the hero and heroine filled with secondary characters who take on a life of their own.

Along with *The Sins & Scandals Series*, she has also released several western historical romances: *The Salvation Falls Series* and *The Brides of Fatal Bluff Series*.

Currently, she is hard at work developing a new three book series on the Lindwell Family, who were introduced in *The Sins & Scandals Series*.

Copyright

www.ingramcontent.com/pod-product-compliance
Lightning Source LLC
Chambersburg PA
CBHW020540020726
47494CB00006B/1851